T0196622

A DIVINATION OF THE DOG

A.M. FARROW

authorHOUSE®

AuthorHouse™
1663 Liberty Drive
Bloomington, IN 47403
www.authorhouse.com
Phone: 833-262-8899

This is a work of fiction. All of the characters, names, incidents, organizations, and dialogue in this novel are either the products of the author's imagination or are used fictitiously.

Published by AuthorHouse 12/14/2020

ISBN: 978-1-6655-0840-7 (sc)
ISBN: 978-1-6655-0839-1 (e)

Library of Congress Control Number: 2020923165

Print information available on the last page.

CHAPTER 1

December 18th, 2021, prison cell block Four's top bunk, it is Aaliyah anytime anywhere around here, with an exception to when I sleep, I say right as the correction officer passes by. Not that I can get a good night's rest in this six by eight shared living space. And if I somehow fall asleep more than likely I will wake up from a recurring dream, exhausted.

"I always picture God as a dice player. What you think about that?" cellmate MA23154 lining the bedding of the bottom bunk asked me my opinion.

"I bet they are playing cards."

"You gamble?"

I responded, "Only when I can help it."

"Something in the way you said that makes me think you do. Right situation, the right people, and to top it off we get played by those who live by a negative existence. Loved by those who are down to see us smile. My brother made me smile. Though I can't justify the end, only that I hurt my brother either way. Maybe I am delusional, but I always believed big brother could make everything better. Aint no one going to tell me how I raise my younger brother. Partners in crime, an acquiescent Jewel thief as his preferred mentality, the door locked from the inside and my sixteen-year-old brother knew the combination. How he did, I have no Idea, but he did have autism, nonverbal so anything he did was exceptional. Mathematica for him was learning the numbers to the safe listening to music that made him happy. I only desire to see my brother cared for. I would

1

take his hand as he hung on every word, I said to him. I rather die than to lose him. But if I have an opportunity to avoid both scenarios, I am always going to look to the latter and what was in that safe I believed would keep us together. Lord knows I had to make that choice, lonely and cold, imagine standing on the edge of the Connecticut River, looking up wondering if the stars might let you shine. The electricity that opens the door to the marijuana dispensary was controlled by me and another security guard. Both working a double shift during the pandemic, my motive mostly was to feed and shelter my brother and me. I promised the case workers I could care for him when our mother and father became two of those stars in the sky. I had a cousin that lived on the other end of the city who would help us on occasion, when she wasn't having to work herself. This is America, we all must work if we want the bigger bag. I called off for the first four months, second shift, fifth month, I was told I could start to work again, on the condition that I could bring my brother Dawin to work with me. Dangerous, I know but I believe things only get better and I would do it all again no hesitation, only problem was Dawin would not wear a face mask. Instead when I insisted that he wear one, it would lead to a short manic outburst. Sometimes he would wear the face shield if I also wore one, as well I carried around a big bottle of hand sanitizer and sneeze absorbent towels, that I brought with me in my duffle bag. The beautiful bud tenders who beside the occasional fill ins were three ladies that thought Dawin was so cute. They loved having him around the shop, probably because they never met someone so genuine before. They would have taken him home if I let them. The owners were cool, at first. They were these two Albanian guys who loved hip hop more than any brother I met. I told em look, you're really getting two for the price of one because my brother, who was taught by our parents, knew how to read and type. So while I was watching, making sure each customer was respecting the rules and regulations of the dispensary during a pandemic, Dawin could collect Identification cards, type their names into the computer and hand the customer back their I.D., smooth and simple. They may have empathized with our plight, in any case my brother was happy just sitting, sometimes rocking back and forth, listening to mostly 80s music. I also let him watch movies on my phone, specifically James Carey's 1994 classic, "*The Mask*" which he enjoyed more than the rest. For me, it was white noise by the 58th viewing, besides for the scenes that contained Camron Diaz, those always got my attention. The younger brother was so big and dumb. He wanted to be the leader so bad he would make these constipated faces as if he were receiving some divine insight. What amused me the most was the music that Dawin played when the owners were around. I noticed any time the bigger guy was around Dawin, for whatever reason, from whatever song he was listening to currently he would change to Cyndi Lauper's 1983 pop smash "*Girls Just Want to Have Fun.*" I think the big guy became weirded out, once he realized that anytime he asked what Dawin was listening to, I would tell him that "he was listening to some *Tears for Fears* earlier, but as soon as he saw you." No judgement, I just was not fooled by his size. I knew which brother wore the pants in the family. What really fascinated me was the song Dawin chose whenever the older smaller brother was around and what the smaller guy was doing at the time. Behind a plywood door, directly parallel to the check in desk that Dawin collected IDs from, in the back room, was a luxury black German antique safe with refurbished mechanical combination lock. Whenever the door had to be opened, as the cash drawer out front would become full or the smaller guy would leave for home with his personal key, I would detect the word Heindl across its iron frame. More importantly I noted that it collected and stored all monies that the shop had accumulated in a week, maybe even a month. At the same time this was happening, on cue, Dawin would switch to the playlist that had the amazing seventeen-year-old Lesley Gore singing her 1963 rebel anthem "It's My Party and I'll Cry If I Want To", to Dawins animated fingers rhythmically manipulating themselves like that of a rotating three number combination, dubbing it the west side as to complete the pattern. Impossible I thought. Most times I was proactive when it came to managing Dawin's surroundings, usually foiling his plot beforehand, for he never missed an opportunity to snatch a persons unattended beverage. Though more difficult, was managing where others left their coffee, sodas, juices, everything besides a clear bottle water enticed Dawin to taste. I had no issue reimbursing the girl's drink but what initially seemed not to bother her became problematic as the brothers now told me effective immediately, I had to leave Dawin at home or be let go. I could not afford either of those options, feel me. I had to do what I had to do. Twinkle in my eye, one evening I left the music on, windows down and I had Dawin wait in the car, while I attended my last shift. Getting my hands on the key was the easy part. Getting out the shop was a bit more difficult. I got the safe open and everything. Inside was cash, a lot of cash plus an eclectic stone if I ever saw one, that I also grabbed. All I had to do was let myself out. Earlier I let the other guard know that I had everything covered and that he could take his break. As it turns out the same lady bud tender whose drink Dawin drank was also sleeping with the little guy and saw me take the key and also apparently, she was waiting until the last second to tell the little guy. I pleaded with the girl to press the button to open the door. She pretended like she wanted to work out a deal, but I could tell she was just stalling. I don't know, maybe becoming a channel five news talking point was a repressed fantasy of hers. In any case they had set me up.

"Sounds like you had a sure-fire plan. Just one tiny anomaly", In front of one eye, I minimized the space between my thumb and pointer finger, which he could not see. "Here you are roomed with me, inmate MA 17447, Massachusetts State Property."

"What is your problem?"

"I didn't know I needed a reason besides this being Suffolk County House of Corrections."

"We've been cellmates for more than a month now, I have told you quite a bit about me, I told you how I was getting money on the outside, and I just told you about how I got myself locked up in here. As for you, all I know about you is that you go by the name Sam Waters and that you came from Los Angeles and it seems, anytime the moment comes up where you could add in a little more about yourself, you end up referencing some dumb old movie that nobody else has ever seen before and totally change the subject."

"Have you never seen Shawshank Redemption?"

"And thank you for making my point."

"I don't know, I think it may relate to our situation."

"What else you got to do? We aint in super max Sam. Much of our recreation is limited to some quality conversation for the remainder of our sentence. What are you twisted or something? Right now, this very instant, tell me what you are in here for?"

"Murder" I answered.

"No bullshit? What could have bothered a young brother like yourself so much that you felt you needed to take a life that wasn't your own?"

"I am innocent, I never took a life."

"Oh so, your waiting to be released any day now. Probably have top professional's working through the fire, am I right?"

"I probably won't hold my breath."

"Young brother, these top professionals aint gonna free you from yourself. Sure, they may clear your name and get you out from behind bars but if you are not right on the inside, you will come right back here, for the same mistake you swore you would never make again.

"If anything, what I'm guilty of being is anxious."

"Many times, knowing how one gets to a certain point, granted you plan to move forward, you could almost figure what's going to happen next, Feel me. Shit, you must be only a couple years younger than me. What your parents didn't love you or something? I mean you might as well tell me, we aint got nothing but time in here. What are you afraid of?"

In my most troublesome voice, I replied "A positive identification maybe." Seems I was set up by the bigger picture, a love that the older

I get becomes more and more prevalent. Still I don't mind telling you about what happen to my family if that is what you desire to hear. I paused for a retraction that never came. I called back to my memory "If the end of my world were to be televised, it would have probably started the way twenty-twenty started out. What I originally believed to be everything under control ultimately fell on to the spectrum of uncertainty and spread like the Covid Virus. What feels not so long ago, though not any easier to explain, the night my father disappeared. But before I can tell you about what happen on the night of March 20th, 2020, I must tell you about what happen three months ago, Monday September 13th, 2021."

CHAPTER 2

The destination was a nearly empty waiting room to Los Angeles's highly reputable and dedicated shrink, Doctor A.M. Farrow. Brought to me by an early morning tight rope to my mothers' car. I was to call her when I was done, something that she used to say before dropping me off at summer camp. I now ceased to be a child. "To be or not to be", here? A choice not made by these fish swimming around the murky water of this office fish tank. I was hoping that question was less rhetorical and maybe one of these fish would answer me using a form of telekinesis. This was not fact, less because fish have fish brains and cannot communicate with us mask breathers and more because I had to be here whether these fish cared or not. Glancing over at the door, I imaged myself having to explain an early exit to my mother. In a most rebellious fashion, my back slid down the comfortable parts of the waiting room chair. If I wanted to avoid a third appearance in front of a judge and in effect ninety days of mandatory confinement" I had to be here according to the second judge and lucky for Doctor Farrow, my mother's insurance covered priceless advice or else we would have come out of pocket for someone more affordable, someone less published, someone who didn't have radio advertising; Farrow Family Psychology 2400 E. Imperial Highway, El Segundo, California. A corner office space on the thirteenth floor inside the new Los Angeles Times building. Truth is, I was here to receive guidance, recommended by my former 12th grade Critical Theory teacher, Mr. Isaac Burt.

Just then I heard the snap of bubble gum, "You like the fish?" the receptionist had spoke to me with no complaints apparent.

"Sure, what kind are they?"

"That bluish green one there is a Siamese fighting fish. We used to have two. We learned you only can have one of them in the tank at a time or they will fight each other. To the death" she whispered.

By the look of the water, it was most likely a mercy killing.

"I don't know if you can see it but that big black one at the sandy bottom is called a Black ghost knife fish. It is supposedly electric, though I just like to picture him drinking pinacolato and getting caught in the rain. You know which one is the goldfish right?"

"The little gold one hiding behind the plant" I said.

"The plant it's hiding behind is called an Anubias plant. It's like one of two plants that can survive around a goldfish. Personally, the goldfish is my favorite. That unique looking one with the stripes, that is called a *Pterophyllum scalare*, also known as the Angel fish. I call them the loyal fish because they refuse to breed with more than one spouse. Now only if I could find a man with the same qualities."

Have you tried the penitentiary?

"Yeah, the Doctor likes to talk to them as well. He should be here soon. Can I get you any water?"

"Umm no thank you, mother packed me a water with my recommendation letter."

Justified across my misshaped body with the date, September 13th, 2021, the letter read like;

Dear Friend and Honorable Doctor Farrow,

I wanted to thank you again for the emotional guidance that you have provided my wife and I after such an enormous loss. Not once, at our most vulnerable moment did I feel as though your wholehearted feedback misunderstood our suffering. Since the last time we spoke, my wife and I have eased back into society with a new appreciation for things

8

that truly make this life worth living. Like you had previously emphasized "when there is No problem too small, who are you gunna call?" Dr. A.M. Farrow, that's who! I realize the answer that you so poetically were steering us to, was one to be found within "ourselves". If we want to find meaning within the madness, we need not make unimportant any small matter and to take responsible our own outcome. Words to live by! Therefore, it gives me absolute pleasure to recommend Samori Waters, a talented and bright young man who under your accomplished tutelage, would benefit immensely. As you are aware life after the 2020 pandemic has not been easy for anyone which brought new meaning to the slogan "We Are All in This Together." Although this continues to reign true, I have also observed that some more than others were immersed deeper into consequence, this including Samori and the Waters family. As a former history teacher to Samori at University High School in Santa Monica and friend of the Waters family outside of school, I find without a doubt the troubles that have plagued the Waters family since the first week of quarantine will not resolve themselves without a great deal of professional unearthing. I suppose therefore I feel obligated to write this letter and ultimately shepherd Samori into your direction.

Sincerely your friend,

MA, BA, Isaac Burt.

"My father would always tell me how privilege I should feel to be seen by those who genuinely want to see me and that I should keep a good attitude to be viewed in the highest regard. He said a lot of things that stuck with me. This included him telling me that most of these so-called professionals could just take it all back once I walked out that door. In some cases, I think it must be in the job description to be good at pretending. Still it was up to me to decipher which valued form of advice was fair to apply to this situation. I guess worst case scenario I was just going to have to beat them at their own game. He aint the only one that has read a book."

"Mr. Waters!?" Again, I was redirected to the receptionists' vocal inquiry. With warp-spasm, I reassemble my body before responding with a sharp,

"Yes!"

"You may go ahead and have a seat in the room directly in front of you" the receptionist announced.

I raised up from the chair looking down to realize that I must have left my bottle of water in my mother's car. I returned the receptionists off putting exaggerated smile with a halfhearted one of my own just in case she hadn't already figured out about my boyish displeasure. Four ordinary steps later gripping the knob with my right palm, combined with a clockwise rotation, I open the door to nobody.

"Take a seat please. Doctor Farrow will be with you in a moment" she reluctantly emitted.

My sizeable head and lean body snuck through the door frame. The smell of new air combined with an incessant wind whizzing under the half-cracked window was cause for my hesitation. Stepping into the room with the door now closed behind me, I surrendered to the feeling of emptiness as I caught my reflection escaping the perfectly placed gold trim mirror that protruded from the white wall. I winced, viewing the improbable still tender scar, extending diagonally across my left eye. Above my eyebrow, glistening ointment blanketed dry blood where the last few stitches remained. An instance of pain flashed across my subconscious. Also protruding was that of my hair which resembled a jail break, each hair follicle out for themselves after escaping from underneath my black raiders hat with no definite plan. I folded the paper into the new era cap and then folded the cap around the letter. My mustache curled and pierced my upper lip persuading me to shake my head with disapproval hoping to witness my reflection agree. It did. Below the mirror was a solid antique working desk also with gold trim twirling down its front leg which supported all the typical office materials; a framed picture, note pad, a lamp, pens, pencils, and a landline. The office ornament that stood out to me was the life-size, gold crested owl figurine perched at the top of a bookshelf. The bead of its preeminent and possessive eyes whether I chose one of the two soft centered leather chairs, or the no armed sofa extending adjacent, I felt as if it were watching me. I Chose to sit upright.

The phone rang. Just then, I recounted an eerie moment my father told me happened where an ominous thunder cracked open the dark clouds above his childhood home. As he stood over the caller ID, like how I was standing over the office phone now. His phone displayed seven 7s and moments earlier he said it was nothing but clear sky. In my case the phone stopped ringing.

I placed my hat next to a box of tissue's I would not be using, no sooner my seat secured does the door swing open. Flipping on the lights with a disheveled tie, none other than a GQ suit wearing, two tone, sun burnt brown skinned man with expensive black plastic framed sunglasses and with shoulders that made a degree the same as a triangle coat hanger. His early middle-aged face with obvious stubble said he must have been too busy to shave the night before, and the gelled part in his nearly slick back hair which resembled one the likes of Fredrick Douglas except more down the middle, said that he may need to get his priorities straight. He removed his sunglasses from his face where I could see the bags under his eyes looked as if they were newly acquired. While his gaunt cheeks exhibited, what he probably still refers to as dimples but at his age possibly in his early forties, were more like wrinkles. Behind his abrupt movement I was able to trace the overcompensation of cologne that delivered a sort of peppery musk to my nostrils. In the short time of me sitting I concluded that he was either a poor pretentious psychiatrist or a hugely misunderstood one. With words of remorse "Sorry that I'm Late", the man with a brown leather satchel thrown over his left shoulder, newspaper wedged into his right armpit continued straight toward the antique desk, ignoring eye contact or any form a professional courtesy, "LA, right?" A digital clock lay atop a handmade shelf that suspended to the right of his desk. It indicated a time of 9:06am but I knew that it was in fact 8:06am. With a low-pitched north-eastern drawl, the six- foot two man went on to voice what I first recognized to be rhetorical.

"Did you get to meet the fish, he asked. I suppose I have Sheila working two jobs, one of which is my secretary. "No" he said I guess being sarcastic. "She loves them, and she does a great job for me as well. I swear it's these mystery phone calls that pop up on the caller ID, somewhere like Phoenixville, PA. I don't know, but they have me questioning an individual's purpose on this planet. She really is a lifeline in this business, and I am thankful she stuck around." Not until his brown satchel was dropped sloppily near the bottom of the desk, and his now connected laptop, propped open and fully booted, did he first look up to see that someone else was in fact in the room. The dark sunglasses in his hand were then placed in the top drawer exchanged for some expensive looking eyeglasses.

"And when you pick up it's like hello, this is Vanity calling how can we get your last dollar today. Next thing you know, you are to be a big music producer about to break into the music industry. But we know that's not true." He paused in his chair, newspaper in hand and more to say,

"You must be Samori Waters, my name is Dr. A.M. Farrow. Do you read the newspaper? He continued without my response.

"Well there is a real tragic story on today's front page about a college girl who had been sexually assaulted and then murdered at her campus apartment. The police have no suspects in custody but of course a witness identified the perpetrator as a colored man running from the scene. Normally a single witness account of a crime is not enough for a conviction. Except in the court of public opinion. In this story" he held up the newspaper signifying its importance, "the journalist uses descriptive words like monster and predator to reinforce an image of a savage," A savage witnessed by one Caucasian woman, puts the entire black race at threat level red until said individual is caught." He culminated his point by tossing the newspaper on the top of his desk.

What I then believed to be desolate banter, soon became less rudimentary.

"So tragic" he pointed out. "This leads me to my next question.

Do you believe in God?" Doctor Farrow inquired with a sudden shift in focus. Caught off guard by his seriousness, all I could mustered out was a simple, Yes. First feeling confused and then fortunate that my answer of yes also indicated that I was indeed Samori Waters.

"It's ok you don't have to answer that" he conveyed. "I am just saying there has to be a higher power out there that each person may want to account for, do you know what I'm trying to say?" In agreement I reported back to him his exact words "That there has to be a higher power out there that each person should account for."

"Right. Something that holds us responsible. Would you rather me call you Sam or Samori?" he followed with.

You can call me Samori.

"Okay Samori, he said leaning back into his chair business like, "this is how it will work, today is somewhat of an intake period or trial run for both parties. If at the end of the session it is perceived that I am not able to help you and someone else might be better suited to help or you feel obligated to seek an alternative support, then you are free to do that, and it will no longer be necessary for us to meet after today. Today's Insight-oriented therapy session was supposed to begin at 8:00am and end at 1:00pm but since I was a few minutes late we can push our session later. There is no one else on my schedule today until 3:00pm and if you need the full 7 hours today that is not a problem. If you get hungry there is a vending machine at the end of the hall, if you brought a lunch feel free to eat at any point. Last but most important, Don't Lie to Me. Do you have any questions?"

It wasn't the Psycho Neurotic Institute of the Very Very Nervous. But I was Listening. "Can we smoke in here?"

He said, "You smoke?" clearly confused.

I said "This would make it plausible me asking if I could smoke in here."

"What do you smoke?"

"What do you got?"

"I mean I've been known to spark a Rosschild on the right occasion. Do you know what that is?" He inquired reaching into his bottom left drawer to pull out a pack of Newport 100 menthols.

I impressed with confidence "Davidoff or Robusto?"

"Oh, so you know about cigars. Your father must be a smoker?"

I hadn't seen him smoke much, occasionally I would leave an end of a fiscally smoked blunt hidden behind some garden appliance to later find it withered to roach size. But I know he knew the difference between a quality cigar and a Newport 100.

"This is what I call my emergency stash" he touted before walking me over a Lucy. "You're not worried about the impotence?" he asked me,

"No, why is that what happen to you?"

"No."

He then wanted to know when I started smoking, but I hadn't yet.

"Got a lite?"

"It doesn't say anything about you smoking in your file and that's something that would have been in there."

"Yeah well it does not say anything about me needing to speak with a Psychiatrist either.

"Yeah it does actually."

I played naïve, "Does it really? And here I was thinking that you were the crazy one whom needed my help."

"I get it. The last couple of people you spoke with didn't have the answers you were looking for, can you really blame them though?, It wasn't their world that was flipped upside down, the way yours was. I imagine it's a lot easier to deal with keeping it close to the body." But I assure you Sam, my qualifications precede your average listener."

"Is that what this is? I excused. "You show me a couple of Psychiatry certificates and I am supposed to just open up. Quite the unique strategy I must say."

"I am a Psychologist not a psychiatrist, and yeah your file highly recommends you seek professional help. Maybe not entirely from me, maybe I only give you a minor push in the right direction, but it will be one less obstacle later."

Cigarette hanging off my bottom lip, I let the silence in the room speak for me.

"You want to take that chance?" he said.

"Does the Pope turn water in to wine?"

Tossed me a two-inch yellow Bic Lighter I caught first try. Doctor Farrow evoked my best James Dean persona.

"Looks like this is going to be One terrific day!"

"I Never underestimate a man who smokes. Not that I advocate for it because it can be a real nasty habit. Maybe because it's a hallmark of a man who has nothing to lose. Nineteen is kind of young not to have something to live for, wouldn't you agree?"

"What If I don't think about the consequences until after the fact?"

"If that is true, it may explain why you are here in my office today."

"I don't know you tell me, you're the doctor."

"The piece of paper you are holding, is that for me?"

"Oh right. I have this recommendation letter my mother printed out last night from Mr. Burt. Seems someone else believed you helped them" I explained walking over to hand Doctor Farrow the letter. I called attention to the digital clock on the shelf that I saw was an hour fast.

"Do you know your clock is an hour fast?"

"It is some Psychometrics and a bit of Signal Detection Theory that I use with some of my other clients."

Not up to date with my psychology terminology. "Psychometrics?" I repeated back.

"Have you ever heard of the Bayesian and maximum-likelihood procedure?"

"Is that where they stitch a person headfirst to another guy's ass?"

"No, that would be the Inhumane centipede, not medically recommended. What I am talking about is a way to objectively measure individual differences, using experimental psychology. We use it daily to recall a person's memory, to measure someone's emotional state, possibly one's perception of events, a person's behaviors, even an individual's underlying motivation. I use the clock to measure reaction time. Nothing that should interest you, just some Psychology Mumbo Jumbo. We can move on unless you wanted to go over to the clock and change it to correct time." He stated pen in hand, measuring my level of doubt.

Eager to move on and to not be included in any further experiments, I simply walked back to my seat.

"No Worries, in two months it will change itself." Deviating back, "I see he has taken quite an interested in your wellbeing. Don't you think?"

"How I got to be so fortunate, I do not know. I wish we could have just shaken hands, well maybe not shaken hands but parted ways like a normal student teacher relationship. I mean yeah, he was a cool teacher and all but now he is calling my house and making personal recommendations. What does he think he is the first male teacher to put a move on my mother? I am sorry that his marriage is a work in progress, but I don't think that's any excuse for him to call my mother at all hours of the night. Selfish much. He's old enough to head into the bathroom with a magazine when he gets lonely. I know for a fact before my dad went missing Isaac Burt wasn't about to call my house any time of night, unless my father knew about it first. My question is, when will the grotesque face of misogyny cease to implement our children's curriculum. What never did no one a disservice, if you ask me, is minding one's own business. Though, I did find his class kind of interesting." Looking uneasy, Doctor Farrow squirted a dollop of hand sanitizer into his palm after first putting aside the recommendation letter.

"In any case, Mr. Burt, I'm sure has plenty of other students that he could have been helping. Seems like he went out of his way to connect you to me."

As I Looked to ash my cigarette somewhere, "He sure did" I replied.

"And here you are." Silence divided our session as Dr. Farrows attention was focused to the screen of his black acer laptop.

"Mr. Burt assured me that you are no dummy."

"Well he aint no professor himself, I commented before what apparently fell to def ears, me asking if there was a place that I could ash my cigarette. Again, my focus was drawn to the judgmental depth of the diamond eyed owl. A memory of Jada accumulated in my mind and then faded away like the ash of my cigarette which fell to the carpet. A mistake that I wasn't about to step on toes to fix.

Breaking the silence, "Is that real gold?" I exhumed, before ripping another puff.

He swiveled in his chair to face me, removing his eyewear that he preferred to have on while staring at his laptop screen. The hearing of the doctor now appearing to be in full effect.

"What the Owl?" he answered. "Yes, that's real gold. I won it in a card game, some of my old college buddies."

"You must have quite the poker face doctor. It makes me want to ask, what type of person gambles with something like that?" Your friend must not have been too happy to see that go. What would that even cost, something real like that?

"My wife and I knew a couple of professors in the archaeology program at Harvard. We would have them over our house once or twice a week for a friendly card game. My wife rather I commit carless consumption under her watchful supervision. She would worry about my drinking, then my driving and when I finally made it home the next morning, the amount of money I had spent. Understand, that just because we can do something, doesn't mean we should always do it. Easier said than done, I know. Especially, if you are a gambling man like me. It is a shame not to play the cards we were given. You win some, you lose some. Yet we all have a hand to play. It's the collective consciousness that won't allow us fail. Though, some more than others have a direct line and therefore, you are here taking a chance on me", summed up nicely by the doctor before one final confirmation. "In any case this person lost, and I won this beautiful golden owl. Moral of the story is, know your limit." Dr. Farrow made the universal drinking sign by folding his three middle fingers and then putting his thumb to his lips.

I lifted my head in acknowledgement at the same time Dr. Farrow reached into the same drawer the cigarettes were in, pulled out a glass ash tray and slid it to the edge of his desk.

"Ash into this instead of on the floor. Contrary to what you might believe the custodians do not enjoy cleaning up after you."

"Sorry", I said feeling slight unkempt shame.

I spotted a blonde hair woman mounted on the torso of an immense proportioned, thick neck, elongated face horse which was framed upon the desk. Is that a picture of your wife? I inquired.

"Yes, it is" he said now tilting the picture frame toward himself. After silently reminiscing for a moment he continued, "She used to love to ride horses around Europe's longest water way depository, the Tara River Canyon. This picture was taken in Montenegro. The fourteen-hour flight from Boston to Podgorica, Montenegro, with a stop in Bogota, beauty worthy of the experience, if you have the euros. If you ever get an opportunity you should travel. Early in the morning we would ride up the narrow riviera side eventually tying off old Whiskey and Jack for a scenic picnic and a little wine tasting. She called every horse she rode Jack or Jackie renamed after the soul singer Jackie Wilson. It was our first time on the trail alone without a guide, and the horses must have known that they could take advantage of some tourists wet behind the ears, because they flipped us both to the dirt soon as we were out of sight of the camp ground. "You Got Me Walking" by Jackie Wilson came to her mind and then it played more than a few times on our stereo. I on the other hand needed a drink after that."

Sentimental, he stared at the photo. "Ten years ago, today actually" it appeared to register. "She loved how inaccessible Montenegro was, Boston as well but Montenegro for considerably seclusive reasons. So much so she wanted to move from the US.

"Oh yeah and after the pandemic, is she enjoying the respectable prices, overcrowded beaches and mask littered Los Angeles streets?" The doctor pushed the bridge of his glasses closer to his face. "Change is inevitable, which makes it all relative my dear Samori" he remarked at my perplexed expression which also personified my witticism.

"You know from the Sherlock Holmes stories?" apparently Doctor Farrow was waiting for me to acknowledge his poor attempt to claim that "It's all elementary my dear Watson" the actual catch phrase that he insisted on butchering, and even that, I believe to be a member of Mandela effect. You know the one where everyone thought Nelson Mandela was dead because it was too terrifying to picture a black man alive with major influence?

"You don't know what I am talking about do you? After sherlock Holmes use to find a clue he would say it's all relative my dear." He paused. Your file says you like pop culture. It's probably before your time. Never mind, forget about it" he yielded. I got up, stubbed my cigarette in the ash tray and returned to the couch,

"Rest in Peace Nelson Mandela."

I was more so concerned on why he kept addressing his wife in the past tense. "You said that she used to love to ride horses. What, does she not love to ride horses anymore?" I questioned glancing over at the digital clock still an hour fast. Dr. Farrow insisted we move on.

"Here I am thinking I was going have to pry your mouth open to get you to speak to me but here you are with all the questions but how about we talk about you today and if everything goes well, I'll let you know a little more about me next time" he explained as I felt a lack of transparency in the room.

"She left me. It was a while ago and it's something that I am still currently dealing with."

"Please tell me that my psychiatrist is seeing a psychiatrist."

"No but that happens sometimes. Professionals who seek help from other professional is not uncommon." The faded tan line around his marriage finger made apparent he was not over her. Again, with attention to the laptop screen Dr. Farrow Pivoted the focus toward my issues,

"Now here it says you've had some recent trouble with the law"

I brutally cleared my throat, as Doctor Farrow's face was left unimpressed by the nasty sound I had made.

I interjected "Sorry, do you have cups for that water bubbler behind you?"

"They are in the cabinet to the right."

"Fantastic", I said as I sauntered over to the water bubbler, "You do know I get awfully thirsty right? That should be in my file as well", I said. In the cabinet I grabbed a three-ounce Dixie cup, drank a shot of water and then took one for the road, returning to my seat. As I sat back down, I saw that Dr. Farrow was about to start talking again so I took the shot of water and went straight back to the bubbler as to feature our sessions logistics. I disposed the cup into the trash and returned to the chair saved by my cap. With Impatient restraint in his eyes,

"You good?" said the doctor accepting my stillness as reciprocity before he returned to the file on his laptop.

"According to this it says you were cited and detained for refusing to wear a mask when entering a Home Depot back in September of 2020.

"I didn't refuse to wear one, I just didn't have one with me at the time and at that point I wasn't planning on going back home. I did not have the mask to buy a mask, so they kicked me out but not before having to hear what I thought about them first."

"After that, you were then arrested March 17th 2021, for breaking into a laundry mat in Chinatown."

"I like the fabric softener they use."

"In the middle of the night?"

"I don't know, should having a clean pair of drawers be prolonged?", I remarked as I reached for any excuse.

"My real question though, does either one of those two incidents have anything to do with your father's mysterious disappearance the night of March 20th, 2020? In which the police report states that you believed that your father was trapped inside the basement of the Tower Theater in downtown, LA. Your friend Jada Shepherd made a similar statement. Unfortunately, there was no evidence found by either you or law enforcement upon returning to the theater." A memory of Jada again popped into my head only lasting a few seconds. I said, "these cuties have no seeds in them." My mom thinks they must have some special additive which would explain the heavy promotion of cuties outside the fitness center.

"Do you feel that you are innocent Samori?"

"To tell you the truth, I can hardly remember but I know that I am innocent" I replied.

"Have you spoken to Jada since that night?" Dr. Farrow asked.

I shook my head no, "Her and her mom moved south a month later", I went on to explain. "The way I see it she aint have much choice."

"How about Mr. Burt, have you spoken to Mr. Burt about your father's disappearance?"

"Absolutely not!" I said with snap reaction. "And I don't care that much to tell you either. Me and Jada both told the cops what we saw. Now her and her mom moved to Georgia and I am here with a shrink. So how about you save us both sometime, prescribe me a couple Ferris Bueller's and I promise not to let life moves too quickly."

"That is not my job to prescribe medication and I am not here to make any assumptions or accusations, but it seems to me that your troubles started with the disappearance of your father. Can we agree upon that?"

I sat there in silence.

CHAPTER 3

"I don't know if I mentioned this earlier and if I haven't then I apologize, but everything you tell me today is confidential. It doesn't leave this room" he attempted to reassure.

"Yeah only till the cops need to put me away." What you think, to pass US government it wasn't mandatory to watch Law and Order episodes?"

"No, that's not true. I don't work for the police department. Besides, you already told the police what you believed happen to your father."

"Yeah well everyone has a motive. This includes you."

Doctor Farrow closed his laptop, removed his glasses and sat back in his chair. I won't speculate but he appeared to be contemplating the right words to use.

He opened, "Here me out."

"I believe you didn't have anything to do with your father's disappearance. I have not yet had the fortune of becoming a father and though this pains me to believe I may never father a child in this world, I have had the pleasure of being conceived by a black man. And I do understand the incomparable sacrifice a black man has to make in order to provide for his family and still be considered a man. This world has a lot of temptations in it. Has it yet crossed your mind that maybe your father needed a break? I mean just look how we were quarantined for the first half of 2020. Your mother was expecting a new baby. I can only imagine the stress that could cause a man. Is it just possible that your father had another lady friend he may have ran away with?"

"No. Insinuating that my father cheated on my mother is not going to get you any closer to finding out what happen? But I might think you arrogant if I did not know you were misinformed. My father would not do that to my mother, he adored the ground my mother walked on, since I have been alive. Besides his mother, he has only ever talked about one woman. He would not leave us without good reason."

He said, "Okay so you don't think all of these gorgeous women walking around is a good enough reason." he paused to glance at the laptop screen, "Well tell me this, do you think your father would constitute getting engaged as an act of love?"

I wasn't following.

"It makes me wonder what else you don't know about him, if you were uninformed that your father was engaged to a woman before he was engaged to your mother, back in 1995."

"That is really neat that you have all this information stored in your Hawkins like brain but yet I still have to surmise that I witnessed my father get abducted."

"Right, you mentioned that in the missing person report, that he was taken. In the same report it also mentions that you hit your head. So, should I assume that scar across your face is a new style the kids are wearing these days", he sarcastically pointed out. "Taken by what exactly?"

"I don't know exactly" I said in slow response. Opening his personal black book, Doctor Farrow attested,

"I'm going to need you to try and be more specific. How about even intimately concerned if you would like to resolve this matter."

"I DON'T KNOW!" I impatiently punctuated devoid of etiquette "I don't know what took him. A theater, a book, an old Oriental Janitor. What do you want me to lie to you and say that it doesn't sound completely crazy to even me? And if you think that I am doing myself any favors by not telling you exactly what happen that night, I might as well go next door to the press and tell them my fucked up story," I said as an empty threat. "Tell them how I called upon every God and any God to answer so as to return my father to me."

Witnessing my blood pressure lower "Then tell me what happen! Word for word," he continued.

Humbled by the thought, "Where would I even start? So much has happened in a year."

"How about from the beginning", Doctor Farrow said as he unwrapped a lozenge he popped into his mouth. "Do you know how one gets to Carnegie Hall?"

"I've heard this one before, my father would say "Practice."

"Wrong! To get to Carnegie Hall you need to be able to sing like Aretha. A lot of weird shit happens to people. It is nothing new, try me."

"It was my eye not my head," I examined gently with my hand, the slashing scar above my eyelid careful not to press, Too hard! "It comes and goes, and it comes in bits and pieces. I've been doing my best to deal with what all seems to be unreal but what I know for fact is very true.

"There are things that you will come to gradually understand" Doctor Farrow uttered slowly leaning forward in his chair as to gesture his point across to me. "And then there are some things you will realize with the right amount of effort," he said reclining his body weight back into the seat.

"And then there are things that you will never be able to comprehend" I said before the silence of my dwindling options.

"We have six more hours left of this session. If you'd rather talk about how better your life was before the pandemic, before it turned to shit. I am all ears. Or we can try and get something accomplished together. You need time to process this pain that runs deep inside you, I get it. Though it might benefit you to share it with me. This session is all about you."

I unapologetically rose from my seat to be standing there with intent. As I walked past the gold owl that rest atop the bookshelf, I found myself in front of the digital clock. I set back the clock from

10:06am to the correct time of 9:06am and I again walked back to my seat.

"Conscious not to miss the Adventures of Sherlock Holmes, my father with saw dust still on his jeans would race home from his full-time job as a carpenter, just to catch a half hour episode with me. My father and I have probably seen over a hundred episodes. Though it did not say much about relativity. I thought that was Einstein's thing. The theory that matter can be affected, moved, changed without being physically,

"touched by another object," the doctor took the words from me. "And you know physics, outstanding."

"last I checked Mr. Burt was going over Quantum Mechanics."

"You have a voracious appetite for knowledge, Sam."

"Special relativity, general relativity, makes no difference to me. If I learned anything from my father, it is that life goes on."

"A natural process whose conditions also need to be satisfied, sounds relative to me."

I surmised.

Dr. Farrow pulled open the curtain from behind his desk, that brought forth the morning sun. Like the force of gravity upon my shoulders, the sun's rays hit me with great intensity. The excruciating pressure that pierced the back of my eye just then reminded me how I had to borrow my father's sunglasses on our way to school one morning, forgetting to grab my Ray Bans out mother's car the night before. Not too bright.

CHAPTER 4

It was eleven Fridays from graduation. March 13th, 2020 before every parent got sick of their kid. Maybe a hint of ominous chatter in the air but I couldn't see anything to be so concerned about as what I thought to be a routine morning, my phones six am chimes alarmed my reflexes, just enough to have me reach over and press snooze. What never seems like a half an hour later but apparently always is, had my father ripping the covers from my lukewarm fossilized body, exposing me to the morning chill.

"Get Up, Samori!" my father demanded,

"Your breakfast is next to your computer" which was two slices of cinnamon raisin bread, toasted with butter. Between you and me, when I was not in fear of being ambushed by unmerited reprimand for not being an efficient eater, I quite enjoy it. And since my mother became pregnant, if I forwent the cinnamon raisin bread in the morning for whatever reason, when I returned home from school, I sometimes got another opportunity to experience the soggy bread, in the same spot my father left it. I was not complaining. My mother still asleep in bed on early maternity leave used the additional rest to make the most outstanding dinner for us and we all thanked her for it except now this designated my father to breakfast duties, O Fortuna.

"Do you mind." Moving a seat closer out from around the obstructing desk, notepad in hand. "I'll be a better help if I have something to refer back to, Doctor Farrow explained. "Now your father's name is Thomas Waters, and your mother is Eva Waters." He jotted.

"Yup."

"Okay, continue."

I dragged myself into the shower, and not until my hand wiped through the fog of procrastination, did I twenty minutes later hop out of the shower, Lord knows I was still half asleep while I brushed my teeth. Pulled up over my checkered boxer briefs was a pair of faded blue baggy jeans, which was a Friday favorite of mine, unintended right knee hole and all. Next was my brown leather belt, black "All eyes on me 2pac t shirt, which had the track list on the back, also my black champion hoody, socks and black boots. Anticipating my father downstairs getting ready to call up to me, off balance, I threw the strap to my backpack over my right shoulder. I grabbed my wallet, house keys, last I unplugged my phone which I somehow squeezed into the pocket of my jeans. Out the door into the early morning, I sunk into the passenger seat like the toast that I never savored. For a couple of weeks my father had been talking about an outbreak that started on the Asian continent, but I remember that morning the radio broadcasted in effect, a thirty day travel ban on all domestic and international flights in an effort to combat the global pandemic, apparently underway. Am I surprised I heard this? Yea, being that I was fading in and out of consciousness as we turned down Crenshaw in my father's 2019 maroon Jeep Cherokee. Once on to the 105 freeway, to avoid the blinding migraine I got from the naked sun, I asked if I could burrow my father's extra pair of sunglasses that he kept in the center consul. The short conversation, midway down the carpool lane helped me regain my focus, which most days, not until the highway came to an end next to the Los Angeles International Airport, did I come out from under the morning haze.

Most of the time when driving me to school my father would like the radio off but on Friday's he made an exception. It was rare that we agreed upon a station but every now and then there would be a song that we both liked. "You are listening to Los Angles number one radio station for RnB and Soul, 94.7 the Wave." I'm not the type of person who is going to pull their phone out to secretly video record their father bobbing his head to the beat like a fucking weirdo. I prefer just to enjoy the moment when my father slowly turns up the volume. That morning legendary rhythm and blues group Guy, blessed us with their 1980s New Jack swing hit "Let's Stay Together." With no shame, me on lead vocals, my father on the bass, we pulled up to my school in full concert mode.

"Hey Samori, don't forget I would like for you to help me once schools over." He said to me closing the passenger side door. My father was a carpenter so, I and wood were words from one of my earlier vocab lists.

University High in Santa Monica, California. I planned on excusing myself from Mr. Burt's fifth period AP Critical Theory class to meet up with Jada, who in secret I had been texting from under the top of my desk.

"Measured to certainty, we are forced to surrender to the belief, that a mathematical equation describing the nature of atoms could be proven in our relative time frame. American Theorist's such as Bohm have gone on to describe hidden variables possibly piloting our existence, insinuating that we should be content appreciating the immense discovery a world of atoms provides. Try telling that to a theorist though," Mr. Burt digressed. "The Discovery of Special Relativity; an inconclusive possibility of two particles interacting over a distance in space and time, as well Quantum Entanglement, although certainly imposing, does not bring us any closer to secrets of the ancient ones or a fourth dimension."

Mr. Burt's rendition on loose thinking was quite fascinating and I was kind of disappointed that this was the last week that he would be covering the topic. I guess if I missed it that much, I could refer to the top of my desk, which was vandalized by what I believed the fourth dimension to look like. Not to be confused with a collage of tiny penis's, artwork done during a different class period.

"Check out Charles Howard Hinton's *A New Era of Thought*" on the fourth dimension, *printed 1888*. It was inspired by Plato's *Allegory of a Cave*." Fascinating literature if you're interested" the Doctor recommended.

"Maybe I will have time to read up on the fourth dimension when I'm in jail. I'm sure their libraries have quite the diverse catalog of literature for such a diverse population.

"Let's get back to the story", Doctor Farrow redirecting. "You were telling me how you were texting Jada during Mr. Burt's lesson."

"Yeah like I said it was an interesting lesson, but Jada wanted me to leave class to meet her at the outside cafeteria. She had wanted to speak with me earlier in the school day, but there is not much time to talk in between bells. So, I replied to Jada's text and agreed to meet her in five minutes at the lunch table next to the boy's bathroom.

There was still ten minutes left of class, but I had asked Mr. Burt if I could visit the nurse on account of my almost made-up migraine and he willingly complied. Thanks Mom.

"Next week we will begin reading "The Jewel of the Seven Stars, 1903.", the last thing I heard Mr. Burt say before I walked out.

So, per usual Jada had been fashionably late.

"This is your best friend Jada Shepherd?"

Yes.

"Your friend Jada, he paused, can you elaborate more on the dynamic of your relationship?" he insisted. "For instance, why is she always late to your meetings?"

Jada would carry herself as if someone were always watching her. It always being one of two reasons. Either she wants it to be known that she moves at her own pace and no one has the right to tell her when or how she is to live her life. But the more than likely reason is that she got into some heated argument with one of her teachers, totally forgetting the concept of time, becoming too busy explaining her point of view. Especially this period when I know Jada can't stand her History of Music teacher, Mr. Shoemaker. While instructing us to listen to music he deems as quote "superior", he tends to belittle the music of today as uneducated nonsense. Jada don't even like

29

the mumble music that is put out now a day. Behind a larger motive to perpetuate lies to our community, she thinks it is a platform being wasted for minor material gain. But she would never let Mr. Shoemaker enjoy knowing this. And she makes a good point, I mean, I definitely have fun listening to certain present-day jams but then I remember I don't own a Ferrari or drive up a mansion in Malibu.

"From what your file says, Hip Hop has played a major impact on your life, but let's come back to that later. Anyways, you were telling me,"

"Yeah, like I said she ain't dig Mr. Shoemakers policies an all. She told me that one time, mistakenly, she was talking out loud to her friend Angie in the next row about how much they be charging for school lunch and how she wasn't poor enough to get free lunch but how she damn sure didn't have a dollar fifty every day for three cold chicken nuggets on lump of smooshed potatoes. She would say,

"And God help you if you forgot to grab your carton of milk and have to go back." What was a clear case of multi-tasking in her eyes, that being her ability to listen to a piece of music by French Impressionist Claude Debussy, while also talking to her friend in the next row was sometimes misconstrued as her wanting to be called out in front of the class by Mr. Shoemaker. "Pause the music please."

"Jada, I know you must be a person of sense because you apparently don't need the entire class period to understand this lesson, Do you? Mr. Shoemaker implied. You must be ready for the final exam then. So I'll tell you what, after you let me finish playing legendary composition *Reflets dans l'eau* I will let you describe for me, for a participation grade in class today, what images Claude Debussy was so patiently trying to evoke in you.

"It's like that?" Jada responded forthright.

"Just like that." Mr. Shoemaker replied.

"Press play" said Mr. Shoemaker, to a student sitting closest to the laptop which on the overhead projector, displayed a PowerPoint to go along with the music. "My eyes moving with each shift in tempo,

I leaned forward attentively with both elbows on top of the desk, I focused my attention on the digital sheet of music, out of the corner of my eye I could see Mr. Shoemaker watching me. I knew that Mr. Shoemaker only made this offer to get me to shut up long enough so that he could hear his music that he more than likely plays for his wife every night. What he really wants to know is if I have an ability to fully comprehend. Which is ironic, because the comprehension skills my peers and I are judged on, and are so easily categorize by, are so effective that they let me know, it is actually he who can't comprehend a damn thing about me. Still I listened to every word, every sound and watched every overhead movement like my life depended on it, but just my final grade was in question.

"Lights on" he requested, attention back on me. This piece of music having inspired many great composers, some as young as you, Jada. So, I ask again, what image was Claude Debussy attempting to evoke?"

"Well Mr. Shoemaker, I really enjoy Claude Debussy. Normally I like to listen to Reflets dan l'eau while using colorful pastels to depict light reflecting off water with each harmonic change in key. Otherwise, I am listening to the work of those great composers Debussy inspired such as Olivier Messiaen and his piece on Japanese bird sounds "*Sept haikai*" or my personal favorite, his five-movement piece about resurrecting the dead "*Et exspecto resurrectionem mortuorum.*" I am just saying, I rather not give you a subjective answer, over a complete objective one. I mean, since *Reflets dans l'eau* is the first of three set pieces in one impressionistic volume, which Debussy went on to name "Images"

"You looked that up."

"But if you really want to know what vibrant colors were evoked inside me, I will tell you. Then he wrote me out a pass to the nurse."

Naturally, I asked "You really told him that it evoked your menstrual cycle?",

"More or less. Well, I wasn't about to tell him that I looked it up on my phone. I don't even know why he is so surprised. Is that not what the internet is for, to make our teachers feel obsolete. Anyways it got me out of class.

My five eleven mostly legs towered over Jada's shoulder length braids, youthful smile and five-foot-five frame. They think they know, but they don't know her style. An inexpensive cool radiated from her brown sugar skin, like she had been here before. Meanwhile, her time cost no more than good conversation and no less than a loyal friendship. For me, Jada's almond eyes undressed her creative spirit even if her family could not afford to buy her designer clothes. Sometimes she dressed like a girly girl, mostly she had a tomboyish swag to her. She had on a copper colored blouse with black dress pants, an outfit she obviously borrowed from her mother's adult wardrobe for school that day, still never lacking confidence. Because nobody in the twelfth grade, I mean nobody could pull off hand me downs like how she could. As she approached, I saw that she saw I was walking away from the lunch table.

"And where were you going?" her voice with such charm.

"Presently, I'm pretending that I have somewhere to be."

"Bro Mr. Shoemaker is starting to catch on to the menstrual excuse." Wherefrom she confessed "Good thing it comes with cramps," never ceasing to divulge too much information.

"What, are you afraid that a vice principal will call your name over the walkie talkie? I swear Sam, sometimes you are such a scaredy cat."

"Well that is only because sometimes you are such a tardy", trying to think of an animal with a poor sense of time, I stammered for a second, before I came out with "fish."

"Nice one."

"If you really must know, I was walking to the nurse because I think I got stung in the neck."

"That's what's up! What are you going to do with the stinger?"

"Oh, I don't know I think I might leave it in as a fashion statement. What are you kidding me? I am going to get it removed from my neck."

"If you are not allergic just wait and I will take it out myself. Did you know they experiment with bee venom as to cure cancer?"

"Fantastic. I have become a lab rat."

"So, I take it you and Jada were close outside of school as well?"

"Yeah, you could say that our relationship was well balanced. Me usually screwing things up and then Jada there to come save my effort, from out of nowhere. And then sometimes she would say things out of frustration and I then would have to rationalize it for the both of us.

"Say things like?"

"Tell me why his name his Alexander Kyle if he is Hispanic?" Shouldn't he have a name like Hernandez or something.

I replied "Have you seen his house? "Have you seen the car his father drives?"

"Your right, I do remember seeing his father at the football game and he was quite the dapper fellow."

"Supposedly his dad is a member of the Owen River Valley Syndicate, a committee that manages the growth and development of aqueducts, effectively distributing the flow of water throughout Los Angeles. "Control the water and control the future of California", and for twenty-five million I could tell you which direction the money flows" my father would say.

"He probably has a baby mother in every area code," Jada added.

I added "His pimp game probably has a passport", finding amusement.

"Alexander Kyle", Doctor Farrow enunciated. Another friend to you and Jada?"

"Yes, I mean, kind of. You don't have to write that down though. He is that student whose name you might hear called over the loudspeaker, a minimum of three times a week, in trouble for something deliberately foolish. He is someone we hung out with, to be honest I don't exactly know why, because he always seemed to enjoy my last nerve bulging from the side of my neck. I guess I give people enough time to grow wings and fly away but I was mostly interested in who he was dating. Jada on the other hand, had more patients for him but even that sometimes wore thin. Like when they would compare men to woman,

"Women can do anything men can do, and more!" Jada acknowledged.

And Alex would respond "Everything except choosing at least one more sport to play. University needs a men's lacrosse team; you know Per Title IX."

I then would interject with something like "a woman capable of giving birth is amazing all on its own." No not really but that is what I should have said instead of "the only good advice Alex has ever given another human is when he told them not to wait up."

"I told him to muck off. If he plays lacrosse anything like he plays quarterback, the team wouldn't score a field goal all year." She had no heart for sports, only the muscle bound, no neck, gym, tan, and laundry ripping jocks.

"Of course not, apparently she is more interested in cigars. Do tell, how that came about."

"Well, it wasn't something she learnt from her father, a three-time felon who left Jada and her five-year old twin brothers to be raised by a single mother. Any picture that he was in was locked away in a closet somewhere, just like he was. Think of it as her way of coping with not having a male influence around. Instead of a new boyfriend every month like her mother, she could tell you that a Havana cigar today does not taste the same as it did pre-Castro because of the way it's grown in the shade. And how Romeo y Julieta are two brands

34

established in 1875 by a Spanish couple that produced the cigars on separate Islands or how it became quite popular when the company was acquired by Cubin nationalist Pepin Fernandez, who traveled through Europe and the Americas promoting the cigar on his horse, Julieta." She would say,

"I bet Alex is too pussy to even smoke a Toscano with me. He'll probably make some excuse like he has to stay in shape to throw a football."

"I've had one. They weren't as deadly as they smelled."

"The sale of the cigar in 1899 represented the end of the depression. A working man's cigar. It would signal the status of a countries economic upturn and would help to ease trade relations; it being a good representation of a free market." Doctor Farrow added. I wish I known this earlier, I would have stocked up on my favorite Dutch wrap.

"Impolite and against the law my ass. There were nurses who smoked too" Jada said rehashing the Victorian era.

"Were you and Jada ever intimate at any point?"

"You asking me if Jada and I ever" he interrupted before I finished.

"Had a casual dating relationship, it does not have to mean sex" he clarified.

"Nah, Nope, No, Uh-uh" I shook my head. It was clear from the beginning that we were to be just friends. Maybe at one time I had a crush on her but like I said, she didn't play sports, she played the jocks. After all, there was not an Olympian around who didn't want to feel her Mitus touch. Anyways, I've had my eye on this girl Lisa for a while now, the only problem was she was dating a poser and didn't know it yet.

"Now that I can clearly see you had no feelings for each other, lets discuss why leaving class early was so important."

"Well let's see, before you started patronizing me with questions. I was telling you that the whole point of me skipping class early, besides us trying to avoid the stampede, was also to hear what Jada had planned for tonight.

"The reason I wanted to talk to you Sam, is that I wanted to see what you had planned for tonight", She said a moment before the bell rang.

"Nothing fun. I just promised my dad, after school I would go to the store with him to get some supplies"

"Sounds like some serious supply gathering. I'm confused didn't you tell me that your mother is on early maternity leave?"

"My dad doesn't want her to leave the house, her being pregnant and there being a virus spreading."

"Oh, right the virus. Does your father think it will be that bad?"

"Whoever said to keep your friends close but your enemies closer must have been referring to my father in front of the T.V."

"Oh Damn" she replied. "Hopefully, it doesn't affect us too bad. I had my heart set on it being the first summer having the house to myself. My brothers were going to be at summer camp or sleeping over their stepdads house most nights, while my mom was going to be working evenings. I planned on twisting up some Flavor."

"Or instead, why don't you get a Job this summer or enroll in school."

"Because I'm not meant for college like you" she responded. "I'll end up going to night school for a couple years just to end up at a Job without benefits. Let me enjoy my last summer of freedom. Besides, I won't get to see your stupid face anymore when your off at Georgetown in the fall. By the way how did your father take the news when you told him that you chose Georgetown over Harvard?"

He always wants me to strive for the things that he wasn't able to accomplish in his life. It can be really annoying sometimes. I could tell that he was kind of disappointed, but he told me that it was a good school. Though, I know he had yet to see me as the primary advocate of my own life.

I believed him to be mixed up in the juvenile chaos on the total opposite side of the school at this time, but to some unforeseen logistics, Alex Kyle like the Neanderthal he is, open palm fire smacked the back of my neck into next Monday.

He opened with "What up Sam? I'm sorry, that was totally necessary" he found amusement in being taller than me. I found amusement knowing after high school that Alex Kyle was a person that I wouldn't have to hopefully deal with anymore. He would be going to some division one school on full scholarship for football, basketball, whatever, then graduate with a BA in criminal Justice and if I had to take a guess, go off to become a cop. If I played my cards right, Alex Kyle's ADD would be introduced to boredom this summer and while he left Los Angeles early for a new Brocial network, I could shoot my shot with his soon to be ex, Lisa.

"What up Jada? I heard about what happen in Mr. Shoemakers class. He can be a real douche sometimes. Anyways, did you relay the message to Sam, about tonight?"

"I was just about to" she said.

"I'm sorry. You now have my unsatiated attention, as I am curious to know how this involves the three of us walking to class together."

"Chill wit the brain", Alex Kyle gestured. "Isn't your favorite rapper Tupac?"

"Since 5th grade or whenever the first time I could comprehend my surroundings" I proclaimed.

"Oh, that's right I remember you use to wear all those Tupac shirts, right." As if he could not see I had on one right then. He deviated ever so annoyingly "I saw this really cool Tupac shirt, had him and Biggie standing back to back like on the covers of the Lethal Weapon movies." I almost bought it to", he said.

I'm not surprised, might as well wear Nipsey Hussle on a t-shirt next to Shitty Cuz.

"But I went with big pippin, H to the O to the," he digressed no cap, just now realizing he couldn't spell so well.

"You know who I mean, Jay Z muthaa fuckaa." Vulgar words he extended to try and play off his illiteracy.

The final class bell rang. Avoiding a polymath of stairs, we took the ramp up back inside the school building. Alex continued with a barrage of adept mischief, ripping down taped flyers as he walked by that students skipped class to put up. Flirting with any girl that he deemed worthy of his affection, with success I might add, and also making clear his presence in every doorway, of every class room with a high possibility there being a friend or teacher in them that he wanted to disturb.

"For God Sake will you tell him already!" Jada spoke up.

"You aint never lie sugar foot, my fault Sam." My hands in my pockets and my backpack leaned up against the locker. "Anyways what I wanted to tell you is that Rome's older brother Rashaad, you know the one who thinks he's Don P on chill. The one with all the chains?

"The one who DJ's on the weekends?" I had him clarify.

"Yea well, when he's not doing that, he's night custodian for the Old Tower Theatre off Broadway. He told me that in the basement of the theater, there is a monumentally fresh image, you know the album that says Exit Tupac, Enter Makaveli?" he said with an exasperating tone

"Makaveli tha Don Killuminati 7-day theory." I said moving the conversation along.

"Yeah, the cover with Tupac on the cross."

One of his brother's coworkers told him that the Death Row office would move from time to time and then when Death Row Records had gone bankrupt, I guess a lot of valuable items got lost in the mix. One being, a painting of the album cover sitting ambiguously, like the smile of Mona Lisa in the basement of the Tower Theater. My interest like the arch in my brow, piqued.

"Now this part is major. To forego the alarm and sneak away for a quick smoke break on the days my brother works, he'll leave the back door propped open and anybody that had information like this, could walk right in, no problem.

"Tonight, we are taking Rome's early graduation present, a raspberry red 2019 ford mustang to go check it out. Alex chuckled "You down? I know Jada's down, aint that right Jada?"

"Oh, what up Drip Dog?"

"Oh, what up Rome?"

"Sho nuff. Yo tell me why I was the last one to know that Denzel was blind at the end of *Book of Eli*. I am here thinking that he just like to read books in braille. Man, Denzel is such a good actor."

Rome's presence ventured into our circle of loitered souls pausing the discomfort for a moment while I waited for our conversation to be broken up soon, anyways. I heard a teacher on hallway duty just then declare "Get to Class or start walking toward the cafeteria!", that is where you went to get your full name written down as well as receive a late pass. None of us yielded to the threat.

"We on for tonight?"

Jada stepped in "Sam had told me earlier that his older cousin, the one who makes fake IDs was in town for the weekend and that they were going to check out a lounge or two." saving me from a critical response.

"Ask if she got an ID for me" Alex Kyle pushed.

Adding shade "That's it, ruin your scholarship" Jada remarked.

"You four!" The same teacher forcefully scolded from down the hall, "Get to class!"

"Congrats on the new ride," I said.

"Thanks" replied Rome. "Alex, Lisa, Jada, if you're down and I were going to take a ride later, first to get some food, then to see what is up with this Tupac painting. If you change your mind Sam, holla at one of us. They can miss me with the bullshit because I'm gone."

Hearing that Lisa was going to be with them as they went to see the Don Killuminati, while I had to help my father grocery shop, almost broke my heart.

"Im going Miss Crabtree, I just stopped to ask for directions." Alex said to a teacher I do not think went by the name, Miss Crabtree.

"I'm going to class Sam, I will call you later to see if anything changed", Jada said to me before saying to Alex "Why do I feel like somehow I'll be squished into a back seat", as they split.

Adding salt "Not true, I'll let you have the front seat while me and Lisa chill in the back," said Alex Kyle's fading voice.

I could hear the school television, which was fastened to the top corner of the Main office wall report "The United states is declaring a National Emergency in order to combat this global pandemic, or something of that nature" said the president. I then thought, Lisa need not fear, someone was always going to want to be around her, virus or no virus, that I knew.

"Excuse me. Young man. Go get yourself a tardy slip at the Cafeteria. I will walkie to let them know Tupac is on his way."

CHAPTER 5

Doctor Farrow was able to rest, not quite in the palm but in the webbing between the index finger and his thumb, the left side of his face, like that of an intellectual thinker, who before speaking to me, crossed his left leg over his right knee, prudently.

"A requirement for a first time author with a PhD is to study research already researched by such indelible minds as Psychoanalyst Harry Sullivan, who once wrote that psychological stress on the body can distort our perception of others solely based on the projected fantasies we have for them. It's somewhat of an immature defense mechanism."

"By the way, Congratulations." I said his face confused, "For your book being referenced in my theory class", I remember Mr. Burt saying

"Okay class have a good rest of the day. Hey, if you want some light reading for the weekend, Sam. Check out Doctor A.M. Farrow's book "You Might Not Agree with Everything I Say, but You Need People Like Me to Support Your Fucked Up Existence."

"A mere poetic line composition from my earlier work, that's all that is. Sadly, it's misquoted too often. I thank you for your recognition none the less", Doctor Farrow said with humble pretend.

"Yea" I said still not believing myself to be crazy, "well the next time you speak to Harry, let me know what he thought about 2020."

"He's dead." Doctor Farrow quickly responded.

"I guess there's our answer."

"The choices we make today are always going to determine who we are tomorrow, and considering it a sensitive matter; your mother almost in labor and your father wanting to take the necessary precautions to protect his family, you must have been in a state of great frustration to learn that your friends were planning to experience, an important figure in your life without you. Or tell me, were you able to seize on this obstacle as opportunity? Doctor Farrow investigated.

Needless to say, the conversation went nowhere. My father picked me up at 3 o'clock inside the gated back-parking lot of the University campus. He seemed a tad more anxious than usual, so I started with some small talk as he pulled out into two-way traffic.

"What is mom making for supper? I asked.

"I don't know, you didn't finish the breakfast I made for you this morning," dropping his gaze, as if I were really going to eat the cold piece of toast wrapped inside a grease-soaked paper towel resting above the cup holder.

"That's right, I remember turning the time back on my dad's digital car clock as well."

"Go ahead and change it", he said mostly focused on the road and the way they were talking about the virus on the radio."

I said, "When did you need my help?"

"Right now," he said. "I wanted to stop at the Lowes and the grocery store. Your mother wanted you to remind me not to forget food" for our dog Ace.

I was waiting for the right time to ask, "What time do you think we will be done?"

"I couldn't tell you. There are quite a few things we need, just to get by right now."

"Right. But maybe the two of us together, finish early."

"Cmon now, step up and say what you want to say. I raised you to speak with purpose."

"Well Jada heard that inside the Tower Theater there was a Don Killumnati painting in the basement." I only mentioned Jada because he wasn't that big a fan of Alex Kyle and he didn't know who Rome's cousin was. "She has a friend that works as a janitor in the theater and they said that if we wanted to come downtown to see it, it would be alright" for the most part I told my father everything.

"Jada heard what?" he rephrased in a question always making me have to repeat myself anyways.

Jada heard that inside the Tower Theater there was a one and million rare chance depiction of our favorite revolutionary, Tupac Amaru Shakur.

"Listen to me, Samori" he named dropped, I could tell setting me up for some Quasimodo speech. "Now's not a good time, haven't you been listening to the radio, there is a serious virus on the way about to change the world, and you want to go to downtown Los Angeles, the epicenter of disease?" I knew he meant it rhetorically.

"Mind the fact your mother is eight months pregnant. God help us if you were to bring something home."

"I have been listening, they said they are shutting down transportation and that the virus is like the flu." My plea, a falsetto coax, carried down the aisle of Lowes and then to the front of the checkout line of our local supermarket, where it was so easily discarded by my father.

"I will be incredibly careful, I said. "Don't you trust me?"

"Let it go Sam. And don't you have that same Tupac poster on your wall at home? Don Killuminati 7 day theory, was a 12 song masterpiece and the last Tupac album intended for release prior to September 13, 1996. You might have to be completely blind to say that there is not great mystery surrounding this album. "Going anywhere unnecessary is out of the question," He said.

Knowing how my father grew up, how he raised me to stand for something and to never be silent about the things that matter, it was difficult to imagine I would hear him use Tupac and unnecessary in same sentence.

Out of my frustration "What is Pac not that important to you anymore?"

"I really don't think you are hearing me Samori. This is not about whether I trust you or how important Tupac is to me."

"No, it was about purchasing a new first aid kit, a flashlight, double A batteries, a portable radio, 9-volt batteries, gloves, thermometer, vitamins, a manual can opener for the; canned beans, canned corn, can vegetables, soap and our fair square of shit paper, and bottled water as if the water in the tap wouldn't still be here a few months from now.

"Why this is a debate, I really don't even know. The answer is No."

"What am I not supposed to have a social life ever again, all because of some unseen threat that has that yet to affect anyone? How is this fair!" I complained.

Once again Doctor Farrow altered the placement of his legs to reestablished authority. He said, "Although wise considering the events that followed later in the week, your father's decision at the time was an apparent act of expediency in your eyes. A disagreement, one of which also brought you feelings of anger and disappointment. Him not wanting you to visit the Tupac mural, caused you to doubt his authority, which ultimately effected a future decision." He paused to catch his breath, "So, tell me where the hypocrisy lands in all this. What about your father's past relationship with Tupac, one that largely influenced you, were you having difficulty respecting?"

"First I'm going to need another cigarette" I said.

He pulled another cigarette out of the box handing it to me as he put the ash tray down on the arm rest. "Said like a true king Edward, and I quote *You may Smoke*, Again." A plume of smoke from my lit cigarette circulated the room.

"Let us just say that the parental guidance on Pac's albums never stopped my father from lacing my environment with his presence from an early age. He had the posters, I had the posters, he listened to his music, I listen to his music, no matter the song and no matter how intense the subject matter. He would say to my mother,

"It's something that he should know. The earlier the better." That's not to say plenty of other artists, based off their poor image, were not discriminated against in our household. But I'm pretty sure if my mom would have let him, he would have named me Tupac. Maybe not. I do know that there was no doubt in my father's mind that Tupac Amaru Shakur was one of a kind and at one point he meant the world to my father. On days, my father spoke about his childhood he would always need something dark and potent in a tall glass.

My father on the death of Tupac Shakur "I was about twenty round the time Pac was staying at the Luxor Hotel. Seems God made the world not to be enough for us two. But I think that's all I would like to speak on that matter."

In the eyes of my father, nobody knew better than Pac. He would say "he personified a love in the physical form, a miracle, a product of prism, a maleficent mirage to a half-hearted humanity, who's unconditional suffrage surmounts to a system of stars, and the ghost that swings in the dark, smelt pine oil separating, the constellation of a prince so palpable for his people upon return, and a possible lawsuit for the police department, all who perpetuate protocol. I really did appreciate every moment I spent listening to his spirit orchestrate a plot of all plots, he then say "and for the powers that be, I salute your plastic judgement, unprescribed of course and raise thy rose out from under the concrete into the sunshine of paradise. Who do you believe in? Hell, if I know, us waters we plead the fifth in the court of public opinion," next he would raise his glass.

"I remember, way back when being whatever I wanted to be depended on how good I could play pretend, POPULAR TO ME. Baptized in a wave of seawater from out the womb,

"What's the matter?" I said seeing my father's thoughts become distant.

I remember when I was younger my family took me to the beach and a freak wave took me under where I nearly drowned if it wasn't for my mother praying for me in mass every Sunday. Anyways that is when my faith fell silent following behind in the rear view of my mother's fire red Subaru hatchback. At one point I would ask my mother every single morning on our way to school if everything would be alright that day and of course she would say yes and of course everything turned out okay. I always made it to my after-school sports or back home to my afternoon cartoons. Inside my childhood nativity, a twenty-one-inch colored Hitachi television set, which I sat too close to influenced my cognitive development through; epic fantasies of mysticism, cartoons layered in sublime messaging, to framed black families with rebellious grooves extending into my adulthood, how things change. For years while I was away my mother would text me "I Love You." Every single day. I know it made her feel closer to me even though some days I would say it back to her, but my mind would be somewhere else.

"Cheers."

"I couldn't really care too much though. My world wouldn't let me. But Life Goes On is how I went about it. Just another day to make things right. Now picture me never wanting to break my mothers' heart. I had no choice but to grow up.

Then I had asked him if his friends growing up listened to Pac like he had.

"No not like me. Though I am sure they listened, like they would to whatever was hot in the streets at the time. All my friends really did was play basketball, so I played basketball you see. Being a student athlete, a purple knight, meant you did not have to try so hard to fit in. Yeah, I knew early on making the team each year, however likely would not propel me up the same ladder of success as it did basketball super elites, Kobe Bryant and Allen Iverson. I name these two because If you caught any of my games, you would have seen from the bench, me advertising a pair of their sneakers. The ladies might have noticed that I was a well composed baller, but the truth is, I knew how to face defeat with grace or maybe it was pride, any matter it's probably the reason why I was named captain my senior season. My status as an athlete spoke volumes to many bored conversationalists, wondering if I were thinking about attending college or if I cared whether I got a c+ grade or D- average. Do skip class and don't do homework, I should have said. That part was easy. After that, now all I had to do was tread water for the remainder of my high school career and hope for my SAT scores to get mixed in with the salutatorian's.

"Drinks were plentiful, but not cheap. I ate my dinner at an Irish catholic table, though I do not remember each meal, only that it was less important to the fact that I always had one. In a city always on the cusp of redemption, if you were not Hispanic and just Irish or even sometimes black, you were probably me. A half ass crook by way of sexual deposition. Depending on the time of day, the crowd, the way I wore my cap, could one bet on what side was about to walk around the paper city, and commit what they would say at each court hearing, and what they wrote on the affidavit as "disorderly conduct." An oxymoron used for a bender spent in the clink. Between the time it took for the verdict and the judge to dismiss my case but not before the bang of her gavel, did I find myself able to breathe again.

My father would say "Until you have children of your own, I do not expect you to understand what it is to have everlasting love in your world. The fears that once drove the younger you, aint the same anymore." Oh, and trust me, there is a hard way. I had to experience my fair share of growing pains, to say the least"

I was beaten up the police one Saturday afternoon. At the road race I found myself at the front of the food and beverage line, on a day I thought I was allowed to celebrate part of my heritage, instead I found myself in the midst of a love triangle gone awry, a petty drunken dispute I had no business being a part of, especially since I hadn't reached that level of inebriation yet. "Yeah that's the bastard" I heard one of the pigs say. I thought, "How did he know?" Before he closed the paddy wagon door in my face. I finally understood the proverb you are what you eat. While cuffed to a metal bar outside the holding cell, waiting to be processed into the system, I devised a plan, an old basketball injury which allowed me to dislocate and then reset the ulna in my wrist. Twenty minutes earlier I had just popped the urinary seal, but it's not like they cared whether I was able to hold back the flood doors or not. I was exhausted playing by these rules. I freed my arm that was cuffed to the pole with relatively painful ease. Now I just had to wait for the doors that only open from the outside, to open on the inside, in order to initiate my escape. Clang! Boom! The door screeched open to a plain clothed officer pushing the door as far as his scrawny arms could muster. I kept my head down as he pass only looking up to see his back. Here it was my chance, my mind already out the door, just waiting for my body to say, "fuck it." As the door closed slowly on my window of opportunity, "fuck it!" there I went, making a run for it. Out through the main doors. In the corner of my eye I could see the uniformed intake secretary, looking helpless with her nose pressed up against the glass. "Fuck outta here" I laughed. There was a park across from the station that I made an aggressive sprint towards. In this park there was, according to a fifth-grade field trip to the hall of records, one of oldest Merry Go Rounds in the country and at this moment happened to be fully functioning for a twelve-year old's birthday party. It was a Puerto Rican celebration! My skin was lighter, and I could blend in as a Dominican relative, so it should have been a smooth transition. I had just realized, syphoning in small breaths of air, that they made me lose my Memphis Grizzlies snap back, as I casually walked into the party.

"Hola, how are you?", I said before grabbing a potato chip from the glass bowl. "Too bad about the clowns, huh?" I said evidently touching on a fear.

"What Clowns!" the unsuspecting woman responded. "I'm sorry, who are you?" she then asked.

"Speak of the circus performers," I looked behind me and saw that the clowns had arrived.

"My child's the one going through your bags!" I said leaping over the guard rail on to the merry go round platform. The police were hot on my ass. I saw that most of the horses were straddled by children or both parent and child. So that's what I did. That very instant I became a parent to an unbeknownst child riding on a horse. I quite easily blended in as I came around the first turn. Jimmy, Jimmy, I could hear fading out as the horse went around for a second time. Jimmy, Jimmy I heard once more this time I noticed an Asian lady in panic mode as she pointed the police officer into my ever-fugitive direction. Assuming that this must be little Jimmy who was sitting on my lap unaware that I was playing the role of his father and him my son, I leaned forward to get a look at his face. Yup, I picked the only Asian boy at this party as my pretend son. Shit! I said jumping off the back of the horse, leaving Jimmy's mom to tell him the story when he gets older. While the cops were still trying to figure out how to stop the merry go round, I dipped low in between the horses to avoid further detection. I could see that a plain clothed officer jumped on to the merry go round as well. Thinking fast as the horse came around the bend. I attempted to pull off my best pole dancer impersonation now. I grabbed, with both hands, the iron pole that was impaling the horses' decor. Using all my upper body strength to perpendicularly hold myself up across the side of its body, I believed that I was hidden from view. But apparently they could see my feet because I overheard someone say "I can see his feet! He is hanging on the side of the horse" and that was in fact what I was doing. I let myself drop to find a new hiding spot, not knowing how long I could keep this going before I was shot. I reached one of the chariot chairs they built for lazy merry go round participation, to hide under. "Maybe they will give up" is what I said to myself. That's when a pigeon from hell descended from the collar beam and landed next to my face. Was this a sign? Well that was right before the merry go round came to a complete stop and Nine officers', guns drawn surrounded me, "Don't move scumbag!" one of them said. While I could hear and see the feet of parents and children exiting the merry go round. I realized I might have reached the end of this adventure. In a last stitch effort understanding that this was a predominately Irish city whom most of them also believed could play for the PGA tour in their spare time. I skeptically blurted out, what I believed to be the universal term for do over, "Mulligan!?" That night as I slept in my cell, I dreamt about different geometric water shapes, burning images projecting from my mind that quite possibly were based off the head trauma and boot imprints the cops symmetrically pressed into my face. Soon after I made up my mind, instead of a 4-year school like some of my friends, I decide to become a Damage Controlman in the United States Coast Guard. It gave me carpentry as a new occupation and allowed me a fresh start on the west coast. Some days I could coast by being part of the group and on others I barely made the boat, just the way I like it. In the end we all have the pleasure of seeing God by ourselves, so be careful who you follow Sam." He would say as his resting face had him always looking angry.

"And this must have been disappointing to find out that your father did not move to California because of Tupac, he moved to escape something from his past. Problems", Doctor Farrow added to my second halfway finished cigarette. "The ego is our imaginary childhood friend, one who notably conforms our Id, as natural acting boss in a chaotic society. It protects us from a world of criticism."

"Whatever. It didn't mean that he wasn't still interested in Tupac's life."

"You are going to learn that life's not about being fair, it's about staying on top of the curve. Besides your mom and I talked about having a movie night, just the three of us like we use to."

"You mean the four of us", I said correcting his error.

"You're right the four of us. I am going to have to get use to saying that. Anyways, you can make the popcorn."

CHAPTER 6

"Well son, we're all set" my father voiced feeling accomplished as we made are way through the Superior parking lot and I pushed the shopping cart full of supplies while my father rustled around in his pockets looking for his car keys. "listen I will let you work at the docks this week, make some extra money. This company from Asia wants me to do a job for them, we worked out a deal."

My dad mostly took on the housing and apartment contracts for the residents of southern California who decided to build a second floor on an already solid one story rather than move a market down. When something needed to be personalized to eschew the red tape, you called my dad. But my father never cut corners, he just was in business for himself. Sometimes he would let me help him with a project. Cleaning, cutting, sweeping mostly just learning the ins and outs probably because he was hoping I might want to follow in his footsteps one day. I didn't mind working with him sometimes. Hundred dollars for a couple hours of manual labor was better than sitting in a classroom, ten out of ten times. He makes sure to check with my mother before giving me any money and she is good at keeping track of my previously forgotten screwups.

"Aye what up king" a man confidently approached my father in front of our car. "Hey yo can I holla atchu for a second? At all possible my father gave everyman the opportunity to speak their mind. Of course, if it weren't a good idea my father wouldn't shy away from letting that be known as well. A stack of CDs incased inside white envelopes were in the man's left hand. "Hey man I got this album for sale, see I just got done doing a five-year prison sentence for a frame up and I'm out here trying to sell my story. "Your name is Sci-Fi Onjahbo?" My dad responded reading the envelope. "The name is Sci Fi guy, a nigga can't reach me 555, fuck a 5 to 9, I just did five in a five by five. There is more of that on this CD. What I am going to do for you though is let you keep the sleeve. It has my cover artists name and number on the inside, he paints living room walls as well, nurseries, everything custom for only Fifteen dollars or however much you can help me with g." The cover was what looked like a diamond with wheels driving through the streets of Medellin. My father was always willing to give, spare some change, lay down some advice if the opportunity came about. "Here is five dollars, as you can see, we just spent a good amount of money and this is what I have for you."

Thank you, brother. Here you can just have the CD, I aint trippin."

"I can't take your CD from you."

"Why not?"

"Because by you giving me this CD for less than what you were originally selling it for, your devaluing your word."

"We all have to start somewhere, as long as they are hearing my CD it will be cool. I got my Instagram account on the back. You can see at the bottom," he pointed.

"Brother, do you want people to just hear you or do you want them to listen to you? Because there is a difference. I could walk down the middle of Crenshaw right now screaming at the top of my voice, so that everyone could hear me within a twenty-foot radius, but that doesn't mean they are going to listen." We all hear. That is a function of human nature but to listen, that takes conscious action by the individual. Sci-fi Onjahbo investigated my direction,

"Do you know you got Larry Fishburne as your dad" he said.

"I think he prefers to go by Laurence" my father answered. And the one word my father truly disliked being called was "King" as he would often complain to my mother about being called that. "And please brother, I prefer not to be called king. I don't have say over anyone else in life but my own and my families, he said looking at me. Never give yourself completely to your people because they will eventually take advantage of your status, that's something Pac taught me. Also never compensate lies with more lies. Five million kings in America and not one piece of land to call our own.

And just like that "Ima pray for you brother" the man said on the way to a new business opportunity.

Doctor Farrow "It seems like your mother set your father's mind at ease. Sounds like you had a real loving family."

"That is what I was telling you earlier, he would never just leave us!"

Back up a bit "Is that all you got from Home Depot and the grocery store, some flashlights and some can goods?"

Lowes and No. I'm glad you asked because I almost forgot the; canned meats, canned juices, canned soup, garbage bags, 100 sheets of Premium Standard and Better Douglas Fir Lumber, that I still to this day do not know what my father planned on building. Oh and, we remembered dog food."

"Did your father ever tell you how him and your mother met?" the doctor requested.

"Well after my father left the coast guard, he found part time employment as a lead carpenter on the set of film and television production, mostly constructing small scenic props; doors to houses, drawbridges to castles, water towers, projects like that."

"It was called Crocodile Dundee lost in LA or something like that. Where I met your mother. I had developed the skill and the reputation of a reliable carpenter soon after leaving the Guard. At that time, everything in my life seemed to be going well. I had money in my pocket, a roof over my head, a good Job and then one fate filled day I ran into the woman I wanted to spend the rest of my life with. For this Job there was a scene where the actors were about to take a ride on like an Amazon themed rollercoaster, next to a waterfall, and different tropical animals were supposed to surprise the unsuspecting patrons. Earlier in the day I had constructed the outside of water tower that was to hang above the scene until the director or stage manager would press a button releasing the flow of water down on to the set. See anything that involved wood was under my jurisdiction. The mechanical aspect was discussed in segments, in part because the production team was always trying to meet a specific deadline, or they were worried about who flipped the ketchup bottle the wrong way. Birds have become quite the constant in my life, I must say. They said that the lever was too heavy for a bird to land on and release the mechanism holding back water. But they had not accounted for the lever, whose fulcrum pivoted from the middle of load and effort being struck by a bunch of birds ascending from the studio floor up into the ceiling like spirits playing me for a fool.

> "Can we get this shot people? The caterers don't get paid our overtime. For crying out loud, I walk around with a Fendi purse. They have families just like us, who are probably at home waiting for their dinner, while we continue to mess around!"

"Maybe we should get those birds out from above the set. That lever they keep landing on is all that is holding back an onslaught the water", I failed to coerce.

> "I appreciate your expertise opinion, Mr. carpenter", she said apparently reading my name tag, "but wasn't it your job to make sure the set is safe so no accidents like that happen? If you are not satisfied with your own work then I don't know what to tell you, you might be in the wrong profession and you'll possibly be hearing from my lawyer if I get so much as wet."

"I am not in charge of the lever.",

> And I can't stop my Pitbull of a lawyer from dragging me along when he sees something he wants to bite."

"Save me your thorns", I said walking to the back of production.

> "Jerry can we lose the anaconda. My third grader knows its

fake, I think a hunter of crocodiles would be able to spot the difference. What millennium are we about to be in?"

That was not your mother, your mother was the one standing next to Cruella Deville.

What your mother said was "We will not be standing next to anything electrical in this scene, if that helps any. If anything, I will make sure to push her out of the way before she gets wet." As the stage crew hurried her to the next shot.

Action!

"If that water tower opens then it will take down the whole set" I immediately got another crew member's attention. "What do you know, right on cue, these two white birds split from the flock smack dab up into the lever like geese flying into the engine of a Boeing 747. No time to say I told you so, I raced passed those not paying attention, watching the water engulf a thirty-foot wooden dinosaur. I saw your mother with her back turned to impending doom, so I threw myself completely at her. Literally, knocking her over as water and wood tumbled down, breaking across my back. Next thing I remember, I am waking up in a hospital bed to a beautiful long-haired brunette woman with arching brows to match her personality, gliding into the room with a tray of coffee. I sat up.

"If those are for my enema, you can forget about it!"

"I wouldn't worry too much; they'd have to remove a giant wooden T Rex first."

"How did the scene turn out?"

"Terrible" she said. They had to stop filming for two weeks. They ended up cutting the entire scene from the movie, probably for the better but,"

"Wait a minute, how long have I been in the hospital?"

"Two days. I'm just saying the whole incident really put a delay on the production, but as well I should be thanking you for sacrificing your body to protect mine. So, thank you."

She continued, "the doctors having been trying to get in contact with your family,"

"I don't have any relatives close by."

"I see that" she observed. "Do you need any money, Thomas?"

"Stop."

"I would just like to repay you something, for saving my life."

She hadn't look like she showered or retouched her makeup in a couple of hours, "did you sleep here?" I asked.

She said, "Just the Night." with me pausing a moment to absorb the genuine feeling.

"We're even" I continued. "You slept a night in this hospital looking at this stiff mug, as long as I am not being sued, were even."

"You're not getting sued; on the contrary they were talking about you being the guest of honor at a dinner party sometime."

"Probably at some big wigs fancy home with an indoor stream that leads to a pool that I lose my two-hundred-dollar shoe in, no thank you. Let me take you out to a nice Italian restaurant?"

"We can, but I just left a pretty serious relationship so, I am not looking to be romantically involved with anyone right now."

"Wow am I that ugly."

"No, I am just saying," she paused to partake in my awkward silence.

"I'm kidding. I always wanted to test out my acting skills on a professional actor. How about we pretend we're this power couple while truthfully we only want something to eat other than hospital chow?"

"Yea that will work." She laughed.

I said "Here I go" before attempting to remove myself from the hospital bed.

"Wait, not this second! You just woke up out of a coma. Let me call a nurse."

"Say I am a secret agent who needs to protect his Identity, who do I make out the reservation for?"

"You want to know my name?" I waited. "My name is Eva Venco."

"Venco. Is that petroleum?"

"No, I think it's Dutch."

"Then the rest was history. Eighteen years later."

"I no longer waited for love like the strings on a Spanish guitar. In fact, it was a couple years later the last time I waited for that same gorgeous woman to walk down an aisle of pink and red rose peddles, dusted ever so gently along a silk carpet that a select few of our guests, who were seated front and center could follow to the back where your mothers figure, wrapped in a tight white wedding gown waited for her father's arm to escort her casually down to my adamant unease. Where then the cameras captured the California sun, a yellow sky which bound our unconditional love." "Be with me forever" were the words that I heard her say. Sticking with tradition she ended up taking my father's last name, Waters. For whatever reason after my mother became pregnant with me, she felt comfortable enough to retire from acting, then decided to open her own bookstore. A hobby my father fully supported he said one day.

CHAPTER 7

Back at home which was a house that from the outside looked like every other house on the block as far as a single-story ranch with spear point window bars for security goes. Except the houses on our side of the street were up a little higher on account of an uneven topography, oh and my father, he built a second story on top of our single story which held up my bedroom where I lay my head every night." "My King" my mother said opening the front door to my father carrying a massive bag of food for Ace.

"Funny."

"First it was all 100 sheets of wood that I walked up the driveway, retrieving four or five at a time from the trunk of my father's jeep which was parked in the street. Instead It was my mother's car parked in the driveway that I had to maneuver around each time, dropping my arm full of wood off on the side of the shed. Finally, at the front steps to the inside of my house, no sooner does my dad open the front door to tell me that he appreciated my help "You were a big help Samori, thank you" and then to bring in the remaining grocery bags he neglected to remove from the backseat." His bad back correlated to this somehow.

"So, I take it your father also did some carpentry at home?" the doctor figured.

'Yes, in the back of the house inside a woodshed."

"Would you ever help him build things in the woodshed?"

"Build? No, not exactly build. But whenever I got myself in to trouble, he would use stacking and reorganizing wood as my punishment. Only if my mother somehow could not get me out of doing the task.

Now inside the doorway "Mom! What time is dinner? I yelled to the left of my father standing in the front hallway, not exactly knowing what part of the house my mother was in, but I guessed that she might be upstairs.

My father asked, "We are going to order a pizza, what do you want on it?", before he made a move for the living room television set disregarding my response.

"Well played, I thought as I headed into the well-lit kitchen looking for something to hold me over, while I waited for the pizza to be delivered.

My mother "Don't be eating Junk food before your dinner" creeping up behind me just as I opened the refrigerator door. "I ordered a pizza baby. How was school today?"

"Can I graduate already", I replied.

"Soon enough, and then you will be at college, and I am going to miss you like crazy." The root of the moisture might have been her pregnant hormones in full effect, but her eyes swelled as she said, "You'll always be my baby." Like the subtle thickness of her tiny expression, there was no hiding that my mother was indeed pregnant. My dad knew to use the word firm instead of fat. With her free time, she would mostly either paint pictures on an easel my father built or be in the bathroom giving herself a haircut. My dad would joke with her and say that she is one battle with the scissors away from looking like Pat Benatar. You could tell it did not bother him but honestly, you couldn't tell my mother anything when it came to her looks, unless you were looking for problems. I thought it brought out her face."

Switching up "Here's an apple, eat this for now" she tossed to me.

I could hear my father in the next room putting everyone on the television in check. Sound effects included."

"You know why American's love sports so much? Because we get to know the players. You cannot compete in this country if you do not know all the players of the game. "Take this assembly room for example;" "Starting off the 2020 economic crisis, we have the manager and connoisseur of McDonalds secret sauce, number forty-five, the President, someone get him a map please, of the United, States, of AMERICA!" "And leading off the recession, at the center of high tax and poor trade relations, put your wallets together for, Internal… Customs! Boo! Batting second for the private sector and playing the country against itself one race at a time, dating back to the ancient wall painting's, it's your fake friend, never the one and only, the… Media!" I suppose it was the smell of fermenting grapes that had my father standing in the middle of the hardwood with his piano playing fingers wrapped around a glass of red wine. It's funny because my father drinks red wine and my mother drinks one-part Alize and one-part crystal, when she is not pregnant of course. Thug passion, Tupac. If you do it right, you should have neon piss for a week my dad says. "Now batting third and crushing unsuspecting companies not willing to consolidate, we have Maritime…Merger! Of course, only under suspicious circumstances." I didn't know who half of these people were. "Batting clean-up, known for a buy low and sell low strategy, with a onetime, one point six five percent fee of the funded amount, as well, eight percent to property managers, two percent of which are African American but will soon change like the wind, we have… Real Estate! Finally, batting fifth designated in certain civil jurisdictions as Intellectual rights, still indivisible as well as confusing, number one, section eight-clause eight, let's give a big congressional welcome to INTel.. LEctual… Properties!"

I said, "Vin Skully must be turning in his grave."

"Don't get me started on the Dodgers. World Series Champs, Ha! Yeah, right. Maybe in a different world. One in which you wouldn't need to cheat to win." I took a major bite out of the apple as my father's head turned from the television to see me standing in the doorway.

I spewed out "Maybe you should speak with someone", along with small pieces of apple that had been obstructing my words. I could see my quips were not landing by the exhausted expression on his face, Therefore I decided to excuse myself to my bedroom to inform Jada that I wouldn't be Joining them tonight as well I had to remove my laundry from the dryer in an attempt to fold carefully on the edge of my bed. At times I was able to multi-task using my feet to catch the loose laundry about to hit my dusty floor.

"You did your own laundry?" Doctor Farrow asked sounding surprised.

Why, wait did you think my mom did it? Don't be so frigid to the times doctor, men are starting to pick up the slack" I promptly trolled.

"No of course not, I was just wondering if you did everyone's laundry?"

I started to do my own laundry when my father and I agreed that I should help out around the house, especially while my mother was pregnant and by taking some initiative when it came the upkeep of a few of my favorite spots in the house, he also believed it was helping to building my character, one sock at a time. The truth is, I wanted to do my own laundry because my clothes would smell like smoke. I did not need my parents to stress out over me and the last thing I wanted to hear before bed was some old angry adage.

"And your father? Where was he while you were burning the evidence, as they say."

My thoughts, he spent the hour working in the shed, standing next to the table saw caressing the wood like it had a soul. Or he was sitting with his sander, smoothing out the plain of wood before taking a hand saw to the pencil markings. "All Great things take time" words of a true craftsman. What I love about this skill, the trade of carpentry, is that when you fail, and we all fail from time to time, the wood will continue to be whatever we want it to be. To a certain respect, it's our dreams carved out to our own reality. A union of all matter. It also keeps me unafraid at night because I know that I could build a shelter for my family with thy own capable hands if worse came to worse. Maybe, possible remedy to a broken heart? Wherever the groove takes you" my father would finish, pun intended. "For a balance cut you should use an eighteen-inch tenant saw with a ten PPI, that's points per inch and a three fifth's cut."

"Let's fall back to the previous axiom," Dr. Farrow contrived. "You mentioned to your father that he should possibly speak with someone."

"Yeah but I was just trying to get under his skin, I never believed he needed to see a psychiatrist."

"It was a year before he joined the coast guard, when your father was engaged to another woman. Did you know that she got pregnant but lost it, stillbirth? The woman, without your father's considerable knowledge, decided to move to the middle east, Lebanon. Thomas Water's was ordered for a psychiatric evaluation as he became quite depressed and almost had a complete mental breakdown. Some reason or another these files where sealed and your dad was able to join the Coast Guard, no problem."

"So how are you able to have these files?"

"Once you go missing or get charged with a felony, federal employers with certain clearance are able to get access to your file. Though I have the power to access such information, I am only telling this to you because you are his son, and if someone was to have judgment over the matter it should be you" Doctor Farrow disclosed.

"I guess we all have a past" I said.

Doctor Farrow possibly empathetic "I would be remised not to mention that if I were to be glued to the television all day while this whole pandemic was going down, it would make me a little uneasy as well."

"I was only joking with my father", I said. "I get it, what he means, in times like these we need builders to build, painters to paint, writers need to write, singers need to sing, nurses need to heal because we are all in this watery descant together", I summed up no bullshit. "You read the newspaper right, does that mean you are losing your mind? I reversed the interrogation "So let's hear it, your psychosomatic analogy between television and the newspaper."

"Psychosomatic? Good one", Doctor Farrow emphasized. "To my understanding most people feel that reading is necessary to the fundamental human development, whereas television, not so much. Is this something your father might agree with?"

"Yes, he would. My father loves to read."

"What about you. Do you like to read?"

I mean, it's not so bad. I explained how "I probably wouldn't choose the book over the movie, but it has its benefits."

Besides furnishing a new hole in the house, in the den my father built was a carved-out entertainment stand, a coffee table, and a couple of wooden coasters that my mother painted. Later that night we gathered in front of the T.V. with my mom sitting firm pressed against my father and the remote in his hand. They sat at one end of the brown L shaped leather couch, while I sat at the other end. Ace loved to sprawl out on the shag rug while he'd wait for me to massage his back with my socks. And if he wasn't careful, he'd easily become my footrest for the night.

"You there? Yeah you Dog! Listen, do you own a Dog that barks incessantly at the wrong times and just won't listen when you tell him or her to stop right away? Does the doorbell give you anxiety, whenever it puts your dog into a panic? Are your doggy treats just not working like they use to? Then this Bark-Be-Gone is for you! Hi there, my name is Jordan white and I'm the inventor of the BARK-BE-GONE. A battery remote powered non-lethal sound that tells your dog that you mean business and enough is enough. Imagine having human ears like we all do and then having to listen to the copy machine chew out paper while you are forced to eat a tuna fish melt made on week old pumpernickel bread, for your thirty minute lunch break that started ten minutes ago. Sounds like a headache waiting to happen right, believe me I know. Well worry no more because the only disturbance that is going to be coming from your dog's copy machine is going to sound to him like neutered. Tell me, are you sick of your dog barking in at all the wrong times? Barking when the pizza guy comes to the door, barking when you and your partner are trying to eat at a fancy restaurant? Barking when you're trying to worship the almighty? Barking at the wrong race of people? Then BARK-BE-GONE is for you! Just press the bark kill switch on your remote and it will release a sound that will have your dog knowing when to shut the hell up in no time. Then all you have to worry about is, does my dog deserve to get my wife's leftovers tonight. We have a sense of humor over here at Barkquarters. It is policy. To make you and your dog friends forever! From the makers of Belt-Be-Gone, the pants where one waist size doesn't mean choosing a hernia over public embarrassment. Now bring you, The BARK-BE-GONE! retraining your dog for the quiet you know they deserve. Batteries sold separately."

"Ace is such a good dog. He did not need no BARK-BE-GONE. Anyways, the fireworks heard around the neighborhood worked just the same. Poor Ace, I tried to drown them out with a Tupac album. I listened to Pac every night during the pandemic, and if they had their window's open, so did my neighbors."

"Who's a good boy, you're a good boy, yes you are, you ate all those nasty mushrooms off my pizza for me, yes you did, oh yes you did" I said in my best dog voice as I rubbed his domesticated tummy.

"Honey that is the remote for the stereo, this is why the TVs not working," my mother communicated to my father as he was having a difficult time changing the channel.

"We obviously don't know how some things work around here" I said.

"Who said I didn't want to listen to music?

"Well then you need to point it at the Stereo", my mother added.

"Where's the television remote", he submitted.

"Have we checked the stereo yet?" I suggested.

"I don't know, why doesn't your smart ass go check."

That's my cue. From their angle they couldn't see the T.V. remote in fact on the stereo.

"That reminds me Hun, did you find out what time your sisters' plane is landing next Saturday?" My mother said to my father looking to check the batteries in the remote. My dad's half-sister was going to be staying with us.

"My sisters plane landing!" he questioned as both batteries dispersed from the remote to the carpet. "In Which state?"

My mother's sweetness displayed a glimpse of her white teeth I saw while she slapped my father across the chest in a you so dumb flirtation type of way.

Both batteries that my father dropped he picked up from the side of the couch and placed them back inside the remote and then altogether on to a small bureau, that I think he bought. "OH, that's right I forgot it was next Saturday", he knew how to save face.

Not fooled "You better have been joking, she is staying with us for a month," my mother said.

"A Month! my dad said shocked." Doesn't she know it's not safe to travel during a pandemic. At minimum, loud enough to hear himself, "Yeah, she does that's why she decided to stay locked down at my house" he accepted under his breath.

I had said "Auntie Sherri sure does make the best biscuits."

"Nobody asked you who makes the best biscuits and give me the remote."

The channel surfing was fun while it lasted as I passed the remote to my mother who then passed it to my father.

"Look at this commercial here. This is what they don't want our kids to see huh? Then why are you the only one showing us! I swear the Anti-Tobacco company and the Tobacco company are the same conglomerate" my father ranted.

"You two better get along when she gets here. The baby doesn't deserve to be stressed out over whether the bread goes in the refrigerator or it doesn't," my mother stated.

"If she likes soft bread, she can get a job at Sunbeam Bread Corporation. In the Waters household a $2.55 cent loaf of bread last longer in the fridge."

"I'll just give her some of my money if she wants to get her own loaf of bread."

"See there you go."

"Can someone tell me what we are going to watch?" I interjected. Robocop was on Starz.

"Parasite" my father said.

"ewhw, I like how you said parasite right there. That was sexy."

"You like that?" "Parasite." he whispered out loud.

"Should we go upstairs?"

He said "After." Identifying my presence in the room. Man, their humor made me uncomfortable.

"Can we focus on the movie?" I insisted.

"I don't know, can we?" my father said like a super villain about to reveal his master plan.

"Wait a minute. The movie is in another language!"

"Korean."

"This is a foreign film!"

"We got ourselves a real-life Sherlock Holmes babe."

"What's the matter Sam? You know how to read. My baby was Mrs. Gates 5th grade spelling champion, two months in a row" my mom proudly reiterated.

"That doesn't mean I want to read as I'm watching a movie. How am I supposed to read the subtitles and see their faces?"

"Then you better learn to speak Korean or Learn how to read faster. "Hey babe" he said to my mother, "How does someone make it to Carnegie hall?"

"Here we go again."

"Practice" she finished.

"Reading builds comprehension."

This was not my idea of a fun Friday night. A trip to the kitchen for another slice of pizza and two bathroom breaks later I was bored and wanted to go smoke a blunt in the backyard. After my fourth time looking into my father's direction, he finally realized I was no longer interested in staying in the same room as them."

"Fine go ahead and leave" my father said.

Drawing my mother's unconcerned attention away from the movie.

"Sam can you Save Seal the rest of the Pizza and put it in the refrigerator please?" My mother ordered.

"Yes", I replied to my mother.

At the kitchen counter I cracked open a Dutch and dropped the guts inside the steel swing top trash can. I could hear them talking in the next room "this just means we can save what we would spend for him to go to college. Take a nice vacation to Bora Bora like we always wanted to." I quickly broke up the weed into the leaf for fear that I might have been scammed, I guess the nuggets were just dense because it broke up nicely.

"Yeah I'm sure you will like it better when he is stuck at home with us until he is thirty."

A few licks later and I was good money.

"Your right. You are totally right we would be turning him into a Parasite" he said.

"Legalize it" I sang.

"Babyy."

"Parasite."

"It looks like we are alone but if you want to take me home you better make moan and groan." my mother sang,

"If you need it, need it, need it, it's right here" they sang a duet.

Ace was a good dog that knew who his true caretaker was. "Save some money by having another baby, yeah that makes sense" I said to Ace before leaving him inside as I walked out into the backyard.

CHAPTER 8

A moonlit starry nothing like the calm before the storm, for it illuminated a dark sky, the passing airplanes, and my solitude which I relished for the time being. It shouldn't take this much time to breathe in a pure thought. Ironically, it stopped there because I was about to inhale all the smoke that I could afford but first, I wanted to avoid my footsteps being detected by the lawn sensors. I walked to the corner edge of the half acre backyard before reaching in my pocket to take out a mini lighter. I made sure I was back toward the furthest corner of the yard before I Lit the blunt so that the smell would not miraculously reach the den where my parents were watching a movie. The tweed; long, skinny and brown I sparked with my Bic. I remember I happened to have a permanent black marker in my other pocket that I planned on using to deface some of the cement wall. Letting the next people to own this house know that some talentless jerks use to live here, and this is there warning to get out while they still can. But they will probably be jerks like us and add their name to the wall of shame. I said "I will depict my emotions with the laugh and cry faces. First a laugh in representation for my love of weed, then will be the frown of my youth" which I never got to as I was obstructed by the feeling that I was being watched. I looked up to see a black cat with its yellow eyes staring at me from perched atop the cement wall that separates us from our neighbors.

"Didn't I see you in the driveway two weeks ago?"

"Lucky Ace aint out here, he would make you his new play toy. Is there something that you would like to tell me?" I could make lemonade out of the dullest moments. "Oh, you wanna hit of this blunt don't you my feline friend? Well cmon sister or maybe you a brother, I don't really know how to tell but if you want to smoke you are going to have to move down from off that wall or even just move in general because your starting to creep me out." A moment after, the cat took off into the next yard as this one was becoming congested.

"Boy I know you're not smoking weed in my back yard right now!" my dad hollered from the sliding door.

Ok I wasnt.

"You don't have a job so I know you can't afford to buy weed" he sniffed out getting closer "yup, it's starting to smell more and more like punished for life. Give me that."

This was the first time that I ever passed the blunt and feared that I would not get it back.

"Don't you know there is a virus attacking the lungs?" he made it seem like he was ok with me living in fear for the rest of my life. Worst of all I knew him to be a hypocrite when it came to Mary Jane. "That's who he was engaged to" I said, pointing to the computer with the file. "That was the other woman in his life, and If I hinted in anyway about his obvious preexisting recreational affair, he denied her like a stepchild. In his case a stepsister."

"What is wrong with you boy?" he said waving his hand in my face, "Aw see the weed gave you a lobotomy, I knew It."

"I smoke weed because I'm dumb and I'm dumb because I smoke weed, it's a vicious cycle" I confessed walking back toward the house.

"Your slow because your mother sent you to the preschool where you only rode a tricycle all day, but I got something that can fix that. Oh, I got something for you." is the last thing I heard before I closed the screen door behind me. I remember thinking that I should have locked it.

My mother in her comfiest maternity apparel "Do you want some Ice cream baby?" she said standing with her back against the kitchen countertop holding a bowl of chocolate ice cream.

"No thank you." I kindly replied.

"Where is your father?" she inquired.

"He said he'll be inside in twenty minutes."

"In twenty minutes! I am going to have eaten both these bowls of ice cream. He's messing with his wood again, isn't he?"

I said "You nailed it mom. I am tired, I think I'll go to bed."

"Okay baby, Goodnight." she would say with such soft speech as if chimes followed her cadence.

"That's what I meant to do" she said viewing her cuticles. I walked upstairs to my room usually to look at some retro comic books withs tommy guns, treasure maps and group adventure on the cover, before I fell asleep of course.

"Apparently, your father's complaints were justified because things had spiraled out of our hands quite abruptly", Doctor Farrow said in a manner slow of speed. "Seems like there is always a price to pay. It may be why we value currency so much. When you hear the word suffering, do you picture yourself wanting to help others or do you think about getting back to your everyday normal routine?"

"Now? I think about my own mistakes more than anyone else's", I paused. "Consequence might not have taken such a toll on my world if I hadn't done what I did. You ask me when I hear the word suffering if I picture myself wanting to help others, but the truth is, when I hear the word suffering all I picture is myself."

As cynical as she was at times, like taking pleasure in some of her classmates not being able to walk across the stage or attend their prom, Jada's thoughtful and witty observations usually helped a population most in need of some support. I on the other hand was ready to finish out the school year and then try to enjoy my summer but that's not what happen. Schools closed, stores were bombarded with people panic purchasing, I took a quick glance at Doctor Farrow's clock, it read 11:30am when I concluded the thought with "Mandatory lockdowns in Los Angeles county took effect."

Friday, March 20th, 8:00am.

Sunlight peaked through my window refracting off the glass covered I-phone lying next to me. Projected on to the Makaveli seven-day theory poster I had taped to my wall, was a beam of light that called attention to the parental advisory sticker that cast over where a brutal puncture wound would have been. As I laid still, but wide awake, I thought "people can be so cruel sometimes", that's before I got up out the bed and moved on with my day.

Every now and then I caught my father looking at himself in his bedroom mirror, obsessing over a receding hairline which he believed to be prominent, like anyone besides my mother should care what he looks like. To me he had wild black hair like a member of Tears for Fears or even a Christmas tree farm, which he tended to push under a flat cap most days. You were more likely to notice his snub nose, dark eyebrows that invaded his cornucopia of pulsating forehead or his pirate like red and black beard depending on what light you saw him in. That's all before anyone is to notice the parts of his hair, that he enjoyed combing with his fingers, thinning to the point where it would be no longer able to hide his big ears. My father gave me a list of chores that he wanted me to do throughout the week. Clean the debris from around the tree; he said I should know what debris he was talking about. Take out the trash, hose down the back wall; he said I should know what wall he means. The stereo downstairs was playing Michael Jackson's *Thriller* while in the kitchen once in blue moon my father would dust off his red leather thriller jacket to try impress my mother, I think like for the forty fifth time.

"Babe, remember this Jacket!?" he proudly presented. "This reminds of the time, back in 2002 when we went downtown to the annual thriller parade and everyone chose me to play Michael Jackson."

"I don't think that's a question Hun. I remember almost getting into a fight with three dancers and you threating to take the jacket home with you if they didn't let you perform as Michael."

"It was tailored to my shoulder movement and I didn't need Frankenstein stretching it out. But yeah, that might explain the hostility I felt coming from some of those zombies."

"You mean ripping it."

"The man who sold it assured me it was genuine python skin."

"Babe, you're not walking around with snakeskin leather on."

"The Man in the fashion district who sells fake Stussy?" I made my presence in the room.

"Whatever" my dad reasoned. "Yeah, well, remember when I busted into that abandoned house to come save you though?"

"I remember you drinking too much, trying to take a leak outside of a residential building and almost getting arrested as a sex offender."

"So, we agree that I should probably tell the story?"

My mother, diverting her attention away from my father as she removed the silverware, the Tupperware, the tableware cutlery, and the good China from the dishwasher, before reorganizing the cupboard.

He said, "We had a good time though, right?"

"Yes, we did." She agreed. They would start dancing than my father would try to seduce my mother as would Fred Astaire do to Ginger Rodgers.

"Babe don't forget your sister's birthday is next week." My mother's mind always on the move as well. My father had it in for birthday's though, I don't know if it was simply because he hated the feeling of being surprised by an upcoming event or that it was just something else that had slipped his mind. In his defense he could complain with the best of them.

"How could I forget it seems like we celebrate it every year. Not only do I get to remember all the birthday beatings I took to the face, but I also get to feel like shit when I try to forget it. Trust me if she knew that, we would't need to buy her a gift this year. A matter of fact, it probably wouldn't hurt my pocket the least bit to be a little more upfront. What am I supposed to remember the birthday of every person that makes it into my phone? My mother never needed the last word to make her point because she would use the previous seventy-nine words to stick a spike through his heart, metaphorically speaking.

"You are not that funny" she said. "And no not everyone who makes it into Mr. Water's very special cell phone needs your attention on their birthday but your sister, yeah it would be nice if you took the time to wish her a happy birthday. If you would check the calendar that I fashioned so nicely on the wall behind you," which I saw also apparently took eight tacks to hold up. "What do think maybe at least once a month? Maybe then you wouldn't need to feel like shit Hun." Not that it was a big deal or anything like that, but my mother's unstable smile said enough to dead the issue this time around. My father looked back at the calendar and then again at my mother.

"That's why I love, I love, I love my little calendar girl." He would somehow always find the words, it was disgusting.

Doctor Farrow, shaking his head in acknowledgment of my knowledge "Fred Astaire, Ginger Rodgers" he repeated.

My father took a couple years of tap dancing. He could be a smooth criminal, too hot to handle when he wanted to be. I wished I hadn't of seen them kiss though. It was a prelude to my father giving me my biggest chore yet. He wanted me to stack all the wood next to the shed. A time when a please to get my way was traded in for a chance to just to kick it and the tiny sympathy that went in one ear and out the other of my mother's middle-aged bob, I was able to catch and save on the other side. I was down for something other than the Waters family motto of your father does this because he loves you.

"Good Morning Sweetheart," My mother greeted me.

"Your son is grounded by the way. He is not to leave the house and he is to complete everything on that sticky note. I am going to run a couple more errands, I will be home around nine. I want that wood stacked the way it says on that piece of paper.

"Don't look Hun but the garner is peaking at us through the window," my mom said. Of course, my dad turned to look.

The Gardner had his entire family standing on the patio staring at us through the sliding door.

Trippy.

"It's your mother, she's an extraordinary kisser, you should see how the birds behave."

I pleaded to my mother as my father went to see what the family wanted "This was not fair. What was he going to keep me locked up forever?"

Evoking the file he now had stored in his head, "Had your mother mention to you of your father's whereabouts earlier in the day?

"No not exactly", I answered.

"Do you know if your father even mentioned it to your mother?"

"I think I heard him say he needed to take the car in for an inspection or something like that."

Again, he wanted me to continue, "I feel like I'm on the public transit we keep stopping and starting."

Doing my best to procrastinate on the inside of the shed, I was going through some of my father's books. He had books on carpentry, books on birds, books on philosophy, books on the black struggle, books on what makes governments, Cd's on top of a boom box, books with guns, books about trees, I haven't found not one Hustler though. Must all be in storage. I do remember seeing what looked to be, if I know my numbers like I think I know my numbers, a billing statement for thirteen thousand four hundred and twenty-five dollars made out to Thomas Waters. The company's name started with a T. It was like Tet something. I thought it looked Japanese,

"They were definitely manufacturing something big if they were going to pay my father that type of money for a five-month job. I think they'd pay him in advance." The Garage Band ringtone I created specifically for Jada's call went off in my pocket.

"What up foo. How's quarantine life treating you?"

"Just great, my father the tyrant is doing his best to suppress my fun.

"That blows, my mom is making me help out as well. So much for my summer aspirations."

"Hey what did you think of the Don Killuminati, was it framed in gold?

"Oh, that's right I forgot you missed it! It was the greatest Pac Mural ever! Alex didn't even end up going, it was just Lisa, Rome and me."

"Bullshit. Why wouldn't you call me?"

"Psych" Jada confessed. "How would it look if I went to see Tupac without the biggest Pac aficionado?" she said playing with my emotions. "Why wouldn't you call me" she mockingly laughed. "Not like you would have showed out or anything like that, show her who the real Samori Waters is."

"Wait, so you guys didn't go?"

"Alex, Rome and Lisa went, I think. This weekend, I'm down to sneak away to check it out, if you want."

"My dad's not going to let me go downtown Jada. Not with this covid-19 virus getting worse."

"Are you supposed to just stay locked up forever?

"Not unless they want me to uphold teenage rebellion. He surely can't expect me to stay home and meditate like my mother, as she would try to convince me in doing so. For two months or for however long this thing lasts, I want him to know, by all means I'm going to make it as difficult as he is making it for me."

I read somewhere that like the kids are struggling to find a daily meal since the outbreak and if it weren't for these special lunch programs, some kids might not be able to eat food, which is so sad to me. I never would have thought I would be missing those two dollars and fifty-five cent lunches. I think I will volunteer to hand out food at one of the local middle schools. Why don't you help me Sam, it will get you out of the house and possibly keep you on your fathers' good side. As far as he is concerned, you're only expressing your front-line civic duties. Say seven Hail Mary's Sam and let's go do something.

"Yea I might be able to do that."

"Do you have gloves?"

"I think my dad does in the shed."

"Be ready at 6:30, dress respectably."

"Don't I always."

"I'll twist one before I pick you up."

I said, "I have to be back before nine."

"No problem," she said.

"Jada",

"Sam."

"Park on the next street over behind my house," I said.

"Cool ill text you when I am outside.

I didn't even know why I had to finish this today, if I'm going to be quarantined for the rest of my life. I said to myself, when my father gets home, I will be sure to let him know about all the changes going down. I put the wood down and went to my room to get ready. My mother had just started painting something new on her easel, so I knew she would be distracted.

CHAPTER 9

6:25pm, I unplugged my phone. I borrowed some of my father's protective gloves. I stuffed those in my back pocket, as well a small bag of chocolate cover raisin for when I got hungry. I climbed out my window and then crab walked the side of the roof, jumping down to the damp grass. I was careful to avoid the earth worms and blood suckers out at dusk. It was the same spot on the wall where I saw the black cat, where I used my right foot as a lever to push off the lower stone connected and intersecting with the larger part of horizontal wall. Then using my upper body, I pulled myself up and over, eventually falling back down on to my feet in my neighbor's backyard. Because of Jada's comment about how I normally dress, I decided to wear one of my better pair of sneakers. They were the ones where the outside got effortlessly dirty if you were to say walk across a neighbor's wet backyard at night. Since she has a tendency to make me wait, I timed it so that I would arrived on the next street one minute to the time she told me to be ready and if she wasn't there, I was just going to stand in the middle of the streetlight until someone called the cops. A moment later I didn't have to worry because I looked up the street to a crème colored 1998 Buick Regal with Gold BBs rims, that's the car Jada's mother drove. I removed the bag of chocolate covered raisins from my back pocket before I hopped in the passenger side closing the door behind me. I saw Jada had been wearing what looked not to be her mother's style, an emerald green Criss cross sundress shaped to her natural curves with a thin spaghetti strap a top her shoulders for support. Around her neck she had a relatively frail looking gold chain with a tiny heart shaped amulet that matched the color of her dress. Then on her wrist and on like six of her fingers what only I can describe other than that of several shiny pieces of Grey Poupon worn as polygonal decoration, was in all likelihood more gold Jada garnished below acrylic dark blue nail polish. I also noticed that she had on canvas slip-ons in funeral black.

"I didn't forget the gloves" I said.

"Gloves for what?" her face bewildered.

"Jada, you asked me If I wanted to help you pass out food to the middle school, and If I had gloves." Jada had good belly laugh,

"You thought I wanted you to pass out middle school lunches tonight? Friday night.", Again she laughed which for some reason made me laugh.

She had already pulled off "Yeah I did, because that's what you told me" I said with patience.

"I never said it was going to be tonight, fool. I do like the gloves, though" she silently rejoiced now.

"Are you serious. Then why am I even here?"

"I wanted to hang out with you, and you were having trouble overruling your commander and chief, so I gave you a little assist. You were talking like you were going to do something drastic anyways. Don't you feel like things are more under control now that they are out of your control?

"No not really", I said. "Unlike you, I have to deal with being in the same house as my father," to a moment of silence blanketing over us.

"Your right Sam, I shouldn't have assumed I was helping you out."

"I didn't mean it like that, Jada."

"I will bring you home then."

"No, I mean I'm here now. "I have to be back before 8 pm but what is it that you wanted us to do." I settled for the bag of delectable stomach sticking chocolate covered raisins.

"I thought you said 9?" she remembered.

"That was before I knew I was going to hell." I said trying to pour a handful of raisins into my hand unsuccessfully.

Jada watched as several brown duds fell in between her car seat. I had said, "You want some Candy?" pretending to be unaware of the mistake I made, "The names Jada and you need to relax" she said. "We're not going to hell. We are going to a house party in Lemert Park, tonight."

"Are you not hearing anything that I have been saying to you?" I wasn't dressed up for a party even though I suppose my acid wash long sleeve denim button up, black raiders hat and black dress pants would suffice. Not that you care what I was wearing I'm just saying, I had dressed for something different.

"Listen, it's probably going to be the last party we attend for a while. My mom says we are probably not going to graduate or even see some of our friends again." Then she hit me with it, "Tell me, when is the next time you are going to get a chance to see Lisa?"

I honestly believe Jada could sell mayonnaise to white a person, She did actually, she worked at the Grocery Outlet for two months before she quit after the store manager took up for a customer that said Jada had shorted him his change. Also, I believe that she could careless whether she saw another student from University after this year. I wouldn't say she was pessimistic, just that she takes pleasure in some of her peers pessimism, especially when she found out that a couple of her classmates who bragged about buying their cap and gown already, weren't going to walk across the stage after all. "Guess their parents are going have to decorate the back window of their SUV, class of 2020 followed by a question mark," I heard her say. And you don't want to get her started on prom.

"This is not even the way to Lemert park," I realized.

"I told you I was going to help out my mom and bring my grandmother her medication." At that point all I had to do was stare at her if I wanted to get her attention and when I eventually got it, that's when I chose to look elsewhere. Somewhere in Compton, we pulled up to a house with the front porch light on.

"You can just wait in the car and I'll tell my grandmother we are in a hurry"

"Whatever" I said as I listened to the radio broadcast announce that at "10pm tonight the state will issue mandatory lockdowns for all non-essential businesses and its residents."

Jada medication in hand, rang the doorbell. I saw the curtains move then I saw Grandma Coral poke her head out between them to see who was ringing her doorbell. Jada's Grandmother greeted her with a big hug as Jada was then shooed quickly into the house closing the door behind her.

As I sat alone in the car with only the radio to comfort me "This 94.7WBLM inside your night at the quiet storm taking your *Soul for Real* with "Your love is Calling Me" what is now nineteen minutes after 7 0clock thank you for your phone calls as we get you closer to your request and dedications. Phone lines are open to send the love and to let that special someone know that there is always a place where they belong, leave ya love note, dedications at 6449393 call me, coming up we will head through your storm with; *702's* "All We Got to Do is Get it Together", *SWV*, I Think You're Going to Like It", Then "You Know What's Up" by *Donnel Jones* and more of the selective, most seductive and most relaxing sounds of Bang! Jada knocked on the car window. Shit aint scare me though, I was just about to sit up anyways. I was on a dark street in a neighborhood that I didn't know but all I could think about is how my father was going to kill me once he found out that I was gone.

"Hey! She wants you to come inside for minute. You can say hello and then well go."

Sure, I haven't seen Grandma Jacobs in a while.

"You better not call her Grandma Jacobs, It's Grandma Coral!

I thought her first name was Jada like yours.

"It is but everyone calls her Grandma Coral."

"Isn't your mother's name Coral?" I asked confused.

"It is but for some reason my grandmother likes to be called Coral and fair warning, if you forget it she will be sure to let you know" Jada explained making a threatening gesture toward me.

He was shot on the 7th, died on the 13th the 7th day, 4:03pm, seven, at twenty-five years of age, seven.

"Whoah."

"Tupac."

"I said Whoah."

"Right. My father was listening to this album in the woodshed. I do not think he's listened to this album since I was."

"Let me guess, seven," she interrupted.

"I was going to say fifteen." Which at that point I said to the back of Jada's head with her box braids pinned to the right, which also covered a platinum gold hoop earring and on the left side of her head was decorative violet flower attached somehow behind her left ear. Outside of an older tan house I saw that a few of the flowers in Grandma Coral's flower bed matched the flower that was on Jada's head. I was surprised not to see bars on the windows out front. Grandma Coral in a floral house dress was standing under the porch light with the screen door partially opened, but not until she saw the whites of my eye was I welcomed by the smell of aromatic spices and Bengay that consumed my nostrils. But they did not hold a candle to Grandma's Coral's warm embrace, "It's so good to see you babies" she said before using the palm of her hand to secure her salt and pepper wig atop her head. "Such a kind face you have Sam", she seemed like she was still with the business. In a Claire Huxtable type of way. Earlier Jada had remined me that Grandma Coral was raised for the most part in the states but harnessed the ability to call upon her native afro Caribbean' islander dialect, Jada believed mostly used to make an impression while displaying ancient authority.

"Come in baby. What ya think dat yah could stop by wit out seeing Grandma Coral?"

Oh no, I didn't know you were home, and I thought Jada was just going to drop off....

"mmhhh save ya breath" grandma Coral insisted. Weh yuh ah seh, Sam? How ya parents?"

They're good, still krazy as ever.

"Hail up dem, yea?" I agreed. "And if you aint the prettiest ting walking around with Confed`once, ya here dat" she said to Jada, looking her up and down. "Skinny as a stick both ya, have ya two become valentines yet?"

Jada laughed, "We are just good friend's grandma."

"Nuff Love Pon your dream, girl" she said to Jada. "Nonsense, I see dey way you look pon each other."

"Grandma, you haven't seen both of us together since we were like fifteen." Jada explained.

"Oh, hush child, you cannot fool Grandma Coral. dhey be two things you should know about dis world sweetness, never cheat the man upstairs and don't you be too womanish baby, before mi tell your mama", she said squeezing Jada's cheek and leading us down a hallway into an outdated living room.

"Do you guys need any toilet papers at home?" she asked.

"No Grandma we just wanted to drop off your medication", Jada reminded her.

"Jus a word J, mi can get mi own damn medication. Mi don't know why your mother always has to struggle with ma. "Come n sit, I had just put some biscuits into the stove when I heard you were stopping by" Grandma Coral said pointing us to the direction of a floral crème colored sofa with its cushions whose softness was probably debatable back in the 60's. The whole scene was vintage to say the least.

"She worries about you Grandma,"

"Oh sweetness, mi luv you guys as well, mi do appreciate you helping Grandma Coral out but im not afraid of no virus. Mi ahrite baby. God will protect you, have faith. Mi just went to Bingo last week and all mi needed was mi canister of Lysol disinfectant and mi lucky marker.

"Yeah but you can still spread it Grandma."

I picked up a picture framed with Grandma Coral and her friends at bingo night.

"Oh to hell wit all dem, mi think they drinking mad here dat" Grandma Coral swatted. Small up dem heavens, couple dem ladies badmind, for attention yu dun knoa!"

It sounded serious so I put the picture frame down.

"Besides mi real bredrin are all dead, yu knoa."

"I thought I was your friend, Grandma?"

"Mi know, Mi sorry child. Grandma just hasn't taken mi stupid medication yet today. Mi should go do that now. By the way how is mi Buick treatin ya?

"I think it needs a detail but it's still working, praise to the most high" Jada turned her head slightly to see me handling a porcelain unicorn figurine that by its weight, felt to be fragile.

Grandma Coral said "Amen" clasping both her hands together. "Let me go take mi medication and then I'll be back in a minute with some wicked biscuits" she said with a smile before walking out of the living room.

"Ya hear that, I never had a wicked biscuit before. What she use like some secret Jamaican cinnamon or something?"

Please, they are regular black grandma biscuits if she was even in the mood to bake at all. If not you aint getting nutin but some Pillsbury dough, boy.

"I thought the buick was your mom's car" I said gently placing back where I found it, the porcelain figurine.

"No, it's my grandmothers' old car that she gave to me. My mom doesn't have a car" Jada explained.

"Oh" I said understanding it was probably time to stop prying. I picked up another picture of what appeared to be a 70's pimp next to a pink Cadillac.

"Who is this?" I asked.

"Oh, I think that was my grandfather who died before I was born."

"Wow your grandfather looks like a real boss playa."

"Here babies, here mi Grandma Coral famous biscuits" Grandma C said reentering the room. "Oh, you like dem Photograph dhere? That was mi late husband, Jada's grandpa Laurence J. Logan Aubrey Cornelius. Up to di time God take his soul he was mi love of mi life. He had lovely green eye like Sam" she said staring at me for an uncomfortable length of time. "He was a real go getter ya hear, he said mi no wait for no lottery to make me a wealthy man.

"He definitely had some style."

"dis was da coolest cat round. Everyone loved him, and he loved everyone. Especially a full woman cuz, he cheat on mi that bastard. That's why mi shoot him."

I put the picture down.

"Oh know baby mi no kill him, what mi leave was just a flesh wound. Two months later we got divorced and he ended up electrocuted at the job in 1996."

"Oh that's good I stammered. I mean that you didn't kill him, not that he got electrocuted" I said reaching for confidence.

"Not a day goes by mi don't think bout him."

Taking a bite of the biscuit I concluded that these were now the best biscuits I have ever tasted.

"Grandma Jacobs these are the best biscuits that I have ever had" I now relayed.

"Oh thenk yuh baby, Grandma loves to please"

"Grandma we really must be going now", Jada stood up and modeled for me the exit strategy, "I am supposed to have Sam home soon" Jada said now implicating me. Actually grandma, can I take these clear plastic cups?" Jada spotted sitting on the kitchen counter

"Yes baby and let mi give you something else before you leave," She said pulling out two pieces of cloth from out an old picture drawer. "These a couple masks mi made, now make sure you keep these on if you are going to be running around. Lord have mercy, mi womanly curse can feel di blood moon, which no pardon any further." Grandma Coral's superstition walking us to the door.

"Baby come here mi like to whisper words to you.

"Te Quiero Cojer" I didn't understand half the stuff she was saying to me and at this point nothing had changed but I made sure to smile.

"Ahrite mi children walk good mi love you" she quickly hurried along.

"What did it mean, what she whispered to you?" Dr. Farrow asked back in the room.

I don't know exactly what she said, I think it sounded Spanish.

"What did she say to you" asked Jada plastic cups in hand.

"I think something about me being a nice boy" I told her.

"Yea im sure that's what she said."

I put the mask grandma Coral made for me over my lips. "Do you think if we walk into the party like this anyone will talk to us again?", I asked Jada.

"Lisa wouldn't."

"We can't have that" I quickly remove the mask.

CHAPTER 10

Now 7:45pm, Down the dark Los Angeles streets; Rosecrans to Crenshaw, Crenshaw to Leimert Blvd, what I called black rain, was enough to put a calm to each major intersection that once contained a plethora of people. The transitory stench of a poor metropolitan being washed not of its past scars, of which engraved in cement leave those passing by to see clearly the stye of its creator but instead momentarily cleanse the community of its pride for it is with their glorious idea of prosperity that we still have yet to contrive anything worthy of our wallow. In fact, it was the fear that something other than a pragmatic return would possibly dictate my future. I thought "He was going to come home, find me gone then somehow show up outside the party to embarrass me."

"All the hardships our people go through in this country, we still somehow always struggle to survive," Jada unknowingly untangled my mood.

"Yea that's something to be proud of" I said. Not until we got to some Leimert park address did I remember that my mother who if she ever left her artistic meditation of a bubble, would most likely join in on the beating I had coming. I guess because of all the cars parked nearby the house that was having the party, we had to park around the corner, down on the next street over in front of a house she doubled back for.

"What's with the cups." I asked.

"I don't like arriving to a party empty handed."

"How considerate of you Jada, you must have some good friends inside this party you would like to appease. I asked "Anyways, whose house is this we are going to?" She paused for a moment, glancing into the direction of the white Subaru parked in a driveway. A Subaru that I had seen before,

"This is Alex's apartment? This is Alex's party?" I said exasperating my words.

Jada said, "I told you Lisa was going to be here." she paused to then clarify "It's Rome's house stupid" before closing the door to her Buick. "C'mon" Jada commanded, "I'm about to flood this party then we're out."

"All this temptation in one night" I slammed the passenger side door. I could tell the party was lit already because there were these two drunk girls sitting on a short stone wall at the end of the driveway, sharing a corner store taco in a gang neighborhood. "Ask him to take a shot with you, of something like tequila, make sure you drink it faster than him though and when you do or he can't finish the whole shot, make sure to insult him with emphasis on pronouns; we, us, our, sometimes even he, girl they eat that stuff up" I heard one of them say.

All around the world it's the same song was bumping out of the speakers to the uneven driveway we were slowly walking up,

"when we get inside how about you roll a blunt with your delicate fingers" she suggested.

"What happen to I'll twist one before I pick you up" I asked.

"I forgot to stop at the store. I texted George before we left grandma Coral's" she said.

George was the typical twelfth grade pot head, who more than likely had some type of wrap on hand. "You the one who gots the cigar cracking nails" I told Jada.

"Transference" Doctor Farrow pointed out before writing something down on to his notepad.

"No, I just didn't want to be the one doing all the work."

"Transference" he repeated. "Carl Jung stated that both you and Jada experience a variety of opposites but are still able to endure the tension without abandoning the capability of growth and transformation. That is more than you can say about our government's bipartisan dialogue", Doctor Farrow stated which I felt indirectly praised Jada and I's relationship. Doctor Farrow removed a shiny quarter from his pocket. "There are two sides to a coin, similar in the fact they are a part of the same coin but each with their own view of success, if you look close enough they are quite different in texture, symbol, as well, one side up" he said showing me the head side of the quarter "opposes the other side." Then two fingers to rotate the quarter to an upside-down bird. "I'm afraid most recently, in history, the side of the youth many times gets stepped over", Doctor Farrow said as I caught the quarter, he threw over to me.

"You got all that from her asking me to roll a blunt? And how do you know Karl Young from miss Ganders third period algebra? Does he come here also?" I asked hearing a needle confidently scratch across a record.

"There is a coffee machine at the end of the hallway" Dr. Farrow said adding a vice "Some say coffee goes good with a cigarette. Personally, I try not touch the caffeine too often, but in season a cup of green tea will do the trick."

What was this the nineteen twenties. I told him I wasn't thirsty.

"Okay then, continue."

"Well the party was packed because outside by the trash can, it started to become a destination for some party goers looking for a quiet place to chat about something sexual. Students gathered with nonstudents upstairs on the back porch which was also where the entrance to the real party was at, which was also being blocked off by the likes of Jack and Diane, kissing classmates who might have been better suited over in the corner somewhere. "It means im from the dirt, the nitty and I should be treated as such, respectfully." One juvenile said to another while displaying a bicep tattoo, that I fortunately could not make out. Inside the party the heat was wall to wall. I remember drifting across a room full of dirty dancers whom besides your popular sexually active couple, who prefers to simulate intercourse in a room of their peers, all else was just some good clean fun and weed smoke completely in synch with the positive vibes. At least for the moment I thought. Jada was a risk taker grabbing a beer that was left untended by two drunk juniors deep in conversation. On our way to the kitchen, Jada with her cups in hand had to curve a couple of drunk guys eager to dance with her. I can't say the same happens when I walk through a crowded party as far as drunk girls wanting to dance with me. I did run into a drunk guy willing to share a bowl of popcorn though. The party was kind of dope but without the masks. In the kitchen Jada spotted what I thought was her friend Angie Fox with a couple of her weekend girlfriends standing back while she was speaking with two boys that she apparently had been playing against each other to the amusement of the ladies.

"Look at this bitch" Jada said directing most of her attention toward Angie. "Pulling these boys strings like a puppet. She doesn't even like them that much, but I know they both really like her."

I passively responded, "What are you gunna do?" And that's when she said,

"I'll show you what I'm going to do."

Jada had walked across sticky kitchen tile to the group gathered by the refrigerator stopping only for a moment to glance at Angie whose face absorbed all of Jada's suspicious behavior, as well was witness to Jada's sensual hand grab the kids face like how a grandparent might do a grandchild's upper cheekbone, the face of one of the guys standing vulnerable without passion before Jada planted a kiss square on his lips for two maybe four long seconds. Then immediately walked away into the other room like there was nothing more to see except I observed for a moment both guys take their attention off of Angie, especially the one whom was in wanderlust after possibly experiencing a kiss that would of hurt the hearts of many contenders and the other guy who was now jealous he didn't receive a kiss. Last I saw Angie and her girlfriend's faces looking dusted and disgusted. "Bitch" is what I think I saw one of their mouth's echo. See you must get your two main species straight. First you have your traditional jaw dropper, the Quercus Pedunculata. And then you have your Quercus Sessiliflora. Pedunculata have sprawling wisdom, rough ends, and wide bottoms. I only have eyes for Pedunculata's, but Sessile's I give them a twenty out of ten. Now Sessile's are a little bit taller, more upright with smooth skin and roundish acorns that make up about fifteen percent of our class. You will have no problem singling them out if you pay attention. My father would say no matter what position life chooses to arrange for you to the start from, at the end of the day we are playing the same game. So lost Doctor Farrow just shook his head in agreement.

> In a room that was more friendly to the people who just wanted to sit and chill, I saw Jada sitting on a worn out sofa with a cigar wrap she found somewhere in the dimly lit smoking quarters that had the Tv on mute while subtitles rolled across the screen. I took myself over to where Jada was tweaking with mind control vibes so, I sat next to her. It then Dawned on me while standing under the door frame just watching; if men were from mars and women are from Venus, then Jada had enough juice to convince me she was from Jupiter. People like me will always remember the ones who move through life fast.

> "Relax his name is Shawn, he has been wanting to get with me." she said as I approached not judging.

>> "I wasn't even going to say anything except. You need me to do something?" I asked her. Which meant either to crack open the Dutch or to pull apart, into a fine row, small nuggets of weed.

> "Break the weed down" she said please.

> I then heard "what's goin on in here!", which I followed up to Alex walking into the room with a stemless shaped beaker

aka a bong, which meant that he was in the right room for that type of recreational function.

"Yo Sam, you missed it. It was crazy it affected me mind body and soul. The Tupac picture, has anyone else seen it?" he looked around as if he was wet behind the ears, as if he didn't already know "It was dope, Aint that right Rome?" Alex said with Rome now stepping into the picture.

"Hey what up Rome?" I said.

"Playa" he replied.

We were speaking kind of loud on account of the music. It was alright though because Alex could speak louder than two ten-inch woofers.

"I will show you some pictures once my phone is finished charging" Alex assured me. "Hey what up Jada?" Alex redirected his attention. "You want to smoke some bong?"

"Hey Alex, No." she said underscoring her intention, made apparent by a crack of the cigars outer casing. It was the momentum she carried with her from the kitchen that was getting harder and harder to keep up with, Jada being adept in subliminal sarcasm but that soon didn't matter once I spotted Lisa's symmetrical smile light up the other half of the smoke filled room. What could only occur in slow motion was the way Lisa gained the attention of her peers either through caring gestures or just her flat-out great sense of humor. I never got the sense she spoke for a self-seeking purpose and I really like that about her. The few conversations we had I could tell that she had a profoundly serious and determined side, however I also believe that could be incorrectly overlooked while she stood next to University high's class clown of 2020, Alex Kyle. I undoubtedly was attracted to her almond shaped eyes, the way she wore her bangs covering one side of her face, even the way she could burp louder than any of the eleventh-grade boys. What some might consider a lack of decorum from a girl pretty as Lisa, I on the other hand believed it just showed you how down to earth she was and able to relate to individuals outside her social circle. I didn't understand what see saw in Alex Kyle that she couldn't see in me. Who am I kidding, she was like a social butterfly and I preferred to carry myself under a radar of stereotypical teenage conformity but the one thing that I did not doubt was, that she knew what was best for Lisa. I myself had a specific list of my ten favorite things about Lisa that I'm sure nobody had time for.

"You wanna come to the store with us Sam and I'll show you them photo's" Alex said suspending my fantasy.

"Not really", I thought out loud.

"Aye George, this Dutch is way too stale. I can't roll up with this" Jada complained across the room. Alex placed the bong on to a short glass coffee table that sat above our feet "We were about to grab some more beer if you want, we can grab you a wrap, like a White owl?" Alex offered.

"A Dutch Master" Jada said looking to me for resolve.

"Fine, I will go with you guys" I surrendered. "But first I'll have to take a leak" I divulged if anyone cared.

"There is a bathroom out the other side of the kitchen, up the stairs and to the right. If that one is occupato then there is one off the back porch, down the stairs and on top of my neighbor's miscellaneous garden furniture," Rome, the orchestrator of this party advised. "My father's been going ape shit over the eye sore," he upheld.

"I think I'll try upstairs first." I said getting up from the over used couch to head toward the yellow kitchen. Up a short winding staircase which creaked all the way to the top floor, I had no intention of waiting in the dark with a full bladder. A soft chatter could be heard off in the distance probably coming from one of the three rooms with its door closed, a hint that whatever was going on up here, was separate from the rest of the party. The door to the right is where Rome said to try first which thankfully had no line in front of it though I did see a light on under the door. So, I knocked twice before attempting to turn the cubic zirconium doorknob, where I then listened on a higher plain of self-awareness.

"The nerve" I thought I heard whispered.

With damn near all my strength I began to bang on the door and then listen for what sounded like a female voice yell "What! Who is it?"

Starting to sweat, I kept my composure standing silent with my back against a wall and my eyes closed. I must have been praying for a miracle.

"The party's that lit it has people passed out standing up." I heard a female voice say as my head dropped and my eyes opened to Lisa standing in front of me. The smell of an ice cream cone on a summers day was to permeate in my sinuses while her euphoric aroma which was my third favorite thing about Lisa, after her personality and her style, immediately became then the second thing to almost have me prematurely soil myself.

"Oh no, im just patiently waiting here for the bathroom to become available" I said stammering to the truth.

"Right. Are you sure it's not because you had enough to drink?" she asked with an almost professional smile.

"Oh nah, I don't even drink like that. I am more of" I hesitated in fear I was revealing how much I tend ramble,

"Occasional smoker, me too" Lisa identified. "Im not Judging you, I planned on taking a couple of hits of the bong when I came back from the bathroom, speaking of that."

"Listen", I said resigning my efforts, "Maybe you'll have better luck, I'm just happy it finally stopped downpouring outside."

"Sam" she said with soft pouty eye's, "Us girls don't need luck when it comes to the bathroom", out from the back of her glistening brunette bun, Lisa pulled a bobby pin she then lengthened "Unless we can wear it somewhere on our body." I figuratively stepped back, figuratively. Then there was a scream from behind what I presumed was the bathroom door, which swung open a second later to both our surprise.

"What is it?" I asked.

"There is some pervert watching us from a tree outside the window" two overly terrified girls testified "Oh my god, my mom was right all men are animals! Lets get out of here Bri" one of the girls said, leading the even more petrified girl expeditiously down the stairs.

"I don't care he can look; I have to Pee Wee Herman" Lisa said stepping into the well-lit bathroom. I Thought, that was either the best or the worst idiom I had ever heard. "What am I thinking, you have been standing here waiting" she realized.

"You know what, how about I go downstairs and get that guy out of the tree, so you can relieve yourself in peace and while I'm down there I'll just find a bush, no problem" I said.

"Really Sam, thank you" Lisa said with an honest expression across her face and a hand on the door that she started to slowly close.

"Hey" I said stopping her from completely closing It. "Do you still have the same number?"

"Yes. Cinco, Cuatro, Tres" she said with a smile before closing the bathroom door.

Downstairs I had just missed the rain again not that it stopped a couple of horny freshmen in a tree from crashing the party, in the only way an immature preteen brain would think.

"Hey perverts" I yelled up. "That's a quick way to never get invited inside the party" I said examining an embarrassed look upon their faces before I saw up in the dark of nothing, the shining silver of a crescent moon waning the night sky, talking to me like it was alive. It was perfectly placed so that you couldn't miss it, if you happen to be standing there picking up its message like I was. What it said was that I got a condition? I got some relief knowing that it didn't look to be a blood moon which we were told to watch out for.

"Has Jada ever asked you what you see in Lisa?" Dr. Farrow said changing the subject.

"No not really only because I assume, she thinks I like Lisa for the same reasons that most guys in my grade like her, but Jada more than anyone should know how much I care about an intellectual connection."

CHAPTER 11

It was Rome and Alex that met me outside after I at last was able to relieve some of my built-up pressure out behind a piece of a broken palm tree. The three of us, like in some ghetto stand by me moment trekked through the dark street on a quest to the corner store for some further party essentials and a Dutch cigar that I told Jada I would grab for her. Alex made sure to remind us that this was gang territory if we hadn't already figured.

"Aint this a Blood neighborhood" Alex mentioned to Rome whose father was a Crip by birth but owned a tenement in a Blood neighborhood." Rome responded "Man, I go where I want. These people know me that's why I can walk around here without getting checked anytime I have to go to the store" Rome said stepping into the middle of the street to avoid a parked car, as us on the sidewalk attempted to avoid hidden puddles. "I can't speak for you guys though" he laughed.

"They know your father that's why you haven't been jacked yet", Alex Kyle said returning a laugh. "The only ones who know you around here are the Korean store owners." He continued as I now joined in on the laughter.

"He is Vietnamese, the store owner" Rome rectified. "Anyways my father says that bloods and Crips are predisposed to a warrior's mentality because of some ancient genetics passed down. Unfortunately, today we project ourselves under a white man's microscope."

Of course, Alex had to say something "Well my father thinks that if they had a goal other than just to have a goal, he could probably hire them," never sounding too pretentious. I always wonder how one gets to a powerful position such as a water chancellor. Like what type of cutthroat mindset does a person need to have to be able to classify everyday people as their potential competition. And what type of elite menace could spawn a brazen child the looks of Alex Kyle with his slick back hair and future entitlement. I remember I had to spit up phlegm on to the grass.

"What did you get Rogue-19 already?" Alex impertinent to the times asked me. "Don't be getting sick on us."

Rome responded, "My father drunk one night, told me that if I could help it, I should hold down my liquor so as not to regurgitate my own venom. That night he also recommended if I'm having trouble with evil spirits, I should try spitting."

"What you got some evil spirits around you Sam" Alex continued.

"I thought it was only rude to spit around females" I specified.

"I bet you spit around Jada. Don't you?" Alex investigated. "Seriously, how do you do it" he said, "hang out with one of the prettiest girls in our school every day and not be tempted to you know, get physical?"

"I think it's that what Jada and I find important to our dynamic, we both rather not complicate with an adolescent break-up."

"What are you saying, you think Lisa and I are going to break-up? That girl would follow me across the country If I wanted her to. Don't get me wrong college life is going to be an experience of its own wild creation, I just figured in the off season when I wasn't playing ball or whenever she had some time off from her studying, we would get back together because if you think about it, it is only four years of partying and then we are back in the real world thinking about marriage," Alex believed.

"See, me and Jada both don't even believe in marriage. She doesn't because her father was never around and for me, because I don't think

I'll ever be able to afford it." I said knowing that was not completely the truth.

"That's why I think you guys would make the perfect couple, even in your lack of faith your almost as cute as me and Lisa." Alex emitted "Check us out in front of the Tupac painting", he said swerving in front of me with his phone and some out of focus photographs. "This one is not bad except Rome totally left out the whole left side of Lisa's body," Alex pointed out.

Rome then said "I think you would really like it Sam."

I thought at least now I know the Tupac theater thing was not some preposterous ploy to embarrass me somehow.

"Yup that's the one" Rome now back next to us on the sidewalk examined. "Tell me something, do you wonder what 2Pac was feeling knowing that he was going back to jail after they jumped that other guy in the casino? Probably the worst place to attack another person if you were thinking to get away, because all the cameras and such. Of course, that is if he wasn't shot and killed later that night" Rome looked my way with revelation.

"Tell me why?" I said as we all got right.

"Unless he wanted us to see him on camera," Alex got there.

There was no escaping the direction we headed a doomed lit parking lot of shadows. From the back of the building you could hear the clanking of bottles as well wet footsteps around the side to the front, we were alright I said to myself but this time it was different, it felt different. We were not alone.

"My brother just got fired but you still would be able to sneak in on Monday, Friday or Sunday when the church parish meets with coffee and pamphlets. It's in a room on the bottom floor." A stout almost toothless man with a gang of scratchers came out the convenience store speaking some type of ghetto scripture "Don't trust these white devils! You ever type I am able in a word document and see it tries to have you change able to can? Can and Able, Able and Kane. The devil is always at work!" As the three of us continued into the store which seemed to have a brand-new light bulb under each ceiling panel. Rome continued with some directions "It's two rights, then two lefts.

"That sounds simple enough" I determined.

"Then another right and then one more left," he said next to the fifty cent potato chips.

"Is it even in the same building anymore?" I joked.

"Hang chill bro."

"It's an Illusion! It was to the right! Now it's to Left! Two men were there, then one disappears." Alex made some inappropriate joke. We headed through the middle Isle to the back of the freezer section where they kept the beer. "Wait a minute, which one of us is 21?" I panicked for second.

"Don't worry, don't worry." Rome pulled out a little rectangle piece of laminated plastic "Rome is twenty-one" Alex said trying to wink at me without hurting himself, "See his ID."

"I see you'll never be a professional wrestler" I made note of. "Yeah but what if they try to card all of us? Everyone always says I look like I am five years younger than my actual age. I look Thirteen. Really?" I said suspicious of everyone.

"Relax they don't do that over here. Aint that right Rome?"

"It never stopped me before," he said.

We walked back up to the front of the store with some Sweet potato chips, a case of cheap beer and Alex I think had a grape freeze pop in his hand while we waited behind one other person ahead of us in line.

"So, when are you and Jada going to be official?" Alex said relentless. "Can you at least admit to me that you and Jada are boyfriend and girlfriend? So, we know what to call you if someone asks."

"Why, would that make you feel better?" I said looking down at the cash fidgeting in my hand with the thought that would never happen because I planned on stealing Lisa from him.

"Yes, I think it would" Alex alluded. "Next" the Asian store clerk hurried us. Rome stepped to the counter with his beer, cash and fake ID. Alex placed the freeze pop on top of the case of beer then stepped aside with his back to the entrance still questioning me on my relationship with Jada

"Lisa thinks you guys look cute. She bet's you guys end up together, though I don't know why Jada would choose you over someone like me" he smiled.

"Next" the Asian man promptly repeated.

I stepped up. "Let me get a pack of the Berry Dutch Masters" I said.

"You see that dress she had on, I might still make my move if that's the case" Alex looked in the direction of Rome.

"Last one" the clerk said as I thought I don't know why they always do that, say last one like I care how well their business was doing.

"Do you have ID." The clerk asked me with the tobacco product already secured in my hand.

Stone faced I turned to look back into the direction of Alex. That's when I caught entering the store with dark hoodies and with someone is about to get pistol whip face masks on, these two men who had nothing better to do than to craft a couple homemade masks that covered their faces up to the bridge of the nose. One of them was brandishing a pistol.

"Give me all the money in the cash drawer" the guy with the gun demanded. "You have to buy" the clerk said. "You better open this register right fucking now or your family will be the ones pressing button to the incinerator, when they cremate you!" he pointed a very big gun at the man's head. "Hurry up! or I promise you you're not going home" the guy with a gun told the clerk becoming more and more impatient. The other guy ran down one of the isles to the back of the store. Panic in his delivery "Okay, okay" the middle age Vietnamese man said. "Don't shoot," the clerk who would have been up to the robbers elbow if he were to come around the counter, instead he nervously pressed on the keys of the register seeming not to remember how it worked. All three of us were sitting tight, still in the middle of the commotion. Except Alex and Rome were the only ones actually sitting, I was stuck standing with my back up against some of the stores most popular snacks thinking that it might be better if I don't move so much.

"Don't make me hurt you, old man" the masked robber said waving the barrel of his pistol loosely intimidating more than just the clerk. "Give me a couple packs of the Berry Dutch Master's also." I had the last pack squeezed into the palm of my hand that I had yet to pay for when all this occurred.

"We have no more Berry!" the clerk screamed back at the masked robber.

"Why did you stop? Nobody said you could stop. Open the drawer and give me the cash. Now! Guyaka! The Other masked robber was back at the front the store with two cases of beer waiting for his partner to get the money so that they could be out before the cops showed up. The store clerk finally had pressed the correct button releasing mostly small bills to the sound of the robber's apparent dismay. "What is this?" he protested. The clerk said, "just take it and go!" as he handed over a wad of cash and a couple in stock cigarillos. "I should come around the counter and whoop your ass, do you a favor. For this." he said holding up an insufficient amount of cash evidently, "but I'm not feeling generous, so I aint gunna do you that favor." As right then the two masked men raced for the exit, I could feel my anxiety retreat for a moment believing that the worst was over. That was until I realized the ringing in both of my ears and the smoke that floated past by my peripheral could be traced back to an even larger gun in the hand of the clerk.

Bang! The clerk shot again, I ducked frightened not fully aware yet of what was happening.

"He shot em!" is what Alex yelled as I turned from the counter to observe the convenience door now propped open by the motionless body of one of the masked men.

I can't remember the exact words I used but it was probably something like HOLY SMOKE! Before I again glanced into the direction of the oriental store clerk still brandishing his own weapon. Just then out from behind the shelves, I don't know how I could have missed him when we first arrived because he was an extraordinarily colossal black man who could have possibly been between seven-five and eight-feet tall, no exaggeration. He walked up to the counter like a bulldozer with feet and then with his gigantic left hand he grabbed the clerks gun crushing the oriental man's trigger finger in the process and with his enormous right palm he reached over the counter to pick up the man by his neck.

"Ahhhh!" the clerk screamed.

Before the gun dropped to the floor me, Alex and Rome were out the door. I soon followed behind using the door that wasn't held open by the man shot in the back of the head, who I now saw from a part of his mask that came undone, was in fact a black man. None of us stopped to make a statement as the three of us on our way back to the party avoided the small crowd that started to gather in the parking lot.

I don't remember any of us saying another word to each other as we arrived back to the apartment. I could see five or six cop cars with their flashing lights and ten or eleven officers, making their way into the party. We must have split up from there because I ran along the side of the house on to the back porch and up the stairs that led to a door which also led into the kitchen. I saw that there were quite a few people still in the party, and there was Jada still on the couch waiting to roll her weed. That very same moment from one room to the next I saw men in blue enter the party uninvited.

"Who Lives Here" I heard one of them demand to know.

"We gotta go" I said before grabbing Jada's hand lifting her off the couch to her displeasure."

"Wait, why are you pulling me?" she detested.

"No time" I said leading us back through the kitchen just as the music came to a complete stop. Over one of the police walkies, I heard a response call for a two eleven and a possible one eighty-seven with immediate police presence to the corner store that we had just left. Jada and I snuck out the back door, somehow avoiding all the chaos before making it to the same street over by where we last parked the car.

"What the hell is going on" she asked confused.

"Are you good to drive?" I asked insinuating that we should pull off.

CHAPTER 12

It was around 8:45 when we headed down Slauson in Jada's Buick, as the black sky brood a howling wind and a heavy kind of rain fell to a bone chill in front of a malfunctioning car heater.

"What did you see?" Jada asked looking over in my direction every other second her eyes were not on the road. "Sam tell me."

The unease of rueful images replayed as I sat quiet, Jada still looking over at me for an answer that I was having a difficult time to translate. Why was I subjected to such a horrible turn of events I thought to myself? Of all the beauty in this world, why is it that ugliness has longer lasting ramifications.

"Can you bring me home?" I said with my face forward making no eye contact.

"Sam" she said sounding concerned.

"I rather not talk about it right now. It's better probably that you don't know, you won't want to know."

"Did someone get hurt?"

"Yea, someone we don't know" I hoped but still made no difference. I remember Jada telling me that I stink "Why do you smell like smoke?" she asked me.

"Oh yeah that's right," I rehashed what Doctor Farrow asked me earlier. "Remember when you were surprised that I smoked cigarettes, and you wanted to know where I first picked up the habit? Well it started that night." While letting me hold his phone to see the Tupac pictures, Alex took out a pack of Newport menthol cigarettes from his pocket. He slid one to the top of the box so that it was sticking out but not before packing the nicotine using his outside thigh.

"You smoke?" he asked me.

Before I got a chance to decide,

"Sure, you do" he answered. "What would Tupac do?" he said handing me a cigarette.

"Not fold under peer pressure" I said taking the cigarette from Alex's hand. I had told Jada that I smoked a cigarette right before the store got robbed.

"You scared me Sam. You could have sent me a text" she said.

I said "We raced out of there as quick as we could, before somehow our skin color implicated us to a crime and then I saw the cops at the house, so I knew then I had to go get you and get us the hell out of there as fast as possible."

"Freak!" Jada suddenly announced.

"What is it" I said.

"I feel it's better that I keep the details to myself' she said. "It's probably better that you don't know," Jada mocked.

> I know it annoyed her me not telling her every gruesome detail, but Jada had no direct line to my troubles even though the color I saw leaving my face in the visor mirror said a lot. The best I could do for her at that point was put a damper on her night, if I told her exactly what went down. Just another sad story perpetuated by its victims, thankful to have survived a night in South Central Los Angeles while some mother is out there missing her child right now, I shook my head. "This is just the type of thing that would also get back to my father", but I tried to let it go.

Pen placed inside the pad Doctor Farrow paused the session to check on me,

"You okay?"

"This is the first I talked about it."

"How do you feel?" he asked.

"I feel a bit lighter, as far as weight on the conscious goes. I'm just surprised at how clear my recollection of that night has been thus far."

"What did I say, once you get the juices flowing it'll come back to you." Doctor Farrow opened back up his notepad, "let's continue."

And just like that "What were we last discussing?" I asked unfettered.

"You and your girlfriend were power gliding down the streets of LA while she was giving you a taste of your own medicine" Doctor Farrow kindly reminded me. "It is probably for the best you didn't tell her", he expressed. "I mean woman don't need us to keep letting them down, they already deal with us thinking we know what is best for them. Like how we love to define what they should or should not be allowed to do with their bodies. To be frank, I find comfort in knowing that they will be around to put us in our place to the very end. We need not worry about the path of the female, we will meet them where they are and everything else, forget about it. That being said, Jada sounds like an understanding young lady, I am sure she would have been able to maturely handle the sad reality of the situation" Doctor Farrow supposed, letting the issue fade.

While she was not one to suppress her own thoughts "Okay I'll tell you" Jada maneuvered cautiously through the streets, adjusting her windshield wipers to a speed conducive of a thunderstorm "I forgot the weed at the party" she revealed peeping the Berry Dutch Master that I hadn't paid for at my feet. "You grabbed me so fast," she explained. "You want to go home, I will bring you home Sam, but can we please stop at a dispensary first?"

"Sorry about that." I said picking up the double cigar pack from off the car floor, "I panicked."

"It's alright" she said looking more toward the follow up, "Just give me directions to one that's open right now, and we'll be square."

"Did we forget we aren't twenty-one" I said almost forgetting who I was talking to. The story Jada told Alex about a cousin making fake Id's was partially true. There was a cousin who made fake ID's except it was Jada's cousin not mine.

"I'll probably need to smoke if I'm going to get sleep tonight anyways", I said using my phones search engine to locate the only shop open fifteen minutes from us, "Miss Mineola's off West Eighth street."

"At least the traffic's not too bad" Jada said as if I hadn't already been convinced of her talent for persuasion. Consummated with the phrase "Like selling salt to a slug. No wait" I corrected myself, "even better, like selling Rosalita Summers the name on her Id, to any one business without an ID scanner" I said.

We pulled into the parking lot to Miss Mineola's Medicine not fully convinced of whether the shop was still open or not but "the light above the entrance is still glowing and my phone says it's open till ten."

"Are you going to stay in the car, or did you want something?" Jada asked.

"It's probably better if I come inside", I said.

The front door opened on the first try but it took both of our strength to pry it open. Inside it appeared to be completely empty though visible was a blacked out, one-way precession with a round hole in the center to speak into. I was startled by the sudden appearance of a plump set of lips and a voice,

"First time or returning?"

I let Jada handle this.

"First time" she said.

"If you are going inside, I am going to need to see both your IDs and you're going to have to fill out this short form" the lips mouthed. "You need to be twenty-one years of age to purchase marijuana without a medical card" the receptionist said. "Thirty to thirty-five a gram, our eighth's range from forty-five to fifty dollars for top shelf, you also get twenty percent off for first time customers" she added.

"Sounds fair enough" I said. "I don't have money anyways, so who am I to complain."

That's what you said?" Doctor Farrow asked.

"Yes. Why did you picture me throwing a tantrum "This is an outrage! Attica. I demand to see my lawyer right now and he just happens to be inside your dispensary buying some of your finest ganja." I laughed.

"I just wondered why you went inside in the first place if you didn't have a proper identification card" Doctor Farrow probed.

Nah, I really just wanted to make sure Jada made it inside alright. I had no clever schemes, I just ended up waiting in the car while Jada was left to pick her poison, a tough decision made without my endorsement. That is if she was able to make it through without setting off the metal detector, I thought. I did get to read the strains advertised on a white board in the lobby though; Doobie Doo, Thin Mint, Gookies, Gingerbread, Super Sunset, Top of the World, Purple Cookie, Brown Skittles, Cali Cheese, Liquid Gas, Blue Berry Haze...

"That's quite the strains" Doctor Farrow said impressed.

"Wedding Cake, Purple Galaxy, Scarlett Johannsson, Dro", I was finished. I told her "Liquid Gas sounds like it has potential. Potential for what? I did not get to find out, because she chose" I paused on the consonant just where I had enough time to close my eyes and come up with

"Look at that. Your memory is coming back nicely" Dr. Farrow remarked gassing me up.

"I might have made some of those up, but it be like that sometimes," I said.

In what looked to be the remainder of my night, my phone had read a little past 9:00pm, the time my father told me that he was going to be home. I most likely caused a fight between my parents that night.

"And how do you feel about that?" Doctor Farrow said playing to my guilt.

I feel like shit now but at that time perhaps I was naive to the amount of trouble I was getting myself into "what else could he do besides ground me", I thought. I paused to a dreadful image of my arrival home that possessed me to be ever present to an eerie silence that had trespassed to each one of my senses. In the middle of miss Mineola's parking lot, I leaned my back up against the dry parts of Jada's 98 Buick taking in remnants of downtown LA's corroded air, all whilst becoming increasingly more aware of my location. Across the street, a building that looked to have old Victorian tapestry that outlined a marquee which in turn hovered over the main entrance. The street said Broadway.

"Baroque Architecture." Doctor Farrow said in a most Grandiose tone.

"Huh?"

"You are talking about the Old Tower Theater, right?"

"Yeah."

"The designed, a clay-based ceramic earthenware pronounced Terracotta. Influenced by 17th and 18th century architecture called Baroque." said Doctor Farrow who made sure not to cheapen an opportunity to educate me.

I could not believe the one thing that I have been dying to see was now right across the street. Amazing.

Jada snuck up on me after returning from the inside of Miss Mineola's Medicine.

"I went with the Doobie Doo." That was what Jada chose "It's a Hybrid" she said followed by "What are you looking at?"

"Look over there" I pointed with great enthusiasm "It's the theater!"

"Oh no way" Jada said sounding surprised "what are the odds."

Peering back at the life projecting out of Jada's light brown eyes "Apparently it's indisputable" I said before I stepped forward to get a closer look at the theater, "maybe it means something." Granted it was a fair distance away, but from where I was standing relative to the marquee, I saw what I believe resembled an upside down seven.

"Yea it could mean that we should smoke a little to really appreciate this historical moment and to thoughtfully plan out our exploration of LA's underbelly, hopefully sometime next weekend" she said sounding uncertain.

"Tell me you see that?" I said.

"See what?" she replied squinting towards the direction of the theater.

"The upside down seven on the marquee."

"Oh, come on Sam" she said not wanting to indulge me. 'First off, it's obviously an L not a seven. L for let's go to bed we are both tired and we are starting to see stuff. "The least you could do is wait until I'm high before you make me think that I'm tripping" she said. "How do we know it's even open?"

"Alex told me that it is open Monday, Friday and Saturday. And today is Friday so let's check it out!

"Oh, and when did you start listening to Alex? What happen to the only good advice Alex ever gave someone is when he tells them don't wait up?" she said with scathing sarcasm.

"It's already past my curfew, meaning that I'm for sure grounded after this and this might be my only chance to see this thing, in this decade, if I'm that fortunate. So c'mon, please Jada.

"Can't we smoke a little bit first? I get it, I was wrong, and you were right. I should have never misled you" she confessed a tad too late.

"It won't take no more than a couple minutes."
Never again will we get a better chance."

"Is what our headstones will say if we go in there Sam."

"We will be alright Jada," I assured and then I said with confidence we will go in, check the scene out really quick and then we can come back to the car. And I will roll us a phat blunt" I said to her fixation.

"The image of choking on loose weed, doesn't sound too appealing. Thank you but I will roll the blunt" She seemed to be softening her stance. "Whatever, let's just hurry up she said attempting to use the paper bag which contained her weed to block the mist from her hair "let me put this in the car first" she said tossing the medical marijuana bag into the back seat as well my ball cap before we listened to my gut intuition and ran across the dark street. Now under a temperate sky we made it safely to the marquee which became our shelter.

"Have you spoken to your mother about that night? When your Father saw that you weren't home?" Dr. Farrow added.

He had evidently tried to call me from the several voice mails and missed calls I found later that night, after I retrieved my phone from Jada's car. Or was it the morning. Jada's cell phone lost service once inside, but we were able to use the phone's flashlight for a little bit before that also died. "What did the voice messages say?"

He said "Hey Samori, this is your Father, I just got home to see that you are not. Call me back please. Your mother and I are worried about you. If you need a ride call one us, I will come get you. I could hear my mother in the background "We love you Sam", and then my father ended with "please make it home safe." I overwhelmingly remembered.

"He is not answering his phone Eva! When is the last time you spoke to him?"

"Last time I spoke to our son was when he was in the backyard building some character, as you elegantly put it. Then I thought

I heard him go upstairs to his room because you told him he could not leave the house.

"You didn't think to check on him? What time do you think he went to his room Eva?

"5:30 maybe" mom sighed. "Where were you? You have been gone all night!?"

"I am trying to protect him. The governor is declaring a mandatory Lockdown for the city of Los Angeles, as we speak. That's like telling the police have at it, you have free range to pick on a black man."

"Let's just calm down for a minute and think. I will go upstairs and find my phone; I should have Jada's number," is how I picture it going down. I have three more messages like that.

"So did your mother get in touch with Jada?" Doctor Farrow said missing the whole point of my impersonation.

No Jada's cell phone lost service once we were inside, but she got in touch with Jada's mother while my father went searching for us.

Are you going to stop to write in your notebook every time? I asked the doctor.

"You know what, your right" he said closing the pad on to a double-sided pen." I should be giving you my complete undivided attention." He put the notepad aside and said "Let me try something different" where he then walked back over to his desk to remove a recorder from the bottom righthand drawer.

"I can capture it with this and then physically document it after. Sorry, go" he said taking his seat across from me.

"Here it is", I directed Jada out of the cold misty scene inside the surprisingly unlocked main entrance to the tower theater. A promising site was one of decadence, yet alive still warm with soft aggression. I had hope.

CHAPTER 13

"I wish we could do this another night. Can't we do this another night?" Jada said climbing the tower with cold feet, metaphorically speaking.

"C'mon we are already here" I replied. The dimly lit lobby looked like it had recently been refurbished with white and gold accenting the inside walls, a significant difference from the worn down vacant looking exterior. To the left was the main room with orchestra seating where voices were too faint to tell which level they were projecting from.

"Okay so Alex said it was downstairs, then it was two rights and two lefts. Then it was another left and then a right" I said now confusing myself. "Or was it two rights, two lefts, then a left and a right" I said, "Wait. Isn't that what I said the first time?" I turned to Jada hoping for some assistants, but she had deviated from the course into a main performer's cloudscape. Inside the main theater room, I used both hands to direct a loud whisper, "Jada!"

I observed Jada standing at the top the stairs looking down to the stage probably imagining what it would be like to have like fifteen thousand people all show up to see you.

"I think there are only twelve thousand seats" Dr. Farrow corrected tongue and cheek.

"Yea, a shit ton" I agree. Well anyways Jada became spellbound by the room's extravagant energy. "All these velvet red seats and peanut butter brown arches. Can you imagine being on stage, giving a live performance that ended with a standing ovation."

"I probably wouldn't even notice if it happened. Not my cup of tea" she said still not looking to take her eyes off either the stage under the spotlight or the free-flowing curtain. That's when one of the voices that we heard earlier was now chirping into our direction from the front row of the theater. I could see two people but that's pretty much all I needed to make out.

"Can I help you folks!"

"No! Sorry, we were just leaving," I yelled down grabbing Jada by the hand as to remove our immediate presence.

From the top of the stairwell "You could have just called me. You always want to be touching me" she said before berating my taste in movies "like this is some tired old war romance from the forties."

"I think it's down this way" I said ignoring her last remark leading Jada and I to what I believed was the staircase Alex had descended from. I felt as if we had taken the dimly lit lobby for granted as we entered the abrupt darkness, down on the first floor of the theater.

"Damn it I forgot my phone," I just realized.

"The battery in my phone is at ten percent, but here", Jada surrendered control providing us a much-needed flashlight that we used for the time being to see as far in front of us as the little light with tremendous fortitude would brighten. We were just hoping that the battery had enough stamina to get us where we wanted to be and then obviously back to the car. We had no choice but to move with fidelity past the tan carpet under our feet and the crimson colored walls that turned into dark drab almost a greyish brown, reminded me of images I saw when I in the past googled dirty snow. In this case we had neither enough time, enough battery life or enough service other than to continue in the most primitive ways seen to modern technology.

"Okay, he said it was right down this hallway" Jada held on to the back of my shirt as we both followed the light that had me seeing a mere seven inches in front of my face, power gliding as you referred to earlier, down the dark hallway until we came to another even darker hallway. "Seven percent" Jada informed me looking over my right shoulder to her home screen light up. Down this hallway I could barely see four gold objects evenly separated encased under glass. They looked like some ancient military helmets each one more extravagant the further we moved down the line. In my opinion they should have been locked away in a museum not laying around for some teenage kids to come snatch up. We had other intentions though.

"Bye Sam" she said having a bad feeling about this commitment "It's too quiet." "What are we going to do when my phone dies?" Jada felt under pressure.

That is when I conveniently spotted a candle holder with candle mounted to the wall at the end of the hallway. "And there's your answer" I said making a beeline straight to the wax, Jada still hanging close. I dragged my hand along the wall as to guide us through the dark, in the belly of the theater.

"Of course, there is a candle" that is what she said to my elation.

"Let me see your lighter" I demanded digging into my own narrow pockets eventually pulling out one miniature baby blue lighter. I gave Jada her phone back just at two percent as I grabbed the wax by its rustic wood bottom. I lit the candle that illuminated our path, halfway there.

"See."

"Oh, aren't you clever. Where to now captain Waters" she saluted.

"I think through these double doors" I presumed were fashionably structured to open rather than to be a masterfully designed dead end. As an addition to the theme of non-abidance, an enormous vacant dining hall with past elegance coursing through it, showed us inside. I edged forward at once. When closer to the middle of the room, to get better intake of toppled chairs and empty plain cloth tables, I did a masculine twirl. I didn't want to assume "they put away the good silverware because they heard we were coming but damn" did this room look so elegantly deserted. Well except for the recent polished ballroom floor and a massive glistening crystal chandelier, oh and at first what looked to be some type of antifreeze can, turned out to be a can of gold spray paint that I noticed on top of the table dressing.

"They really out did themselves with their security detail."

"Do you smell that?" Jada asked me. I recall not being able to smell much, might have been the candle in my hand.

"What, the smell of Mr. Murray's third grade science class, yeah I do."

"It smells like a lavender flower. I would be able to detect that smell anywhere. it reminds me of my seventh birthday party at the botanical gardens Jada said as her eyes wandered up to the ceiling "That location was my father's idea," she said revaluating past feelings.

"You know I haven't heard you talk about your father in a couple years." an object in my corner left eye paused my momentum at the center of the ballroom floor.

"That's because he taught me that I'm better off alone."

"Get the hell out of here!" I said dumbfounded.

"What's the Matter?"

I slowly turned my body round to a stage where a black cat was again posturing patiently like he had orders to stalk me.

"Oh, it's just a cute little kitty cat," Jada wanted to believe.

That looks like the cat that was sitting outside my house staring at me a few nights ago. In fact, I am almost positive they are the same cat by the way it's staring at me right now. Even the way that it is postured.

"Maybe you have a secret admirer. Come here ashes" Jada called out to the cat stiff as cardboard cutout.

"Ashes?" I questioned.

"Yeah" she said slowly approaching the black cat with bright yellow eyes. "Because you've been dropping ash on to your nice shoes." I looked down to see that she was right, but I quickly picked my head up to tell Jada to,

"Wait!" I said derailing her approach to the cat. "Maybe we should keep going."

"I was just seeing if it was real, look now he's run off.

"At least now you know he's real, but how can you tell he's a he and not a she? I'd be lying if I said I wasn't fascinated as to what determined that for you" I said to Jada as the cat ran off into the same direction that we were heading.

"And I'd be lying if I said that he didn't remind me of the you, whenever Lisa comes around" Jada laughed. "Like a bird on a wire" she said avoiding a look in my direction. "Well let's follow him maybe he knows where Tupac is so I can go home and tell my mother how I wasn't out all-night horsing around." A familiar sense followed my blind inquiry, an endeavor to satisfy marinating in my mind the deep desire to achieve the discovery and maybe some closure to this night. I was not going to be intimidated by any ghostly thinking. Where fear lie waiting for the ones who doubt their future, I had my mind made up. This cat was quick to lose interest in my presence but not quick enough to lose us altogether. I kept a close tail even when its movement became erratic amid the shadows.

"Where'd the cat go?" she said.

"I can feel we're close." I said trying to ease any of Jada's lingered anxiety. "Let's turn down here" I informed her of my intentions which only seemed to make her less compliant.

"It's a dead-end Sam! The hallway ends!"

"We're here," I said.

CHAPTER 14

"Sam, I see nothing! But I hope you remember how to get back to the car because I don't."

I gave Jada the candle "Hold this" I told her taking several insidious steps forward still sliding my relatively long fingers along the wall. I vanished down the dark hallway for strong belief Tupac would inspire to light the rest of the way for me, Candle or no candle.

"Sam, what are you doing? You are not an owl. We humans cannot see in the dark without flashlight. Sam!" Jada called out to me through the pitch blackness of the short narrow cul-de-sac where she received nothing but silence in return. Candle in hand Jada slowly back tracked to where we last made a left turn. Still not yet ready to remove her eyes away from this hallway's dark ambient undertone. A sad surrender washed over me as I believed to be almost to the end of the hall.

"Sam, come quick!" I heard Jada urgently call to me. Running scared back from whence I came, I embraced my lack of vision.

"What is it? What's the matter?" I said in reach of her blank expression.

"I was backing up but still looking to see where you went, thinking that we better be able to skip town in a hurry if something goes terribly wrong and then I hit this." Both Jada and I turned to the wall behind Jada to examine with help from flickering candlelight, from bottom to top, soul to soul, Hail Mary full of grace the image that I have been waiting to see for myself. It was at last the Don Killuminati which appeared overwhelmingly to steal the moment by surprise.

I could not help my excitement, "You are my eyes." Is what I said before I snuck a kiss to Jada's forehead.

"Umm excuse me, you just left me in the dark." she said with pretend hostility as well an astonished sense of relief.

"Makaveli tha Don Killuminati; a thirty by twenty-one-inch golden border portrayal of Black Jesus. Such a masterpiece should be in a museum under twenty-four-hour protection but still visible in the darkest of rooms" I spoke out loud. "Just look at the menacing color scheme sky and the icy moon in the back peaking over his left shoulder", I pointed then to a bandana of thorns. There was a vivid display of bright red blood dripping down his tattoos and finally stamped over his genital region the parental warning us of explicit content, "for it is our sexuality not the depiction of our own sacrifice that threatens the fabric of society," I mocked with a subtle acknowledgement. "His wounds disguise his face, a face that suffers a pain deeper than just of the flesh. To each one of our people's individual sacrifice" I said awakening our inheritance and exorcising any last bit of doubt, "They did not die in vain. But let's just say these ignorant gangbangers need a lesson in anatomy before their next drive by because they missed Pac's heart."

"I don't know who would want to hide something so magnificent but for sake of time how bout you stand in front of it and I will take your picture."

"And ruin the whole image, I think not. Let me see your phone for a second" I then insisted.

You know what, here. When your right, your right" she said handing me her phone of course, that's when a dreadful gust of slighted wind from I don't know where came shivering down and took out the flame leaving us in the pitch black. Jada's phone had a miserable one percent battery left.

"Let me see your lighter" she said franticly.

I thought I gave it to you. Oh no wait I have it" I said correcting myself and slipping out of a scrawny pocket with my fingers was a miniature lime green lighter I now had in the palm of my hand. First thing I saw upon Jada again lighting the wick of the candle were the eyes of Tupac. There was something intrinsically different about the eyes of the painting now than just a few minutes ago, before the lights went out."

"Is it me or do the eyes look almost present?"

"Yeah the painting is really alive," Jada misunderstood my critique.

'I mean seriously the eyes of the painting, don't look like, part of the painting anymore."

I said continuing to keep my gaze centered on the picture.

"It's Alive!" Jada said with a newly found confidence using pop culture to mock me. "No seriously Sam we either take this picture right now or I'm taking this candle and finding my way back to the car. I'll buy a new phone tomorrow."

I quickly took a snap of the mural just before the phone shut off. "I got it' I said proud I accomplished what I set out to do but disappointed I could not make everyone happy. "Where are you going?" I said to Jada as a cold shadow began to darken my circle.

"I'm really getting cold Sam."

"Imagine how I feel, your walking away with the only white heat like we aint finna leave in the same direction. I swear Jada, sometimes you can be a real step up from high maintenance."

"Don't exaggerate.", she said starting to move towards my shadowy self simply to be stricken by a violent pang of compressed alloy along with a seismic wood shift and then a vicious toss of both our bodies on to the rough carpet. I had not enough time to even use my arms to brace my upper half. In defense of this not yet being the end of the world, the surrounding environment we were in at the moment did not help my case.

"Oh, hell no. I'm done here Sam lets go!" I heard Jada loudly proclaim from an even further position.

"Do you have the candle" I replied still trying to gain back my equilibrium.

"No, I dropped it somewhere" she answered back as I began to touch my hand around hoping I would stumble upon the lost candle to no luck of my own but then to my subsequent relief, again there was light. Jada had found the candle.

What would you say, about four point five on the Richter", I communicated from my own two feet to Jada, who I also saw about ten feet from me standing upright."

"Four point five" she repeated in disbelief.

"It wasn't that bad. It barley lasted a moment" I spoke brazenly to the ground beginning to tremble under my unstable stance like two tectonic plates separating themselves and the helpless eye contact I made with Jada which signaled the worst had yet to come. It was unsettling as the floor slowly collapsed around my immediate area but somehow Jada was able to quickly lunge over and grab on to the lining of my jacket. I screamed as my lower body dangling down a hole in the floor.

"Sammmm!" Jada cried out exhausting most of her energy to hold up my body weight through a measly article of clothing while also attempting to use her legs as a type of emergency kick stand to prevent our conjoined plummet. I also reached for any unwavering support to hold on to. I felt the jacket begin to tare through while the unarguable decision to help along the inevitable outcome was made by me.

"Sam I can't hold us both" she said detesting at that very moment, her will power. I forced my other arm from the sleeve of the jacket "Wait Sam", at the same time the material snapped from Jada's grip and I slid down a dusty chute only moments to prepare for impact "Don't Die" is along the lines of what Jada said with what I felt was five to six seconds of free fall before I eventually crash landed horribly into some lush greenery. I promptly figured my gasping for air only meant that I was alive in a, I was alive in something you might find in the middle of a shopping mall and that I had barely missed cracking open my head on to a wooden flower encasement, as I came to witness this new amenity.

CHAPTER 15

Besides some lower back discomfort, it really wasn't too bad, I just took a phantom ride twenty feet through the floor, down a dusty narrow cobb web ridden metal laundry chute on to someone's flower arrangement.

"Yes, that's right" Doctor Farrow recalled in attempt to correspond with the facts. "I do remember Los Angeles recording a seven-point four quake around that time. It caused some power outages in parts of downtown, including around me." What I next observed as one of the most chilling scenes to take place in a basement since *Little Shop of Horrors*. Never in my physical existence did I imagine as my upper half reemerged from a clump of photosynthetic life support that I would lay my eyes on in the distance,

"What did you see?" Dr. Farrow said showing juvenile interest,

"What do you think I saw, some more darkness." In separate worlds again I removed pieces of plant lodged in my coarse hair.

"Are you Okay!" Jada yelled down,

"Never better" I said.

"I dropped the candle down the hole!" what I heard disclosed to which I was fortunate to recognize feeling out of place down by my feet, the said candle. Also, I apparently had two miniature lighters because from my pocket again I pulled out a baby blue. I didn't bother calling back up to Jada as I felt the distance was way too far to have a productive conversation, plus I wasn't sure I was ready to invite just any unknown spirits not already aware of my sudden descent, to me. It was almost unbelievable what I saw next,

"Darkness?"

My legs hanging off the edge of the wood "No at that point I lit the candle." A surge of candlelight expanded beyond the darkness to where I could make out a body of the bluest water, which surrounded by well-polished stone made for a kind of wishing well. At the center of the fountain making its appearance was a shimmering gold statute of a lion's head acting as a spout to which circulated the flow of water calmly and uninterrupted back into the pool. Next to that refreshing sight, I made a short jump down to witness lined up evenly throughout a fairly sizeable hideout to say the least, like something out of the Canterbury tales, I saw nine large bookcases whose collective nature could easily commemorate the life of a celestial outlaw. Though they look like they'd seen better days. I took several autonomous breaths before I walked down past the fountain, in between the depleted bookshelves, one of which I saw had an ancient life size warrior standing guard with a tall sword in one hand and a shield to match, then through my obsessed stare, I saw more than just a symbol reflecting in front of a full-length swinging mirror. There on an old wooden writing desk with a bookmark protruding from its pages which was only visible from where I approached through the placement of the mirror. What lay tattered with practical wisdom, bound in gold all down its solid leather spine for otherwise naked would be simply a brown book with the letter M woven in gold thread as its centerpiece. The Don Killuminati in all its mystery, never more in the forefront of my mind than that very moment, as the thought only added to my intrigue for this book. I could see my reflection as well as the reflection of the water behind me. Still from a short distance away, I was charmed by the powerful presentation of this book. Unperturbed by lose dust particles possibly floating for ages, I inched closer like the cobwebs that stretched across the room. My heart thumped double time as if it were trying to detect a lost stethoscope somewhere in the room, meanwhile I hovered over the book remembering that my father once told me that I should take action as a flower would. And that's what I did. I held the candle low to the binding, careful not to make a terrible error. The books captivating outside energy which radiated like electromagnetic airwaves to my subconscious almost enticed my hand if it were not for the ill omen, maybe even more evident because of the location that this discovery was made. Who would leave a book where you had a fall through a floor to even know exists? Someone who you didn't want to run into. I just had to refrain from making any contact as the temptation to read was not yet too powerful to control. I had my head down but kept my distance for another moment reluctant to have my attention drawn to anything else and by all accounts unaware that in the oval mirror as soon as I lifted my head, to my instant surprise would I see it then reflect the sallow face of my father and his flat cap. I then heard Jada in my left ear say, "What did you bust your eardrums!?"

"Oh shit!" I said turning around to see both Jada and my father standing behind me. "Where did you come from?" I asked.

"We have been calling your name. What other world were you in?" she said lowering her tone of voice.

"How did you guys get down here?"

"How do you think?" my father gestured in the direction from where I fell. "We propelled down by way of a couple tablecloths tied together, anchored at the top by the table itself "my father said pulling pieces of plant out from his beard.

"Of course, you found me" I strongly concluded.

"It was your friend Jada's masterful idea."

"It actually worked better than it did in the movie I, got it from. Thank the Lord."

"Give me the candle" my father demanded before reaching behind me to lite some sort of torch that was attached to the wall. He then walked ten steps to his right and lit another well- fashioned torch in close corner of the room.

"I mean how did you find us here at the Theater?"

"Your mom spoke to Jada's mom. She was supposed to be back with the Buick two hours ago, you know the one parked across the street in front of a dispensary" my father said handing me back the candle. "So, was this part of the plan for tonight? If so, I would love to know what happens next." he humbly stated eyeing the full monastery architecture above all our heads. What could I say to him at that very moment that he wouldn't already know and most likely care not to hear me recite "I am sorry?" Well he could tell I was sorry without me having to say a word just by my underwhelming atonement.

"Fix your face, he said walking pass me around to the other side of the bookshelf close to the edge of the room, in search of maybe a doorway or some kind of alternative exit, I guess.

"Whatchu reading?" Jada asked me.

"Nothing I had just saw this book sitting here."

"Did you get to see the Tupac painting" I said to a glimpse of my father's back in a poor attempt to recoup any lost love, from where I then sought assistants through further eye contact with Jada.

"No candle," She said.

"Was anyone going to mention the double doors at the other end of the room." he said amidst our confusion still somehow able to identify what I lacked to notice during my initial arrival. He again walked over to me and grabbed the candle from my hand before making his way into the heart of darkness with confident certainty or with as little fear a person possibly could have in a situation like we were in. I lost him in the cold blackness, but I could still hear his words of protest as his voice faded in the distance.

"let's just pretend you did something right tonight and knew this door wouldn't open. In that case there is no need for me to even check right", I heard him say only seconds before I then heard the unnerving clang like someone pulling hard on a door handle. He doubted my ability to make a commonsense decision to save my life.

"Can I assume that cell phone service is out of the question?" he said with his voice now getting closer.

"Jada had no service before her phone died and I left my phone in the car" I told the shadowy figure walking towards us. In an act of disappointment, I directed my face downwards which turned out to be a mere neck adjustment for I was fast to pick my head up once father ventured back into my line of vision.

"I'm sorry" he said looking at me dead to rights "I don't think I heard you correctly, were you trying to tell me that you were not ignoring any of my six phone calls and that you just didn't answer your phone, that may I remind you I pay for every month, not because someone robbed you at gunpoint but instead because you were being irresponsible?" Not the way I meant it to be said, sounded like

"No but I really was involved in an armed robbery tonight, right Jada?" I said remembering I hadn't told her much of what happen.

"No this is cool the state can pay for your education. As soon as I get home I'm making a couple phone calls, so don't worry you can keep on with your adventure. You obviously don't respect me or what I know. See I let you get too comfortable, you should be afraid of me as well, it's okay though because I knew God had something in store for me, I just never thought it would be my own family to be the one to hurt me. I mean I never imagined falling onto the biggest fortunes of my life either but look check out this golden sheath" he said as he calmly strolled to the end of one of the bookshelves to find posted, something he could touch. "Get out of here! Look at the blade on this. "he said as I admired the gold shaft glistening in my father's hand moments before he removed the cover to expose the sharp sword. "Can't wait to tell someone about this, if we ever get out here" he acknowledged placing the sword back into its case.

CHAPTER 16

I told the Doctor "The lord as my witness I have never seen anything quite like what I saw displayed in that room. At first it was so dark that we could hardly make out what we were essentially walking past like it were insignificant. Well hidden from the rest of the world, all this treasure tucked away looked like it came from a very distant past, promised me for sure someone or something would eventually come calling. In the meantime, my father was giving us the lavish tour de Thomas on our way back to a more appropriate lighting.

Candle in his left hand, Jada and I followed close behind my father

"Here we have this luxurious wishing well with a lion made of gold perched right at the center to guard it's vivacious waters from I don't know. What do you think, nickels and dimes?" he asked me making a sarcastic transition to some of the lesser sought items in the room.

"What do we have here other than some enriching food for the soul, some lonely writers masterpiece that wound up forgotten to the back of some dusty old bookshelf, hoping and praying that one day a couple kids and their overly trusting parental figure would stumble upon its past glory and for one night only, resurrect some of its knowledge, some of its passion, some of the magic that it once was intended to bring forth. Unfortunately for most of these books they were discovered in the twenty-first century where we neglect to read anything other than a virtual screen.

Sphinx." Dr. Farrow proclaimed.

"Bless you."

"The half-man, half-Lion in gold at the head of the fountain, it's called a Sphinx" Doctor Farrow clarified.

"Yeah part man, part lion," I said.

But don't let me distract you from the real showstopper of this room. "You like gold, don't you Jada? Of course, you do. I don't know why I even ask. If your hanging around my son every day you must really have some expensive taste. I'm not insinuating you have enough money to help pay for this hole in the ceiling or anything like that but come check this out" my father explained as he guided us to a small wooden coffee table that sat in the middle of, if I remember correctly what my father called a Mandala. To me it just looked like some vintage rug.

"I am sure you have probably seen gold many times over but tell me Jada, when is the last time that you ever seen a two foot statue made of Lapis Lazuli; such like this blue faced figure standing so beautifully in front our blue expressions.

"To be honest with you Mr. Waters, I have never even heard of this Lapis Lazu."

"Lapis Lazuli" my father help Jada pronounce. "Its precious stone prized for its deep blue cut, sometimes more than even Gold."

"Why don't we climb up the way we came down" I suggested.

"Because the sheets won't hold my body weight both ways. Not to mention my old basketball injury" he scowled at the same time he momentarily massaged his wrist.

I then pointed out that there was a fireplace behind where he was standing, just beyond the table and the Mandala. I thought at least maybe we wouldn't freeze to death tonight.

"Let me see your lighter" he said. "I'll show you how we do it in my neck of the woods. They don't teach you this at University."

My father told me to "check to make sure the damper was open. "See that tiny loop at the end of the skinny rod? Put your finger in and pull that toward your body" he said. I guess it regulates the flames intensity, so we needed to have it open. He crouched down on to the outer hearth, the name he used to describe a crescent shaped patio in front of the fireplace. "Now I am going to take this sliver of bark and lite the tip as to place it delicately under the rest of the wood. We should be lucky that the wood is not damp or that would be another issue. I am just going to blow some air on in between the logs, and we should be good" he told us giving an instinctive effort. "I'm not making any excuses, but it would be a lot easier if this wasn't damn near an antique or maybe if whoever owns these artifacts believed in gas.

I didn't have the heart to tell him that he grew up mostly around concrete and his boy scout method appeared unsuccessful, but I offered my aid none the less "You want me to try?" I asked.

"I would rather us not blow up if all possible" he said looking up at me before immediately attempting to breathe life into a subtle flame that would not catch onto the bigger pieces. He moistened his upper lip, "It will just take another moment. Come on you mother destroyer of cities, ignite!" my father said once again bringing the lit end piece of bark to the under bottom of the wood, which was in the middle of a chimney.

"You know what, I'm going to need you to step back just a little please, your blocking my feng shui" he said to me in a subdued voice. I didn't think I was in the way but I moved back all the same and then I don't know if it was when he started messing with the damper again but not a moment sooner does the flame erupt with intense heat knocking my father back a short distance to his backside.

He was right about one thing; The University had more trouble putting out fires.

"It's not a competition, as long as you get the job" … All the time in the world to brag about something he couldn't tell anyone, other than the people who were already a witness to the said job but were not bored enough to yet even care why it worked out in the first place, became a distant memory. My father humbly positioned on the ground, had not a second longer to finish his statement before in one spontaneous revolution does the wall that contained the fire place and the outer hearth which my father sat helplessly unaware on, both disappear in a peculiar counter clockwise turn of event. For the wall with a shared fireplace was swapped out for a surround sound entertainment stereo system but I would say more symbolic is what came out of the hidden hallway a head of duel subwoofers, I remember that I was either going crazy or I was in real life seeing a short old oriental man, one of which wore traditional Chinese dynasty eunuch headwear as well a belt full of keys at his waste and a pair of ninety's generation X earphones, appear unexpectedly singing Janet Jacksons *that's the way love goes* totally oblivious to me or Jada standing there.

"Like a moth to a flame burn by the fire, my love is blind can't you see my desire, that's the way love goes." The old man was sticking to the same old two step on his way to behind the bookshelves like Betty Ford. I'm still baffled by what I saw, but me and Jada whose nonliteral jaw I had to scoop up off the floor, had already established a nonverbal line of communication upstairs when exploring through the dark. To where I now found it easier in relative light, to truly listen to what her eyes had to say to me.

"Hey!" she shouted trying to get the attention of the old man who under the ancient law of hidden oriental wisdom held an ornamental tea pot and a book, this one appearing to be dressed in even more gold nestled loosely against his oversized robe. The two of us followed him around the corner as he walked to the edge of the wooden table that stretched along the wall, where the old man then placed the tea kettle down on the wood surface before turning and walking back in our direction to where we were almost positive that he now saw us standing still at the head of the very first book case. We were quite mistaken as a graceful last-minute change of direction placed him in between the first two bookcases, still bobbing his head to the music.

I signaled Jada to go talk to him while she had the same idea softly mouthing off "You go talk to him!"

"Ok let us both go," I said.

CHAPTER 17

"Back to the top shelf next to six ordinary looking covers as he reached his feet forward to the end of a step latter, the old man with a lengthy gray goatee revealed his small appendages that were hidden by a royal shade of hemp garment before he casually placed the glistening gold book somewhere in the mix.

"Excuse me" I said sounding a pathetic attempt to get the mysterious man's attention, made apparent when he stepped down solely to maintain his untiring task.

"Oh, my goodness, that was so weak" Jada scrutinized before telling me to "say it with your hairless chest why don't you."

"Okay, okay."

I said planning my next move in my head while observing the old man with a small torch in hand begin to illuminate the remaining parts of the room from corner to corner, where I could see abstract cave art carved within the walls and on the upper Corinthian order. About two feet from my reach and his back to me, I again looked to gain his attention but this time I decided I would go straight into our dilemma. I declared this time sticking my chest out,

"See me and my friend fell down into this basement, well actually I'm the only one who fell but my dad and my friend Jada climbed down to find me and once we were all down in this, I must say really quite fascinating cellar" my voice getting louder "we then had no way to leave. Oh, and then my father started a fire one hundred and eighty degrees on the other side of that wall you came from behind. Hey mister!" I said beginning to get frustrated as I felt I were being ignored. Still, I was just talking to myself as the old man continued to the furthest corner candle.

"His headphones," Jada explained. "He can't hear you; he's got headphones on.," she said gesturing to her own ear.

"What do you want me to do jump out and surprise him? You see how old he is, that'll kill him" I said.

"Fine, I'll do it myself" she said with reluctant enthusiasm.

Normally Jada would consistently be able to gather the interest of the opposite sex with a mere flutter of an eyelash, a whiff of her sweet scent, the soft contact between her hand and your upper back. A scenario at school where she would have gotten as fed up as she was trying to talk to this old man, would have made Jada quit all together because more than anyone I knew Jada hated being ignored.

"Hey Mister" Jada said mocking me right before reaching out to touch the man's shoulder as he turned in the opposite direction. Completely missing him she stumbled forward into a small set of stairs that I could now make out leading to an above platform where a large titanium door was locked."

"I wasn't laughing at Jada. At least not to her face."

The little old man who somehow wielded a torch without it catching fire to his Komodo, this time as he walked by removed his headphones, only to then begin to start talking to himself.

"May the burden of falling behind no longer impede my readings" he said walking back in between the bookcases, back to the table where he first laid the tea pot. Now that the room was completely lit up he had no reason for the torch any longer so he relinquished the flame onto the wall before picking up a pair of thin clear reading glasses he bent at both ends of the temple, as to place on his tiny nose and then he sauntered down to the other end of the table to retrieve the very first book I saw, the book I had a hard time taking my eyes off of.

"I will read you over some of Mr. Han Wei's warm Red Snapper soup," he spoke before picking up the perfect sized page book.

"Excuse me Mr. Way" I said finally contacting his shoulder, but I found myself quick to regret this as I received a swift jab to the middle of my Adams Apple.

"Who next!? Who want fight with Mr. Han Wei? Come in get it! I leave door unlocked and light on for you." he said positioning his hands out in front as if there were conflict. I backed up gasping for air while Jada had taken over.

"Hey, excuse me sir, we don't mean to sneak up on you we were just in need of some help."

"You need help, 911 good number, you call that!"

"See the thing is sir, when you came out from behind the wall it put someone we came in with, on the other side of it.

"What you want? You want to steal Master Han Wei leftover Abalone?" he slowly walked over to the tea kettle.

I had regurgitated my larynx back into position.

"Listen Mr. Hopsauce," I was mistaken thinking I had caught my breath.

"Mr. Han Wei ears incredibly good. Eyes not so much."

"Incredibly good" I wheezed. "Yeah whatever, Master Han Wei is it" I then somehow manage to get out, "let's just forget you a second ago judo chopped me in the throat" I continued to cough. "Can you please" I said before having to stop to take in more oxygen, "can you please" I paused as he swapped out the book for the teapot.

"Is Master Han Wei a Ghost, you see Mr. Han by the wall? he said walking over with the teapot to some of the flowers that broke my fall.

"You know you're about to pour hot tea on those flowers" Jada recognized.

"Those flowers!" he mimicked. "These White Lavender Lotus, the rarest of its breed can find great usage on any occasion."

"That is Lavender? Jada said sounding surprised "I knew I was smelling lavender upstairs, I told Sam, but he didn't believe me" she said ignoring that I was still hunched over. I'm sorry for the rude introduction, my name is Jada and this who you punched in the throat is Sam," I waved.

"This no tea silly girl this Mr. Han Wei special mineral water." I wasn't upset now I had an excuse not to tell him that I flattened a bunch of his flowers. "Mr. Han actual tea pot have flowers on side, color of Magenta" he explained. All while Jada and Mr. Han Wei were discussing tea pots finally I had the opportunity to fully receive the magnificence that was this room of ancient treasure, from the clay hawk with its wings spread at the very top of the middle bookcase, a gold rams head at the center of the titanium door at the other end of the room, a gold hippo facing us with his teeth the size of tiny bullets at the top of the intermediate platform. After watering his flattened flowers Mr. Han walked back to the table where he put down the pot and picked up the book with the M on the front cover.

All at once I was distracted and amazed that I could fully breath again while asking Mr. Han Wei about the book he first held, completely cover by Gold.

"What was that gold book you had earlier?" I asked.

"Ah you like to watch Mr. Han Wei do you. You obsessed with Han Wei huh?" he said as he then deposited the book with the gold M into his robe and then he again walked on back toward the bookshelf with the book that I was referring to. "Master Han Wei respect the custodial arts. That why Master Han Wei favorite movie *Good Will Hunting.*

CHAPTER 18

As you see Mr. Han also like to read. Well word got around that Master Han Wei carried a gold book around with him while he cleaned toilets and Master Han Wei can't have that" he said back on the foot stool reaching for the sparkling gold book. "So, Master Han Wei had to spray paint *"Hail to the Chins Further Confessions of a Bruce Campbell Movie Actor.* Do you agree this is the sexiest photograph taken of him?" he asked as he then showed me a page in the book with some random guy. I know who Bruce Campbell is now but at the time I was confused. Not until I saw Congo was I able to put the name and the face together.

"So, it was you with the gold spray paint up in the ballroom" I said putting two and two together. He closed the book and placed it back where it belonged right before he stepped down, reached into the right Komodo pouch, and brings out the same can of spray paint I saw upstairs on the table.

"Whip even a galloping horse" he said walking pass me to put the can of spray paint on the long table. "You must try to leave the way you came" he moved toward an old rocking chair I just noticed next to a ten-foot gold spear as well which leaned against the solid wall.

"Your dad." Jada mention.

"I know" I replied to Jada before engaging Master Han Wei again. "Sir that's the thing we want to leave but when you came around the wall singing, my father had just started a fire on the other side." I stood there for a second waiting for him to give me some type reaction instead he maintained silence while sitting with his head down on the beginning page of the brown book. "So, if you could reverse that wall please, we can then leave you alone. Please.

"Good opportunities introduce themselves to those who stay patient." He said still not looking directly at me as I started to move back in fear of what I may do to this man if he didn't start giving me answers that I believed were helpful.

"So how long are we supposed to wait?" I said looking at Jada who saw frustration boil over my face. "And wait for what?" I said to yet again no immediate response.

"I am just going to go over there and start pressing buttons if you don't tell me" I ordered, almost to the stereo. Jada just stood there mute while I had no more to say.

"At times it is better not to intervene but before you waver in the slightest, take seven breaths as my gift of wisdom, never will this satisfy you until your last. Excellent book opens many doors."

"Yea well you just sit there and read your good book" I said with my back to the old man. I will figure out how to free my father without your help. Now which one of these knobs is the play button" I said about to just press the first thing that made sense when all of a sudden the song *Here we go again by* Portrait "blasted out the speakers as the wall began to shift again. I jumped back out of the danger zone in the nick of time. With great relief I observed my father sitting Indigenous style embracing the warmth of the fireplace.

"See" I turned to hear Mr. Han Wei behind me.

"I don't feel it's worth going into right now" my father announced as soon as he saw he was back in the same room as us. "Not saying I didn't deserve it," He then said

"The man with the worried look on his face is my father" I said introducing Master Han Wei to my father. "This is the person behind the wall we were telling you about."

"God is just a little black boy playing with his colored GI joes on the front lawn. Hhmm" he sighed before walking back over to his chair.

"Who is this guy?" my dad with a confused look across his face referred to the old Oriental man who seem to adapt to changes fairly easy.

My dad was now pointing to Master Han Wei's back pausing before asking me whether I knew, if this man knew, how to exit the building. "Let's not wear out our welcome."

"I didn't ask him, but I will be" is what I told my dad before again attempting to get Master Han Wei's attention.

Excuse me, Mr." my dad peered toward me for support,

"Mister Han Wei" I said.

"Excuse me Master Han Wei," I stepped up to track Mr. Han Wei's presence on the other end of the room, Jada as well. "I apologize for our intrusion and I guess I apologize for sneaking up on you,"

"Apologize, no sorry" he spoke still walking away. "Master Han Wei not violent person, you make Mr. Han have to kill like deadly virus."

"Ok I am sorry for sneaking up on you, I really am but we found my father now we are trying to leave. Now can you tell us how to open these doors? I directed with my finger.

"What can Master Han Wei do for you now?" he asked me, scanning me and then Jada like a blind dog in heat. The bush of his eyebrows looked like two white wings and his long gray beard looked just as dusty as the room. At that moment, his eyes resemble what I thought were the eyes of a snake, I asked "What's the look for?"

"This nightmare for you huh?"

"Listen old man," my father had to interrupt me before I lost my temper, "Mr. Gen Han Wei, my father named walking up to our defense prompting Master Han Wei to recognize. My name is Thomas Waters he approached and gave a tiny bow in respect not taking his eyes off the old mans deceptive stance as Master Han Wei returned the gesture. That was your work schedule I saw in the back room. Now you are a janitor, right? You must have keys to one of these doors down here I imagine?

"Ahh!" He said as if he had just become enlightened. "You want Key, why Angela and Rene no say key? Master Han Wei's eyes not so good, he can no longer read lips. You must speak up." I'm pretty sure he was referring to me and Jada as Rene and Angela while it took him several moments to sort through each individual key which was between fifty to eighty keys that were on a loop which he could only extend to about the end of his abdomen, so his upper torso had to meet his hip half way.

I told my father "I can just climb up and go get help."

"Okay this Mr. Han car Key,"

"It might hold my weight" I said just waiting for my father to give me the go ahead.

"Here it is" he said removing a key that looked like every other key from his belt that he just about placed into my father's hand, except right before the key was officially transferred over Master Han Wei rotated his neck slightly to stare into my soul.

"You wouldn't steal any of Master Han Wei's things, would you?" he asked me to my face as to probe any guilt one might find in my eyes which oddly enough made me question whether or not I actually did steal something from him, even though I knew I hadn't. I think. "Master Han Wei could not let you leave if you have taken what does not belong to even Mr. Han. I am merely retainer to artifacts and custodian to Tower Theater, I as well work at Chinese tea shop on weekends and own Han Wash Laundry at end of Broadway," I saw he cached a pamphlet next to his chest which proved he had more to offer.

"I assure you Mr. Han Wei, none of us would take anything from you," I reassured.

"Master Han Wei believe you," he said relinquishing the key to my father's hand.

"Wait a minute. I am confused, was it mister or master?

"Yeah mister. And master. I think it was both."

CHAPTER 19

Just as my father was about to set the key in the keyhole to free us from this fun, Master Han Wei to our great inconvenience disrupted any kind of second attempt we might have had in mind. Before even the first attempt he said

"It will not open that way though. Door open, by voice automation." Both my father and I turned to look at Master Han Wei like, I'm sorry? Jada ain't have to turn because she never took her eyes off him. "Being prepared is Key. One must also be prepared to be disappointed for we only ever find what we are supposed to mean to greater purpose. Which does not intend you all to leave that way."

"We have to get out of here." Is what my father said to us, to himself, I do not think it mattered at that point, but I could tell he meant it.

This time I could see my father shake the locked ram head door handle and I could hear the metallic clang echo off the stone wall which I followed around the room until the vibration ended with the tiniest wobble of a ceramic pottery jar tagged with early symbols that looked a lot like the letters in my name, sitting carelessly at the edge of the platform, which eventually came to a complete stop directly across from the gold hippo.

"What about behind the fireplace" my dad remembered. "You must have another way to exit this basement. My father stepped down from the platform to hand Master Han Wei back his key.

"Yes, there is secret exit staircase in back next to refrigerator."

"But?" my dad optimistic,

"But that way, like this way, no way out. You thank Apple insurance."

Jada wanted to know what that meant "Apple insurance?"

"Apple. You know Apple computer, Apple phone, Apple door.'

"This is an Apple door?" I said astonished by what I heard. "So, what do we have to say to get the apple doors to open?"

"You do not listen to the pandemic radio? Mandatory lockdown. Power out." Master Han Wei said again walking away from the three of us back to his modest amenities.

"So, are we to just sit here and wait until the power comes back on? Of course, that's if the police were the ones who cut the power and not the earthquake" I pointed out before my father. For the time being, I don't know maybe Midnight, Jada had found something that interested her to the other side of the room next to the fireplace. Jada had slid one by one, each of her gold rings into her pocket either for the sake of safe keeping or possibly because the decor of the room left her a little insecure about her past experiences with some of the more precious metal, as would it anyone who had seen the inside. In any matter, where the plastered over stone wall began Jada started to knock with her now bare knuckles to then lean in with her ear pressed against the stone gently, to listen for what I don't know, sounded maybe hollow.

"How does this end, you sit there and read the book? my father spoke back a small distance to Mr. Han Wei's seated attention aiming downward. The old man then looked up at my father to say

"Maybe one of your children would like to read book, Mr. Han eyes not so good." He mentioned more than once "Then perhaps it ends with love lesson," he concluded by bringing his head back down toward the inside cover of his book. My father then turned his head not to look me in the eyes but to make sure I would listen carefully to his next few words.

"You are going to have to try to climb up and go get help. You and Jada."

This was my opportunity to see if the escape gene ran in my family and a chance maybe to right some of my wrongs for tonight. I cleared away some of the first floor debris with my feet, Since the only reason I never made it to the top rope of my fifth-grade gym class was because I had no reason to other than to show the class how uncomfortable I could be with heights. I told Jada that I would first climb up and secure each table knot so that when she climbs up after me, not only would it be safer, but I could also help to pull her up.

"There's that cat!" she replied.

"Did you hear what I said to you? We must climb up this perforation. To the top."

"Yeah Sam I heard you, what about your father?" she asked mostly with her focus on the location of the black cat.

"It was his plan" I said before a stretch and then a short hop up I tugged on the tablecloth to see how well connected it was to the rest of the dining room furniture. By the time I had turned around Jada was completely elsewhere, she will just have to be here in spirit I said as

I prepared myself. It would take a little more than a cat to deter me.

"If this is some type of game, why do I feel like you're making up the rules as you go?"

"Mr. Han might could say the same thing about you."

In front of the fourth bookcase from the floor I fell through, underneath a type of Asiatic shield pinned to the plane wood surface adjacent to a razor-sharp axe, there was a maroon cedar box bench engraved of boats and trees the length of the bookcase's width, that if I stood on I thought might help give me a better starting point up to the top.

"I am a simple carpenter who only wishes to do whatever he has to, to protect his family. I confess it hasn't always been easy, and maybe it didn't turn out the way I planned but it turned out the way someone planned it, someone who believes in only solutions and I thought I could assume someone like you would be able to understand this."

"If you know that Master Han Wei only about solutions, then you never assume Master Han Wei only about solutions."

In the meanwhile it coulda been my stubborn pride that said to me, you're never too busy to dream about somewhere else because I swear I could taste my mother's cooking and that always meant my comfy bed was close by. Of course, if my room were dirty, I would have to clean it before I could relax. Other than that, I think my mom knew that if there was a reason for me to randomly clean my room, there was also a high possibility it meant I wanted it twice as dirty. "Alright" I said as I put my trust in my father's ability to tie and the tower theaters promise to supply guest with solid accoutrements.

"Master Han Wei understand, you want to move mountain at your own accord and when son does same as you, you there to rescue him. But if he has not to fix what you create well then you must fix what you create. Or else you do your family no favor."

I wasn't looking back, hand over hand I was able to pull myself up through this vertical microwave not much wider than my shoulders. In need of a towel to wipe away my sweat and what I hope was just the steady drip of water from some minor leakage that occurred. I could feel the furniture shifting at the very top.

"Truth in one's desires will Lead them to whatever devil they choose or whatever devil chooses them. Your third person narrative is dead giveaway, don't take it personal Mr. Han or Mr. Han Wei, is it?

"Mr. Han very much enjoy Shakespeare; he speaks about difficult choices and consequences intricate to the human emotion. You feel as you don't belong in this Serdab? Doubt is the devil not Master Han Wei. Mr. Han don't have to wish bad things for no man, a suspicious mind conjures its own demons. And Master Han Wei answer to many names.

Moving forward I inhaled then exhaled at each short distance deliberately getting my body jammed in this box to conserve my oxygen and to tighten each table knot. Seizing on this obstacle as opportunity, I let out some pent-up gas, as you could say I was stressed.

"Too great a desire to be free, without successful means to deliver on said promise, makes one no longer available to dictate how one gets to where they will end up regardless. What emerges will be thanks to that which is no longer there, something like everything else you will eventually have to let go. Mr. Han feel we have similar interest."

I was feigning to breathe in the air of freedom, and it was gratifying to see the light up above even if I do not remember there being a light in the first place. I was almost at the top when the water started to accelerate down into my line of sight from where, I could not tell you.

"Sam!" I heard my father's voice call my name from underneath me. That's when the chairs kept together at the top separated from each other sending one chair down toward my head while I fell back before the same chair became wedged inside like how I had wasted my time and shaped this night. Dangerously close I fell about halfway down to my father's panic,

"Don't move Sam!"

> I don't think I could help it much, but I said okay anyways. The water that was still pouring down on to my body as it turns out was also loosening the knot which I found in front of my face. Everything around me began to raddle right as I fell with a little less discretion each time, taking the entire aluminum structure down on top of me. It was probably what saved my life to be honest. Like my mother would always say things can be replaced but I could not.

"Ah right near the rectum! Very painful" he said looking away, "but you must always ask if one wishes to stay for dinner. Mr. Han no like to postpone, fish soup supper."

> I think I blacked out for two maybe three seconds, and when I came to, my father and Jada with the black cat in her arms were standing over me where I understood myself to be lying in the ruin, the seed of disaster.

CHAPTER 20

"Hey Sam! Are you alright?" my father said looking down at me.

"Oh, and just forewarning, Mr. Han things hold very bad curse but Fuk yu very effectively."

"Cursed from who?" my father challenged. "Whose things are these really?"

"Those very good questions. Come over to Master Han Wei domain and he will answer" Mr. Han said walking away from my father.

"We haven't touched anything" my father yelled back.

"Dad" I whimpered. "I used his box to lift myself up" I confessed to the open chest not yet broken but displaying now the gold mask of a pharaoh whose missing eye told me that it may have fractured during the fall.

"It's alright we can clean this up" my father said picking up the mask, then the chest and then putting the mask inside the chest right back to where I had grabbed it from.

A loud popping spark came from out of the fireplace, Pop!

"look it, the cat made it down here somehow. You think it could have climbed down like us? That means there must be another way out of this room."

"Her named Mefdet and she also most usually not like to be moved." Mr. Han seemed to appear out of thin air.

"She must like me than" Jada wanted to believe.

"Or she is frightened of something greater," Mr. Han turned and walked away.

"Where could you have to leave to now!?" my dad declared.

"Much appropriate to make sure host is not predisposed in other duties before self-invite" Mr. Han's voice faded. Another loud pop came unannounced and then the cat scratched Jada's hand before she let it scurry to the floor.

"Ok alright I won't hold you." She said pulling her hand back which I saw was a kind of red.

"You okay" I asked her now standing stagnate after receiving a helping hand from my father whose black bomber zip up smelled like it had been hanging around a campfire.

"Yeah, I'm alright but there is something I have to tell you." she was then interrupted by the incessant crackling of something happening in the fire. Pop, pop.

"I think we should move away from this area" my father said. Pop!

I think there is something in the fire I said watching the flame rise.

"Let me see your hand Jada" I could hear my father say in the background to me alone moving toward the fire. Pop! Pop, pop.

"Sam!" Jada's voice called to me. Then my father "Where are you going Sam!?" curiosity got the better of me as I was just passed the towering Egyptian warrior with Iron sword, when what could wait no longer anymore, the flame exploded with a backdraft bang! As a fiery projectile whizzed by my head which I then heard ricochet off the warrior standing at attention behind me. I felt the left side of my face for pressure marks, as it was that close to piercing the skin. Caught up in what almost just happened, I was not paying any mind to the next moment.

"This room is a Deathtrap," I said reaching down to collect the belt that only grasped the loops as my baggy jeans which dropped to my knees, showing my boxers while my body stood paralyzed for a second by what I believed to be a sign of broken promises.

"Move Sam!" I heard before I couldn't avoid looking up to see the blade of the sword come down across my face and slice my left eye."

"It does not look too bad, considering you could have been beheaded" Doctor Farrow spoke to me. "What happen to the piece of projectile that almost impaled you?"

"Don't Move Sam" I could hear my father's voice again above me as I groaned in poor attempt to conceal my obvious pain. Jada had torn off a piece of her dress to try and stop the bleeding that probably looked a lot worse than it was. The doctors say I have a slim chance of getting my full vision back. That's a good sign as far as I can see.

"Hello again" Jada remarked holding the piece of material over my wound. "I want you to know that I like this outfit. Something else to hold over your head," She comforted me.

"Which one of you owned the priceless artifact that shot out of the flame, causing a chain reaction that almost killed my son!" My father said out loud directed at the old Chinese man. Then to us "listen guys if we have to stay here for a while, I'm going to need you to not touch anything else okay."

"What did you want to tell me earlier?" I asked Jada knowing that whatever she would have said to me would not have made her look any more vulnerable than I seemed right then.

"I can't remember so it must not have been as important as I first thought. Just lay back" she said taking it easy on me.

"Still nothing" my father said looking at his cell phone service. "Hold on Sam I am going to find a way to get us out of here."

"Must move forward to go back."

"Can I get a proverb about what moving forward looks like?"

"You must admit guilt."

"And what are we all guilty of since we are all stuck in here?

"In forbidden book, it tell you everything. Where you must go and what you must do, but most importantly at what point you became lost."

"I'm not sure I need a book to tell me all about that but guess what choice I have. Just leave them out of it. They are children and they should have nothing to do with any of this.

"You must move forward like child must become adult, adult who has no choice but to accept burden of father mistakes or father's glory."

"And what am I supposed to just sit around and watch my family get hurt?"

"No, at your best you will want to intervene and with great vitality however, with excessive knowledge this can prove to be of hinderance depending on the situation. Like no one intervene when Master Han Wei blood sugar need modification. I must now eat, late supper."

"Man, I could really go for a fish sandwich from the Muslim bakery right about now," I said seriously salivating.

Mr. Han have extra of delicious red snapper soup. You try?"

"Sorry I don't have an appetite but if you have something to drink preferably bottled water?" Jada answered.

"No water. Only tea."

"Yea that's fine, thank you."

"I will actually take a bowl of some red snapper soup" I said sitting up.

"Okay you try, you like."

"Nothing for me" the make-up of my father's unreachable expression painted his image on edge.

"Mr. Han be right back" he said walking over to the fireplace to then pull down on the head of an owl which I had not noticed earlier perched on the top left side of the mantel. Like the Owl on Doctor Farrow's desk. The old man disappeared again behind the rotating backdrop.

"I am sorry dad, I never meant for it to turn out like this,

"Forget it Sam. You are not the one who made these rules. You are not the first ones to break them either. I am as much to blame but we can discuss it another night, let us just worry about getting home."

"You called me Sam" one of the biggest surprises of the night.

"Yeah so. Isn't that your name? You're not a little kid anymore, I am just starting to come to grips with this."

"Maybe that book is the key to getting us out of this room." I said. "If not, maybe it keeps us entertained long enough until someone comes to our rescue," I was willing to stay positive.

Ten minutes later Mr. Han who sometimes went by Master Han Wei reappeared with a tea kettle decorated with red flowering in one hand and a tray of hot pot, surrounded by what looked to be old Chinese clay kitchen ware, which I viewed even more of a spectacle by the way in which he was able to balance all that with one arm.

Jada had protested the seating arraignment "You expect us to sit on this cold dusty floor the whole time with no cushion?"

"You ever hear saying, mind over matter? The Master said standing over me and Jada. "Nothing tea wont fix. Let the ceremony commence!" he announced.

"Take small sip, Chinese tea give taste buds, third degree" he chuckled pouring scolding hot liquid into four tiny cups. Jada did not get the message in time apparently as she took too big a sip and immediately regretted it, exhibiting an unpleasant face. "No make ugly face" he said to Jada as he handed me my seafood soup in a bowl. "Pretty girl needs to look more like Janet Jackson less like Peter Jackson." I know in the back of her mind she could have strangled him at that moment but luckily, she instead seemed to enjoy her tea. The Soup was good too.

I Remember saying, "Soups good.",

"This tea is not bad, what's in it? Jada asked.

"Ah thank you. It Master Han Wei special blend of white Lavender, Plumeria stem, snake venom, reticent, cloves, Moxa MugWort, some green tea extract, and some other supplementary ingredients.

"Snake venom!" I said with emphasis.

"Very little snake venom in ancient recipe, no poisonous after Master Han Wei concoct. Have some" the old man offered it to my father next. "The tea help you relax, make you let go of inhibition."

"Won't allow you to let go of that book though" my father speculated.

"Mr. Han must safeguard" my father interrupted him before he could finish.

"I know, I know. Mr. Han Wei must protect what doesn't even belong to him, cheers." my father said downing the small cup of tea like it was a shot of cognac.

"Actually, what is frustrating for Mr. Han to confront is that Master Han Wei eyesight not so good. Make it difficult to read small print without magnifying glass," he explained again in case one of us was deaf, dumb or indecisive, words best used to describe our night.

"And if I read the book in place of you, what will I then become cursed for all eternity?"

"In fact, just the opposite. You will reach inside, another you. One longing to see the light, again. This book is only way to set free. Of course, if this is what you are destined to do."

"What's in it for you?"

"Woah" I said starting to feel a bit disoriented. Jada concurred with my observation and raised me vibrant colors.

"Did you see that?" she was tripping.

"That only temporary cognitive enhancer," Mr. Han soundly convinced. "The tea will cleanse your eyes, incense the nostrils and sanitize your mind. All things needed to live a life of servitude."

To me the tea tasted disgusting, I imagine if I had licked the grooves in the floor, it would taste something like how this tea tasted, but it was warm and it gave the rest of my body a calm feeling, so I continued to drink.

"So, can you tell us more about this book, does it have a name? Where does it come from?" Jada said firing off questions that I was interested in knowing myself.

"Important tasks cannot be accomplished without an element of moderation. Something must come from nothing. First thing little girl must go get Mr. Han chair, then Mr. Han tell you of affairs."

"Wait Jada" my father grabbed her hand before she ran off.

"It's okay, Go! No worry! It Master Han Wei chair, he bought from Pier One Import."

"I will go get it" my father decided. "Stay here."

"What do you mean something from nothing, like evolution?" I asked.

"Yes, evolution. But more!" he said sounding less scientific.

Is this book going to tells us that we came from apes because I do not think a gorilla could knock that door down?

The old man running his long fingernails through his aged beard "No not Gorilla. Where you come from, there are very few trees. Which is unfortunate, Mr. Han Wei revel in shady spot. But you are from a place of sand and water, destruction, and rebirth. Like Mandela. From this book is called,"

My father returned with Mr. Han's chair and placed it at the center of our circle we formed in the middle of the room.

"You must sit, read book," Mr. Han demanded. "Master Han Wei will meditate on floor like child.

"Why the hell not" my father complied sitting down in the wooden chair. "I could have made this chair for a lot cheaper," he said still always a carpenter. "I'm just saying."

"Mr. Han no need cheap chair, need strong chair. Where misfortune have no power over you. Unequal among its peers, the power of not one but two shall emanate within an intermediate vessel while the attributes of pride are willfully condemned and to be expunged from ones character for it would be of great shame to stay as you are now."

"Okay let me see the book" my father said to the old man passing over the archaic scripture. My father opened the hard cover to the inside preamble, you know the writer's foreword. He looked up at us one more time before he went on to read the words oddly still vivid today,

Around since the beginning, left the world as a lesson to an eternal son jealous of his father's favor, guilty the language sentence to reminisce of former glory while he lay defeated, exiled. From where the wandering mind finds its ability to lie, the day its eyes look away, Is the day no longer. And shall it be night that reigns to form the waters who await his return. Before the maker of time, only in the Book of Mercury could history find a full account of the family contention.

"I don't want to even know who had to translate this in 2020," My father stopped reading.

"No one! Deeply satisfying book can translate itself and open any door that the reader wishes." Master Han Wei gave his final passionate point of view as my father was committed by any means, to getting all of us home safe. I notice an addition to my perforated attire as the back of my denim button up had a hole under the arm pit which was smaller than the one in the ceiling but a tad bit larger than the one at my knee.

"I don't expect you to be able to recite the book back to me but if you could, I would be really interested in knowing some of its details." The Doctor said to the act of removing his designer eyewear away from his squinted focus.

"Well I remember I started to get dizzy and I think what happen was that book scarred my memory somehow because it's the opposite" I said sounding strange to my own ears "I believe I am able to recite the passages as if it were a transcript, doctor."

"Amazing" The Doctor had determined. "If you wouldn't mind Sam, if we start to go over the allotted appointment time, my secretary will let me know. Other than that, please continue." My father looked around the room one last time before he continued,

"Where do you keep the Canopic jars?" my dad asked to the unexpected, peculiar smile of Master Han Wei, where only one side of his lips opened up.

"It is here you wait inside one extra-large Canopic Jar and you must read to exit." I figured it was Mr. Han that said that.

"Read to exit you say" my father spoke with a blemish of frustration upon his cheek. "Tell me, how does a fountain in the middle of an oubliette maintain such a steady circulation of water? I'd be fascinated to know since the theaters water bill must be outrages." "Where there is water, there will be life. Water will find its way anywhere and through anything, it was only a matter of what you refer to as, time? Exorcising all demons wherever they may try to hide from view," I saw oriental man again pilot a smirk,

The BOOK of Mercury.

an Eye burns naked for love torn apart

from nothing thy waters still follow.

twice child upon return scorned of heart

for beauty rewarded alone bares sorrow.

then fall shall we to Mourn thy night

And crown thy guilty with thorns of gold.

seek not of him who birth Canaanite

Lest drown as Victory curse of Underworld.

many storms lay down the flag of Chaos

we raise thy waters the clash they sow

till then the spirit does not betray us

give back fair warning thus what you Know.

bring forth thy image through beast I rest

to tell A tale still rise does......

That is where I first started to have visions. A beginning, Against All Odds there was the Attrition from the watery loop of chaos, Ptah, self-created Light from the dark of Nun. From this the creator Ra Atum. Ra Atum the light of the chaotic nothing birthed him two children. Shu and Tefnut, Air and Moisture. Away from their father Ra Atum the celestial rivers drifted Shu and Tefnut lost. Ra Atum, whose only wish was to have his children returned to him generated a cry a wild wind, for it would storm for as long as they were away and not in the grasp of their distraught father. Without vision, no longer hearing, beside a cosmic sea of sadness Ra Atum expressed his love for his children when he created in the image of himself a beautiful long-haired, fire eye temptress named Hathor. It was she who would seek out and find Shu and Tefnut to return them home, to Ra Atum where they belonged. A miraculous recovery, Ra Atum was overjoyed upon the return of the children Shu and Tefnut that he decided to create Geb and Nut. Earth and Sky. A shadow of who she used to be, Hathor saw that Ra Atum had regenerated another of himself, another Ra while Hathor would be reduce to an apparatus of tribute made of less importance. But Ra Atum with no sense, only could see Hathor as a part of him. You are truly special to me Hathor; forever shall I reward you to convolute like a corona around my eye. It is there that Hathor explained to Ra Atum that she could create as she would support her claim by exposing her genitals to a very amused Ra Atum. It was his snicker which put Hathor into a fit of fury. She said to Ra Atum "If all you care about is my beauty, when I am more than only this, then let this no longer distract you." In defiance Hathor cut the lock of her beautiful flowing hair, letting it fall beneath into the Underworld before she too mourned upon the thrown of Ra Atum.

Eons in the past, a world of matter unrestrained like the flow of the Nile River through Egypt. On the support of Geb, the First Dynasty birthed beings made of fresh water and sand that when molded by the hand of nine deities brought with it, Life. This included many different plants and species of animal, birds, hippos, cats, snakes, bulls, cows, fish, crocodiles, and Jackals. But this creation was bittersweet for it was not long before the separated humans rebelled against the Gods. Something had to be changed. Ra Atum decided to start another new beginning, granting Hathor the ability to transition between worlds and the task of relinquishing some of human creation from Geb. Disguised as a primeval beast ripping through every human specimen she came across with an unquenchable thirst for blood. Hathor found a passion for destruction. Ra Atum became worried when it was felt that his entire creation would be destroyed by Hathor. So he devised a plot to transform the water into wine and to render the Nile red, the color of blood so that when Hathor drank it believing it were the blood of humans, she instead became so intoxicated that she was compelled to then return home. "The Gods must rule above and below for there to be order" said Ra Atum. The reunion of Hathor and Ra Atum brought about four more children, two male and two female Gods. Before there was language there was order.

First came an immortal Son, born Osiris. Kind and gentle as a breeze caressing a flower, loved by all created on the sands of the Nile. Then a daughter, Isis. Of beauty and grace her eyes a cure for affliction. A wife to king Osiris, a queen to all of Egypt. Born one night apart, another son, Set. Brother to Osiris of dark and menacing, and strong with determined eyes. To rule the red desert with vigilant authority prepared to rid the kingdom of any untimely invasion, he was forever assigned. Last was Queen Nephthys a breath of fresh air, a sister to Osiris and Isis, devoted wife to Set. It was the duty of these four to return the glory to the Gods and bring the kingdom of Egypt to eternal form.

As the love the four had for each other grew, so did a dynasty. At the favor of the God's in dedication the Kingdom shall touch every corner of Geb. But it was the games of younger Gods that was to decide the direction in which the Kingdom was to reign. Competitive, both Osiris and Set displayed spirited excellence, future order through youthful games such as of hide and seek, all the way up to innocent games of Senet. Usually with Osiris being able to hide in places that Set could never find him. Osiris bested Set often but never strayed away from the morals of good winner. Young Osiris would consul Set.

"Alright Osiris, I give up. Come out and show yourself!"

"We all have somewhere we excel brother, you too Set will excel at something and be better at it than me. It is not in our nature to enjoy the taste of defeat. But as of now I am still your big brother and it is best you take defeat with eyes that listen and ears that see." Set respected Osiris for it. And the kingdom and civilization flourished, and peace reigned throughout Egypt. The Deities were protected by Temples of worship in the hands of the Nubians at southern tip of Upper Egypt. Pyramids as strong as the Gods were built by none other than the tribute of their own creation. In the north, what was Lower Egypt, the four earth deities governed by the source of life which bore

Blue Lilies, Jasmine, Lavender Lotus and Papyrus Reeds, the Nile River ensured that civilization would prosper at its passage. As the four grew to adults so did Egypt expand, where it was then decided almost unanimously by the higher deities that it should be Osiris with whom Isis sits before in marriage, and who then shall rule all of Egypt with virtue and Justice. No mere mortal across the promise lands as far as the eye could see would dare debate whether it was to be Osiris who would be the rightful ruler, as there was no objection from the sky Gods. Although Set, no mere mortal and destined to discipline, felt strongly otherwise. Believing that he was to be the one true ruler and heir to the kingdom of Egypt. Set became adamant in proving to the deities that if Egypt was to provide law over the fertile soil of Geb, then in order to fulfill this highest edict and to maintain model rectitude, it should be Set not Osiris whom the deities put their faith in.

It was a celebration worthy of the exalted order, in accordance of a ritual preservation before Osiris was to marry Isis for the entire Kingdom to witness at the center of Egypt, Benediction, a rare occasion to rival no other it would be plenty reason to share in great success. Gifts and favor were distributed liberally as well a necessary animal sacrifice as to appease the Gods above. For the common people it was a feast of beer, bread, vegetables, and fish. For the royals it was fresh fruit, figs, goose, dates, and wine. On the inside of the palace walls Egyptian felines were never not around the royals so they too would consume the finest foods Egypt had to offer. Towering over their people outside of the palace, a Pharaoh's hand if swept across the sky had the authority to drop the head of every living creature as worship in domino symphonic, a fall throughout the black lands. The air of Destiny past over the tired sun. The games of immature kings were coming to an end and the outset of conception, bare ripe for the Pharaohs consumption, which fell upon the moment. More than just the thrown was of interest to Set, he also had great admiration for his sister Isis.

"The nerve of my sister Isis not to grant her truly loving brother a proper goodbye."

"Hello Set."

"Hello Set!? My sister is to marry the ich on the bottom my

royal foot, to my pent-up Ka and all you manage is Hello Set!? Hello to the blood of Egypt if you are to marry another in my place. Who are they to Judge you!

"If it is to be our last time, that is no fault of yours. It was not in their plans."

"We both know it is possible they can be wrong!"

"They can be allotted unforgiving, cruel, and fair in the same sail but the one thing they are not known to be brother, is wrong."

"If one did not know any better, they might confuse your devoted deposition as anything other than a Despotic inheritance. Come hither sister Isis, protector of misinformed deity, let me foster you some restrain if you are believing our brother Osiris is to keep you.

"You underestimate your brother, Osiris. A mistake your brother does not make about you, Set."

With still enough time for the deities to change their decree, to make Set Pharaoh of Egypt's Blackland's and to take Isis as his queen to live their lives as one. To Set what felt a greater punishment would be to abandon a reckless love than to live with the judgement of a jealous God. Set has grown strong and wise just as Osiris but favor as righteous as its creator, leaves another to pick the bones of its dead like a vulture of the red desert. What would be evening, saw Set generously surround himself with wine and women as to celebrate his brother's final moments, his equal and to embrace a new Dynasty where one would be less responsible to fix the families dysfunction.

"What sours your face brother? This is supposed to be a celebration of the Gods and our eternal reign as brothers in this world."

"While my brother has every advantage, he continues to make mortal mockery of me. You are not the one who is to reign as an outcast in the dry desert with creatures of the shadows as your companion, are you my king?"

"What dominant concern do you reason with Set? Look the Gods granted you drink to calm your nerves and you feel as that their favor is to see you banished. You have everyone at your every beckon call and you still find enough sorrow to chamber a shadow. You have free reign over anything in this kingdom this includes your ravenous appetite for debauchery."

> Thou brother thinks I fear the gossip of a Cicada. None of what you speak is of real tragedy. It is mere reasonable interpretation of events yet to come that you do not find it in bad taste to reward those who are ready to rebel against the kingdom. I find it unsettling that the Gods would see fit to choose my brother, Osiris, the catalyst to chaos over practical permanence. This is not like when we were children where there was a lesson to be learned afterward, brother."

"You have not to worry about contention in the kingdom. Do not stress yourself with talk of rebellion, Egypt is glorious and will remain so. Plus, I have the Gods to thank for rewarding me an unyielding brother to help watch over the kingdom."

> "Yes, from my mouth of sand and death, to your fertile ears. A worthy inheritance to pass on to a son, wouldn't you say so? Leave me brother for I would like to consume my wine and fondle my concubine in the quiet. Plus, isn't it by appointment you are to receive a daily dosage of adulation from those of pious misgivings.

"I leave for upper Egypt after the ceremony and I expect the kingdom to be of order upon my return. I Also expect you to abide to my divine authority over the matter, Set and not to further question my decisions."

> "Thus, you wish and let it be so my Pharaoh."

"Let me go Set, you are besotted by Shedeh!"

> "The foolish believe that Osiris not Set is the true Pharaoh of Egypt. They favor my brother based off games we played as children. I love my brother, but I am stronger. And Father knows this, that is why I am aloud to speak with bare tongue to you, Isis. I have loved you from the very first moment my eyes could comprehend. Denounce my brothers' rule. End this madness!"

"You are with child from Nephthys, so you know not what you speak."

"An obligation I maintain in best interest of the kingdom, but my heart is for your dossier."

> "Sounds more like foolish reasoning. Be careful where that positions you brother. But beneath Sefer, I too will fulfill my obligation and marry Osiris. I hope this settles with in and exudes your future determinations.

At sunrise, the kingdom of Egypt was solidified by the union of Osiris and Isis. Anointed by the Gods above, destined to be a panacea to all ills, as were many spectators to witness Sedans carrying the Pharaoh of gold head wrap, alongside his great royal wife through the middle of city as bodyguards with their swords and the fan-bearers with their golden flabella walked beside the royal cavalcade as everything under the orange sun now belong to the King and Queen. By Aker, the Pharaoh of Egypt had planned to make his journey toward the southern border to discourage any further conflict in Nubia between its Kushite people. To conclude the grandiose tribunal and to consummate the crowning of the Pharaoh and in acceptance to the conditions agreed in the finalized treaty, a few of Nubians gifted the Pharaoh, God King Osiris with a handmade coffer of wood and woven reed, as to show where their loyalty lied.

The Chest

> "Your brother welcomes your return in the courtyard my king. How were your goings with the Kush? Were they servile to you ordain appointment?"

"They are misunderstood Manetho and I am in the position to mediate for the common good of all people. For the love of Maat, we are bound to remedy the ills of the less fortunate and this I shall uphold but as of now I have no more to say lest you have knowledge the where abouts of the queen Isis?"

"What is unknown, I will seek to inquire immediately and then I shall return my king."

"Your loyalty is valued plenty. Let me now go speak with my brother."

A background of the singing birds gathered behind Set and three of his personal council in the drinking court to celebrate what would be another triumphant conquest for the kingdom.

"Could this unhinged celebration which attends to my brother be solely for my return?"

"Ah yes toast to my brother King Osiris he who has finally graced us after another successful conquest, Do I kneel before thee? What story of courage do you reward this royal antiquity you call a brother? Yet we find your return never the poorer.

"To wake inside a civil kingdom is all the fortune one could ask for."

"I too, Set have dabbled in my share of fortune while you were away, presiding over divine responsibility."

"New fortune? I see you have not denounced drink, so I guess it not consist of sobriety."

"Your wit brother, it kills me. But as hard as it may be for you to believe, I do celebrate my brothers safe return, while the people of the court wait to hear about this resolution. Tell me, did you favor the incompetency of the Kushite or maybe the conspiring Nubians.

"I accepted this chest, council, as a peace offering with compliance to my divine authority.

"You except gifts from traitors and I am not to see this as weak?! But I am able to accept this with equanimity. Forgive me brother for the liquor has possessed my lips. But please tell me you have not swapped any of father's riches for this whittled atrocity.

A Set council member had interrupted. "Your brother Set is being humble, king. The Gods have spoken to him as well, they bring other fortune."

"Is this true Set? Have the Gods spoken with you while I was away?"

"I see the wine has affected my council's lips as well."

"Quit the timid confidence brother. What is the good news that the Gods have spoken to you?"

"Will you first remove this ugly chest that my eyes are to aimlessly gaze upon? If they genuinely cared to settle their differences, they could have at least gifted you with a worthy enough coffer. Is it magic? This looks barely decent enough for a child to play hide and seek."

"You defer me to beg Set?"

"Remember us in early youth, when we would play hide n seek brother and you would show me how to hide undetected? You would tell me "the Gods have the ability to take the shape of whatever they will it to be. I truly believe that you would turn into the clay vessel when I could not find you. How naïve I was back then brother, Forgive me.

"You respected my hiding skill, that is nothing to be ashamed of."

"King Osiris, could you teach us how to take the shape of objects?" A council member eagerly spoke.

"He said it was for the Gods stupid!" said council member number two.

"Don't be foolish even a God could not take the shape of that retched thing!" the first council laughed. "Nobody could hide in that thing" said the third council member.

"Enough of your silly inquiry! My brother needs not impress the likes of you. Besides, I'd rather it be for better excuse I explain to the Kushite why their gift was returned in such small pieces" Set and the three council members laughed.

"A wager then?" said the Osiris.

"I am listening."

"I will arrange my form in this chest that you say no God is capable of."

"I meant nothing by it your excellency" a council member spoke out of turn.

"Silence! If I can prove this to be so, you Set will tell me what the Gods speak of. Do we have an agreement?"

"I would not want to be the cause of further strain to you brother. Concerns of the wasteland should not disturb the king of fertile Egypt.

"Set I just as well could order you to tell me?"

"This is true" a tame Set responded. "And when I win and you cannot fit in the chest, what do I get?"

"I will return the chest back to the Nubians along with several gold bars so as not offend anyone, this including my wary brother."

"Then I surely do hope you break it."

"Is this a wager brother?"

"I guess it is."

The Gods saw fit to see Osiris win this bet. One God in particular, and thy name was Set. Set had known that Osiris was going to be able to fit in that chest because it was one of Sets followers who gifted the cedar chest to Osiris with his exact body mold, so as to conspire the God king into his very own casket. Once Osiris was all the way into the chest, Set, with an unruly glance over to one of the conspirators, he had signaled the council to shut and lock the Coffer. As Osiris attempted to get out, Set let it be known what the Gods had told him.

"You see brother, I take no pleasure in this because as you lay confined to your own ignorance, Egypt still suffers. They suffer because of you and now they will suffer for you. Improbable as it seems, losing to you as a child this whole time was only preparing me for besting you as an adult. Why Ennead saw to favor your rule over mine, is something I must learn to contend with but if that is what it must take to save Egypt, then so be it. You all look to forget our father made the Ennead. Ra Atum! And he did speak with me while you left Egypt vulnerable. You want to know what he said? Of course, you do. Well what he whispered to me, like how I whisper to you now, he said Let it be Set whom is to be the God King of all of Egypt, not Osiris."

"Set No!" Osiris's scream muffled by the inside of the chest, could only be heard by the ones in the immediate room. Which was that of Set and his treacherous council.

"Throw the chest in the Nile. Make sure it sinks. We have not seen or heard of his return if someone asks."

"It did not sink!" Old Master Han Wei interrupted my father assisting with some of the narration. "The chest that is. This to Set only meant that if he did not have it, he had not asked for it yet and how he felt in the case of his brother, he did not need it. "It resurfaced though. Turmoil began to fester through the kingdom as to the where abouts of the Pharaoh Osiris, were unbeknownst to those who cared to discover the king. Two seeds will manifest to intersect, "Leaving my brother Osiris's body to be retrieved at the bottom of the Nile."

"Mr. Han apologize for Master Han Wei juvenile tongue, Mr. Han said now holding what looked like some type of prayer bead "Master Han Wei should know that favorite story is long enough as is!" the old man hollered picking up then slapping his bowl of scraps to the floor which he forcefully slid under my father's seat where it reached its destination at the far corner of the bookshelf. There the black cat in the background was seen again, giving the bowl a couple good licks. "I believed he has learned his lesson, please continue."

"Apology is no sorry" I remembered were Master Han's wise words. That got me a grimacing smile in return from the old man, who by the way he was sitting I could now see was wearing open toe sandals made of straw. That is when my father continued to read,

This was not to be so, as when it was discarded in the city of Thebes, the chest containing King Osiris traveled uninhibited down the Nile headed toward lower Egypt before it ultimately washed onto an Abydos bank and ended crammed between the roots of an old tree that leaned over yielding waters. Trapped in clear view of a father and son who had just returned from a fishing trip, to their unsuspecting eyes was a wooden chest made apparent its royal intention by the exquisite hinge design and detailed finish. Still sprightly was the man in his evening years and vigorous was his offspring much to know, yet together they could neither move the stuck casket, nor remove its bolts. The contents were not to be identified until a local pyramid builder who also happen to pass by then joined in the effort

Ready? One, two, three, pull!

"As heavy as it is, there must be a fortune inside."

Using a chisel by trade the brawny man who also came to be a follower of Set was able to break apart the padlock with an impatient strike to open the chest, releasing King Osiris's lifeless body. Word had spread quickly throughout the kingdom, but the news of this disturbing discovery reached

Set before it had the rest of the family. Where then word got to his follower that he was to bring the body of Osiris inside his home to wait for Set's arrival.

"Jealous is Geb of those who denote intolerable remorse on thy infinite battlefield, for what remains despite, is the taste of bad blood ready to be spilled yet again." Set decided it was best that Osiris body be cut into several pieces and disposed of this time with intemperate execution by none other than Set himself.

"Multiple stab wounds to the face and eyes with overall detachment from the socket. Forty-five stab wounds to the chest and thoracic vertebrae, additional disfigurement along the breast plate, including fifteen centimeters of supplementary breakage by way of twenty-two tiny horizontal cuts below the abdomen muscle. Point of bisection, an incision around the navel area and to its entirety the removal of the atrophic limbs as well an adjunct removal of the genitals with further mutilation to the groin, knees, and lower extremities. Number four, a division of the chest cavity in order, to then with my hand gently remove the heart."

Completing the dismemberment of Osiris, Set bribed the accomplice to dispose of Osiris's remains as he himself barely escaped detection when word spread of the holy misdeeds, Set back at the palace in Thebes awaited what he believed would come as rumor of his brother's last known location. Though Set was the first to be informed about his brethren's whereabouts no sooner than Set's mischievous departure does Isis and the kingdom get notified of the murderous treachery and conspiracy to cover up Set's involvement. Though not part of the plan for Set to go into confinement, he was confident that once they were unable to find the body of Osiris, they would then look to Set to reclaim Egypt's thrown. However, as the coconspirator, delinquent of care was caught attempting to transport most of the evidence later identified as the former King Osiris from his home. Isis able to locate the vital body parts and preserve most of the major organs in Jars as King Osiris was prepared to make his next journey. With the promise of leniency and at times compensation for useful intelligence, Set's followers indiscriminately betrayed the Desert deity. More troubling for Set than his admission of guilt for the murder of his brother Osiris, was that of the news Set received of the God King Pharaohs final addendum which saw Queen Isis impregnated with the seed, the divine application and soon to be next ruler of Egypt in the image of his father, came the birth of the vindictive Pharaoh King Horus.

> "We must hide him sister! Set is sure to return to claim Horus's life during infancy while at his advantage." Isis, Horus, Nephthys, and Set's son Anubis headed to the delta Nile to take shelter. The official exile of Set from the kingdom of Egypt came as Osiris's soldiers combed the city with strict ordinance for anyone believed to harbor, to associate in any form or knowingly withhold Sets whereabouts within the Egyptian borders would be tortured and then executed!

Through the years and many failed attempts to assassinate the rebirth of the God King Osiris blanketed under the mystical aura of Isis and what split Great Ennead was by punishable offense, that Geb had to answer for the Empire's disorder and still Set found sufficient favor from his father, Ra Atum. While the deities passed the time on Underworld contention Horus grew to be strong and courageous, a holy metamorphosis was the reincarnation of King Osiris's spirit into the astral body Horus, who loathed the thought of Set never returning to face him.

> The purchase of night, a costly transaction taking place in a faraway dead land, still armed and dangerous, denounced and deprived in shame, Set escaped into the Eastern Desert.

> "Mother try to understand Egypt needs me more than I need it!"

Do you know how much you have made me cry?

> "Mother please!"

On the other side, mourn their Pharaoh Osiris, the people did for many days and many nights with great grief, for the deity Hathor also wept for her son as drought and plague crept in, Egypt without harmony was now to fear damnation. If this world was meant for the righteous to lead, then there was to be no better example than the likes of Horus. The chosen protector of his people, the savior of all Egypt promised since gestation, who ascended with military prowess to the combat ranks in ways never afforded to Osiris. Ready for Set's return for it was recorded on walls of the temple, and then for this Papyrus, there was to be a bout of all bouts, a violent resolution for the throne. To end the holy contention in the Kingdom, Horus would have to face off with his father's killer, a ruler malcontent, hostile to supposed duplicity, the very omen of a sorrow while one could only praise him in vain, the God of chaos.

"Father is it to be true. Why favor my dominion at all if Ennead turns on me? Thy body is a temple son "Some say that I am reckless, but some does not know all. I ask you presently father, what is the meaning?"

God told Set that he must fallback for the time being while the ennead deliberates, and that he would always be in his father's favor, "Couldn't you see that I was the stronger son? You asked me to prove it to you and this is what I did and now you see fit to leave me in disgrace. Is it not my duty to protect Egypt from all threats? And for my potency you demonize me! My guileless brother should be grateful I only disposed of him where I could have bested him and so easily taken his manhood awake. If subjugation be a crime worthy of Enneads Judgment, let artlessness be punishable by death. "Why do I deserve your abandonment father?" Set humbly asked every few hundred miles of staggering aimlessly, days on in without water was sure to cause even the God of the Red Desert to become disillusioned by dehydration, until at last he too would succumb to the exposure of exile, a repercussion of seeking shelter outside the kingdom.

What near for Set in the form of depravity, foreshadowing from the windows of his Ka, his soul, between the waves of destruction when most had turned their back on the God, the favor that lay before Set not at all a mirage of his fate but instead one of fortune. His destiny, while truth promised so little to his insatiable quest, Set found salvation in the first sign of mitigation, where the greenwood resides next to a temperate Shu. It was there his senses independent of light served Set down a dark path to a much-needed promise of shade.

Never distancing himself this far from Egypt or from his family Set, barely conscious entered a land begotten by feelings. In the heart of a forest, here walked a myth with a name that only be whispered, Set hungry and weak and void of all significance was forced to embrace his twisted surroundings as the pestilent bark of an enormous dark sycamore became the foreground for solemn infestation. Difficult to spot in the tall grass when neither the weight of Set's head nor his viable apprehension could any longer support an already deficient Sah. What would have been heard by Set if sound, was the ominous silence in the dark that was fast broken. Broken by the impending ruffled leaves approaching, slicing through the fallen foliage as the cunning ripples came to a complete stop before reaching the motionless Set below a teetering branch.

"Yeah, yeah, yeah, the darkness is undeserved."

"Yah, yah yah may my heart go unpreserved" Set fevered along the roots with a song that did not last long, again he blacked out. Unbeknownst to Set ebbing out of consciousness, what slithered down the curving bough from above his feeble frame with eyes that eclipse its own yellowish red hue, cast in the form of a spell, came to Set a serpent worthy of his unattended desolation.

"Hhhhwhat a ray of light the whirlwind has beset me?" the servant coiled all around the skin of the Pharaoh and then back into the dark green and brown patches of burnt grass where sunlight at one time touched down.

"Father why does it burden you and the others that I follow in your footsteps?"

"Hhhhheyyy there."

175

"Who speaks to me?" Set still in search of something honorable, raised his head only to then drop his gaze on to the hypnotic eyes of the serpent.

"I know you been searching for what only I can provideeehhh. To do a Job that I only wish to do for you."

"You don't know me. You don't know what I have been through!"

"Ah but I know where you are going to be. You are going to be where there is Fame and there is Fortune."

"I've had fortune and I don't wish for fame; I only wish Ennead to respect my power" Set grasped his stomach to shrivel in the pain of his own desiccation. Aptly placed adjacent to the tree he sat against, with no choice but to view what he had not noticed earlier, next to Set's disformed shape lay a waterhole of the freshest drinking water any king could wish of. Plunging into the water was Set's last bit of energy, his face imbued by the liquid that he slurped, and he sipped until the sipping turned into swilling with ravenous gulps, for the ruler could not quench his thirst.

"It shall be as you wish my king and if you wish of it not, so shall it be that as well." A snake of fifteen feet hissed.

The resuscitated lifeforce inside Set exhibited a stare of contempt signaling the Pharaoh was undeniably regenerating,

"Don't be afraid, I am a friend to Set."

"Who are you? What are you?"

"My name is Apep servant to the only God I know, Set the true Pharaoh of the fertile land, as well the marsh. A voice to the formerly banished."

"What do you know of banishment? My family's diatribe word shows no favor, my own father is forced to reject my reasons, the people have turned their backs, and Egypt is predisposed to ruin with Horus at the throne.

"Yesssss and it will be you whom shall rectify so many wrongssss."

"But how, with what army?"

"How any ruler allows their legacy to sustain, by the birth of a new, from out the womb of a queen. A queen fit, for Set!" Out of a dense fog to Set's suspicion introduced a woman so much in the likeness of the Queen Isis, Set at first understood it to be sorcery but as she inched closer he became blinded by her beauty and his belief that each and every one who doubted of Set, would later disavow their judgement. Finally, elation was the face of Set for he could touch and taste what he had been longing since a minor to encounter, the bare bottom of sensual repression surrendered to the way he wanted it to be. In all Sets wicked lust and fury, never did he before release a violent thrust as he did then into the hide of who Set believed was Isis. An aperitif to the crippling orgasmic gyration, Set huffed from behind the woman's delightful aroma which escaped her open neck. It was then that woman's face which only visible to Set from one side began to resemble a woman he had not seen before, though still beautiful. Set continued to push forcefully as the back of her hair bounced wildly off her shoulders, she again turned her head to one side to let out a moan not yet coming to a tolerable tempo, what previously bear a resemblance to a beautiful goddess was mere imitation of form spoiled by the erotic evocation of a beast. A diabolical deceit by the dog faced creature with sharp teeth that would transition back into a stunning beauty at the blink of an eye and even as Set still deep inside the monstrous underbelly tried to shake away the catatonic illusion, however even more bizarre things became as what Set dominated now had the face of Horus. Then the mysterious female face, then again Isis, one more time Horus, again vile beast. Ending with the insemination of Isis's image still insisting on never speaking a word. Almost instantly what descended from the creature into the shallow unpurified pool of misguided evolution, a spawn unfathomed to the outside world. From the womb of a grotesque shape shifter who vanished as quick as it appeared, leaving a hybrid litter of what came with elongated faces, were only part-man to the upbringing of Set. That what is conceived initially without a vertebra.

"What have I created Lord!?"

"What escapes the obvious is the solution to your suffering, the beginning of your army. Your victory my King."

Meanwhile not all of Sets creation was able survive the early stages of growth. "The dead, we need to bury deep inside Geb and deep inside us, we need to bury testimony."

"I couldn't agree with you more my King. We shall dispose of them as you wish for no creation is made to perfection," Instead shallow graves they went. "But as for the ones that remain let it be evidence of your glory. I will not be there with you while you return to claim Egypt, the reason, I will raise your army to be strong so it shall conquer every land from here to foreign waters. And your kingdom shall reign in the prosperity as you wish it, Set. God King Pharaoh of Egypt.

"What shall be the name of this proper discharge?"

"Maybe something representing your authority over the meager? Correct titles depend on many circumstances. How about someone you will conquer? For they too will be taught of their oppression. What can sound like triumph in one place, on occasion becomes a disgrace in another."

"Someone who play the innocent but really is the one responsible for this result. Someone who has not yet seen the best of me. So, I shall name it by his downfall."

"And I shall promise them riches and glory if they follow and all the praise will go to their one true king, Set."

Made twice over at the center of a critical conflict, the creation that lay in the dark for years while Set newly invigorated roamed the heat of desire, to an unseen extent had multiplied, progressed, and grew intelligent to the venomous oracle. While on a mission to strike back at the Empire's disadvantage, Set would return to Egypt alone. Outraged by even the mistaken sight of Set's reflection, Horus a now mature warrior along with his mystic of a mother and her sister, priestess aunt Nephthys, the sister-wife to Set, who all anxiously anticipated the return of chaos but excluded was caution for the vulgarity that lay behind entanglement and as for the outlaw price on Set's head, only could it be afforded a Royal defeat.

Dynasty 0

It was the Day after the thirteenth night and the good people of Egypt continued to live in suspicion, plagued by a fear where even calm waters caused mothers to clutch their children closer at just one ripple. Not knowing what hazardous fate, should they face at early rise, Egyptian cities were barren most regularly. Left was the sudden gust of a sandstorm or a sickly inebriate passing through for the people believed Set could take any form at any injunction. Deceive any being or even God, offended with no discretion, and would murder his own family if he perceived them to be in his way.

As for Horus, every day was another to prepare to take his revenge. Although no such fear course through his veins as he welcomed being spotted fishing at the edge of the Nile by his enemy, but a fool Horus was not as in one hand he would grip the fishing net swooshing through the flourishing river, while the other hand would always be free to draw it's gilded sword from the hip with relative ease.

"I bring news of your uncle my King. He has been spotted two days from here in the city of Edfu."

While Horus stood with his back to the Nile where he received the urgent information from out the mouth of a messenger sent by an anonymous source, who fled as quick as he arrived. Erupting from the constant flow of once placid waters, out of the Nile rose a fiercely aggressive Behemoth of hippopotamus in a pursuit of the blood of prince Horus. It endeavored to take a massive bite of Horus missing his upper half by sheer fate and agility as Horus alluded and scaled the semiaquatic mammal in one heroic feat. Shrewd with his sword Horus struck the humongous animal in the middle of its back once, removing the sword before he fell back down to his feet while the Crimson Hippo galloped craters off into the bush. Behind the hideous stride, shouldering an Egyptian battle axe appeared to Horus, wild eyed with a madding mane, Set managing a distorted grimace as the fire inside Horus climbed to cataclysmic heights. Each muscle in Horus's body seized to care for anything other than anger he had toward Set.

"I will appease the Gods with your slaying."

"I should be so honored by the tribute, for it will be outlined by the edge of my sword."

"Egypt longs to purge the day of Set only than shall your terror recede."

"Egypt will fall in the middle of Set's lap like the apple which rids the day the worm prince thinks of himself other than bait. What so easily leaves your lips, you mistake their friendship for your devotion. You would have only heard stories about honor."

"I offer my penance to my father Osiris while he offers all the vices on Geb, for I would so willingly slay you for Nun." The two warriors with restraint to not make immediate contact gradually aligned their enflamed spirits across from each other. They then produced their weapons while forged in the Egyptian battle stance.

"That's a name I have long waited to hear cut from the tongues of each of his followers. Here I see no better place to start. Tell me peon, does your mother still get lonely?"

My mother only wishes for someone as sickly as you Set to face the Judgement they truly deserve." Silence slid in between the dueling relatives right before the air became thick on the strength of kings and as the temperature deepened, shared on the holy ground a mix of blood, sweat and sand while each divine fall shook the eternal waters of Geb. Down not for long, neither one showed the symptoms aiming to concede to the other but before there could be peace, it was to be a destiny of the vehement Gods which would need to clash.

Offered a chance to yield, Set was repeatedly bested by Horus's fighting skill but not yet ready to resign a corpse.

"You must not expose your chest as much. For I will happily take that instead of your pride." Able to stagger back to his feet to decline the suggestion, Set moved with a nauseating flurry of his sword slicing with brute force toward Horus, nearly decapitating the retreating ruler.

With helmets no longer covering their mighty heads in the midday sun, the two warriors gathered their power and then their shields in a picture of obscenity,

"Let us speak to Ennead before our final claim for the throne of Egypt, you fatherless pudendum."

"Where even the Gods will not save you. We will end these contending's at the temple in Abydos. Where I will cut you down like you did Osiris, once and for all." As the Shadows grew closer to outside the holy stage, the sun Set Inside the sanctuary that no mortal man has ever returned from. Outside the Place of Worship from the dark opening high up where the serving class would only witness what came to the light of the approachable platform, the space where the crowd gathered.

"Holy Father I am a servant to your will. Though I believed you when you tell me that you will always protect me, I do not understand why its only by certain means I am permitted to praise you." The sparkling shine, the light that exited the dark tunnel toward the center of the open platform, unleashed from the dark Iris of Set with a sword in the right and a scepter in the left hand, Set made apparent to thousands who would attest to his supernatural capabilities, that he was ill humored to the animosity.

"Holy Ennead why do you not let me put an end to Set's misfortune, for It never comes alone?" Next exited the prowling pharaoh to his many supporters who upon his arrival lowered their heads to worship or for the ones whom were still undecided, they instead murmured remarks implicit to petty arbitration. Enliven by the divine judgment they had just received both God kings removed what slight armor they wore as their fate was sealed no matter what. For it would be a secret best revealed through honor.

> "One Day you will realize being cheated by you is not evidence of folly but that of Osiris's goodness and Set's ruin."

"Osiris had every benefit at his beckoning whim and all the Gods could offer in return was a babbling son. And is this how you will press the issue if made Pharaoh?" The beautiful goddesses Isis and Nephthys in royal garments cohered to the divine decree, off to the side they stood a royal family whilst they with qualm, watched as the royal opponents traded in uncivil deport for the spasmodic clang of aureate metal as it were a duel nature atop the stairs of the Mausoleum. Attempting to drive him from the cover of his shield, Horus gallantly soared by Set but was left with a slash below his back to remind him of his impatience. Advanced in form Horus again took to the offensive as Set to survive the merciless onslaught, mimicked each thunderous strike with sword, before by the grab of the Gods, Set was able to capture Horus's motion long enough to capitalize with a savage cranium attack.

"Behold, Egypt's chosen king now chooses to kneel at the feet of Set!"

> "Holy Ennead why do you protect a murderer?" For if they were to condemn what still could please, so shall it be memory that plays the villain.

The detached disposition of the two kings with readied shields, just like that shook a once hallow soil underneath as a promise of a new sun above Egypt on the horizon of glory and triumph, was to cast a necessary end. Horus struck a demanding blow to Sets shield knocking him off balance.

> "Holy Father unbreak the spirit of my unrequited love, for my ennui and enmity the Ennead have for me by your side is challenging." Set had inhaled the imputed mist dwelling in Atonement. Of what would come to pass, by authority of the brazen sky tribunal, made

as a recoupable debt to be paid brought on by the dawn of a divided burden. The dawn of the Dead.

Wasting no further words Set a magister of deception scattered a modicum of sand that had amassed at the end of his sword into the eyes of Horus before retrieving his axe from behind his back, that he then tomahawked into the shoulder of Horus. The eternal war continues with Horus first removing the battle axe from his broad shoulder before he then dropped his sizable defense, for an incendiary assault. Set as well resigned a shield to desperately dodged the blade of Horus before he too was stymied by an unforgiving slash to the abdomen. The battle intensified as it spread down the column of stairs and through the servile crowd like the fires that began to blaze around the city amid the contention. Set severely injured remained determined to defeat Horus,

"They will not make me High Pharaoh but father, you too have this authority." Master Han Wei interrupted the story, "God had told Set that there would come a day when he too would relegate his opinion, but this day was not to be without opine, for it would be a toss-up."

Set countered a stealthy jab of Horus's spear to cut the weapon in two. Horus now with a shorter blade that he allotted to himself by the ankle, stabbed the lunging Set between his ribs but again bringing Set close enough to the dismay of the gold like goddess, retrieved by his waste, a knife that he would drive into the neck of Horus. Both warriors close to immortal transcendence, fought to maintain a formidable posture as Horus worse for the ware struggled to fend off a few final blows from Set. Isis not willing to see another King fall to Set, who was presently standing over Horus like a shadow blocking out the sun. She attempted to take matters into her own hands right as Horus made a crucial strike to Set's manhood.

Supported by his own knee, Horus took a wild swing skyward which reached the lower extremities of Set, to remove one of the testicles from his divine vessel. At the same instant Horus looked to counter on the period of fortune bringing his sword above his head only to be struck in the eye by a spear thrown by Isis intended for the back of Set. The enrage that occurred with Horus being blinded by what he thought came from Set's direction led the God kings recklessly wielded sword to strike with a swift cut, releasing her spirit to the Duat, removed from her body was the head of Isis. Crushed with the realization of who he had just expelled with his blade, Horus mortally wounded, languished in defeat as he waited to be cast away by Set. But he too lied in ruin, Set with blood on his face and blood all around, with motive only to heed to the Deities decision.

"The Gods have spoken! Tablets guided by high priests met the acknowledged fate of the spectators, as they mourned the Immortals with tears in their eyes, the word of Ra was read out loud to the public. Separated by how high the Holy temple ascended dangerously into the flames, the new order was presented to the public.

How blind are we to our own existence, that we who sit high above reason, find no fault of our own to be punishable by well-timed removal. Destroy my child I will not. With not a heart of our own, who are we to question its resilience in a land of death and that what remains to be expiated by the foundation of the Red pyramids, to shall be wrapped in royal fabric to preserve its journey to the Afterworld. Set who is guilty of sexual transgression shall suffer the loss of this aptitude, and Horus who could not see his own destruction in the form of retribution will abandon his eye to Set and join his Mother in the sky. As before we are to again be as one, again we must break apart, and with all our impetus to return the guilty home, by increment we will mend the infraction as so will Geb continue to rotate. Still alive, breathing in his final breaths from the inside of ornate sarcophagus with liquid metal lining the inside, to further the preservation, while adorned with gold and limestone symbols on the outside, it was the rest of Set's body that preceded the mummification of Set's face and eyes. What lay past the sapphire and scorpions would be his own reflection that he would last view before the royal priests then shut his coffin, alive for all eternity. And so, shall it be inscribed in the hieroglyphs, the Contention of Set and Horus on the walls of each temple and that of son Set, the unpardonable victor of the Underworld, to be displaced deep under the waters as a Leviathan of the Nile. While his dog image above, drawn on as a demarcation between good and evil. And for the inhabitants of the sunken cosmic water, Egypt's guiltiness would be thy storm that came rolling in with ominous instruments south of Philae. With the promise of riches and glory, Set's horde led by the now human Apopis a top an incomprehensible thunderous steed, entered Egypt with such hostile compulsion that the Egyptian people to avoid further carnage fled south to escape the invading Hyksos people who charged through the center of Egypt. They conquered either on horse with bronze longbows or as they rejoiced in unfriendly Terpsichore, aside a peripatetic wagon. For the entire existence of these nomadic pillagers of advanced weaponry was by way of more than one deity. With a choice between destroying his own son or leaving his son to return as only the lord knew fit, Ra chose to let his word escape him. With this came the darkness that was illuminated by the stars and moon as well what needed to be protected and then return to, by the rightful ruler of the underworld. The Eye of Horus, a Jewell hidden to the average appreciator, in the right hand would destroy the old religious tablet lost to the mountains when they had shot up after the siege and only then would harmony and glory be returned to Geb. "Of course, only with a virtuous heart could this feat be achieved" Master Han spoke leaving my father not much time to even comprehend what he had just read. "With the help of child prodigies. Imagine the campy horror at the sight of life cells unchecked, dressed in all white spreading fear just by the sound of their flutes and their bagpipes." That was Mr. Han referring to what we just heard.

> "Mirror of Mr. Han favorite story is, we who must be setback in time, is great honor, for a lease of the body is of our genetic inheritance."

"You mean moral of the story?" my father corrected.

> "Yes, that is what Master Han Wei said, moral of story. You are about a forty-two, forty- four, no? Mr. Han oddly asked my father. "Your jacket, it is very nice material, what is it made of?"

"Okay so your father had finished the book, but the door still hadn't open?" Doctor Farrow said curious.

"Almost."

> "You told us if we read this book it would free us from this

room" my father anxiously communicated to electrify the chamber to our surprise, with the flickering of static as ceiling lights rolled on above our heads.

"And so, shall it be spoken into existence," The old man uttered.

Jada and I stood up as if the door were about to open suddenly, but still nothing. Except then flames burst from out of the fireplace. As the area in front of the bookshelves lit up like a retail store on the day after thanksgiving, brighter and brighter I could see the dust particles float above our heads. Master Han Wei indicated he would hurry and extinguish the remainder of the wall torches as there was no need for them any longer.

"Is it me or is it getting awfully warm in here?" he answered in typical Mr. Han fashion walking away before I could tell him that I was still very much cold. "I can fix that" he said.

My father kept turning the pages as I kept turning my head, first to see the subtle bubble of water up to the top of the clear blue wishing well and then behind me I turned to the sound of music coming from the stereo system which again took its place against the wall, confused I then turned once more to the sphinx statue that started to slowly sink into the fountain as my father continued to read every last word of the story. Bloop.

an EYE burns naked for love torn apart

from nothing thy waters still follow.

twice child upon return scorned of heart

for beauty rewarded alone bares sorrow.

Bloop, Bloop.

then fall shall we to mourn thy night

and crown thy guilty with thorns of gold.

speak not Of him who birth Canaanite

Lest drown as victory curse of Underworld.

Bloop, Bloop, bloop

           many storms lay down the flag of chaos

           we raise thy waters the clash they sow.

           till then the Spirit does not betray Us

           give back fair warning thus what you stole.

           bring forth thy image through beast thy rest

           to tell a tale still rise does Set.

My father then turned to several blank papyrus pages that were the color of sandpaper. Well at least I thought they were blank. Then standing over his right shoulder I saw an illustration of a tiny hourglass at the footer of the otherwise empty page, where at each time my father turned the page so did the illustration of the tiny hourglass allocate its sand.

bloop, bloop, bloop, Bloop.

CHAPTER 21

Something awoke. Each candle left to burnout spontaneously rekindled at the same time. The water from the Fountain looked as if it was boiling out of a pot. My father stood to see his reflection in the mirror

"What have you done!", Master Han Wei said as he reemerges torch in his hand with a look of disbelief for my father. "You actually spoke the name that we do not speak!"

"What do mean I spoke his name!? I said his name several times already. You said his name!"

> "Never would I say such a thing, maybe when Mr. Han alone in bathroom he may whisper said name, but to repeat it as many times as you did out loud, I think not! For learning how to read is a gift Mr. Han has never received. But he clearly heard verse say, he who shall not be named."

"Wait a minute, that's not what it reads and correct me if I'm wrong didn't you say by finishing the story it would open that door so that we could leave? The whole point of me reading this book!" my father spoke to the unnerving sound of the metallic doors automatically unlocking.

> "Dad the door!" I said pointing out which could not have been more obvious.

> "Apparently, you are free to go" the old man said acknowledging the room come alive.

"Sam go check the door" my father instructed. Jada and I began to race over to the large double doors at the end of the room when I was stricken by a nauseating unsteadiness that I was actually relieved to find was only the ground again tremoring under our feet. While it impeded for the moment both of our forward progress, we were able to sway around the broken pottery which shattered at impact.

"Ah yes, run like dogs in heat toward the door, I believe in you!" the old man whose words supported our escape.

I arrived at the handle of the door before Jada. "It's open" I said first to myself and then aloud "Dad its open!" The horrific scream of my father met me as I turned around with confusion which slowly turned to fear. I tried to comprehend how I was to then witness the room somehow fully ablaze.

"Ahhhhh!" I heard my father for the first-time ever yell with the type of emotion I could not image him conjuring. A pain which sounded deeper than the skin.

"Dad!" I ran back toward him. My mouth fell open as I saw to my fright, the brownish tan pages of the book beginning to wrap themselves around my father's arms and then make their way around his torso as he screamed in anguish. I went to rip the pages from his anatomy, but the searing heat that touched my fingertips at each attempt deterred my aid. "Ah shit!"

Jada had noticed Mr. Han through the fire standing over by the stereo.

"Look, he's leaving!" she said moving my attention again to the back of the room where I could see his mouth and I know I heard him say,

"You will find your faith living under waters!" He said before pressing the play button and then he was gone.

"Get back!" my father commanded slowly being mummified by each page.

"What do we do Sam?"

"Ahhhhhh! Get out of here Sam. RUN!"

"I am not just going to leave you. Master Han!" I screamed to the top of my lungs "Please!"

Jada had run through the smoke and the fire spreading all around in pursuit of Master Han's secret exit but it seemed if we weren't to have bad luck that night, we would've had no luck at all.

"Sam there is nothing here!"

"Try pulling down on the Owl" I said.

"What Owl? I don't see an Owl!" she said as I lost sight of her in the smoke.

I saw that the pages of the book were now wrapping their way up my father's neck and then behind his ears.

"The Water!"

I thought if I could get him into the fountain, we would be able to cool him off enough, so I pushed my father to the edge of the fountain burning both my palms in the process. As the wrap held dominion over his lower half, I was trying not to panic but that became even more difficult when to my disillusion, the once clear blue water now moved more like a transparent lava. He sat upright as the stuff circled down from his forehead and up from his chin. I was able to read his eyes before it totally consumed him. They said to me he had let go trying to fight it, just as he was fully preserved by the pages of book and in slow motion fell back into liquid,

"Mercury", Doctor Farrows said connecting pieces.

"It had a silver tint to it" I said.

"Yeah."

And that was it, he was gone disappearing under the matter.

Jada had arrived by my side in time to see the last parts of my father's body become submerged. "Oh my God Sam, I'm so sorry but we have to go." she said starting to pull on my shoulder, but I had not removed my eyes from the once water. "Sam your father wouldn't want you to die! Please we have to leave" Jada barely finished before she went into a coughing fit on account of all the smoke. She eventually was able to maneuver me closer to the only way out which was becoming less evident at each passing second.

"Oh shit! what about the cat?" she said hesitating with her body partly in the doorway.

"Forget it" I said now assisting her forward progress. "It will find its way out like it found its way down here!"

I felt completely helpless. No one was going to believe us. But both Jada and my father were right, I had no choice but to get back and face the world.

CHAPTER 22

I welcomed the early morning drizzle as is does not usually rain that often in Southern California especially at this time of year, but this also fell consistent with the whole bizarre ordeal. We ran to Jada's car across the street where I saw my phone had four missed calls from my father.

"I think what must of happen is when your father was younger, almost drowning in the Atlantic Ocean more than likely activated his spirit. Then it's like you are thinking about whatever your attracted to, constantly. In this world or another.

"What?"

"Are you going to call the police?" I didn't know what to do. What I wanted to do was run back in there and find Mr. Han Wei, Jada with her legs dangling out the ajar driver side door "Sam, what I wanted to tell you earlier, remember when you had knocked over the chest with the mask?" Just then out of the corner of my eye I see the black cat leap up into the arms of Jada as if it were being chased by a vicious dog.

"Oh my God! She shouted becoming startled by the cat "She made it out!" Jada said sounding shocked but also relieved as she examined with a soft caress from her artful fingers, the ash coated fur of Mefdet. "What are we going to do Sam?"

"Just drive toward my house, Jada."

We all went to the police station together. My mom, my aunt who fresh in town and concerned for her brother, Jada and Jada's mother. Jada's grandmother Coral was up at midnight looking for her granddaughter who never came home. We were headed to the police station and she wasn't feeling well by that time. She wasn't feeling well because she had contracted the Covid Virus and made it home a week later. She died.

"I am so sorry Sam," said the doctor.

The cops didn't seem to care much about the gravity to the story, but they still said they would send someone down to the theater. They weren't moving fast enough because my mother had to be held back by my aunt and then my aunt once my mother calm down had to be held back by me and Jada. "Hold up baby girl, let me talk to them. I'm sorry Officer," she squinted to read off his tiny name tag, "ah well it doesn't really matter. What matters is that a pregnant wife, a son and their family and friends are here looking for someone with some human decency to do their Job, because I assure you there are more of us down for that fuck shit, you feel me? So, can we get it together?" My aunt who was six foot two inches of impatient energy, started to clap her hands in demand of speedy service. We met the police down by the theater the next afternoon where I took the exact route that led me and Jada down to the Don Killuminati portrait.

"no, no, No! It was right here!" Jada attested to my recollection.

Nothing was there. The Don Killuminati painting, the broken floor, the secret basement, the hidden chamber, the fountain, the gold, none of it. The police found none of it. Jada tried her best to defend me but her mother, I could tell was starting to think I was mad. A month after Jada had her grandmother cremated, Jada's mother moved her and her brothers to some town in Georgia. I wasn't given the address. I began to doubt myself solely based off what other people had no clue of. And if they did, I'd be compelled to question what help they would be to the situation. If they were to truly see what I saw, if they knew what I know. I did not bother explaining myself to anymore people. If I was going to find my father, I was going to have to do it myself. At first all I had was a handout advertising Mr. Han's Wash and laundry mat to go on and here I am now.

"Well that might be where you made your," cannot figure why Doctor Farrow reflected peering down at both of his palms, "Mistake. Not that you started doubting yourself in the first place but that a couple of bad encounters where you tried to tell your story disqualified by default, so many believers. That your lack of faith in people is somehow associated with how you keep your own. And then if you knew that to be the truth, would you still liken it as an obstacle every time God puts a person in front of your face? Doctor Farrow not letting me continue "And that's when you got arrested?"

"Yeah."

"Did you find anything?"

"Yeah that I could break the law if I had to."

"Is that all of it?" he asked.

"Is that all of it?" I looked around for a witness, "Yeah Doc, that's it" I said kind of wishing I lied. "So, tell me Doc, can I be fixed?"

"Sam, I want to thank you for sharing your story with me today. What you been through. Wow!" Doctor Farrow who was so touched by my story that he kept having to look down to try and find the right words to describe his fascination. "Do you mind if I turn this recorder off?" I believe you told me everything you possibly would know. And you should realize that if anything, your story Sam is proof that there is a life after death. Absolutely amazing. But I think more important to your predicament is that we share common interest. Can I call you Mr. Outlaw?" we both laughed quietly as he made me feel less like a lunatic and more like a desperate son. "Boy you knock me out! What could you have possibly thought you were going to find at that hour, except someone else's dirty drawers?

"An old Asian man that I need to speak with."

"Well I don't doubt you believed that."

CHAPTER 23

"Right, well not to make less of what you have just told me" Doctor Farrow who was slowly trying to rotate out some of the stiffness in his neck as he had something else to say "but that same night your father went missing, March 20th 2020, I too had an occurrence worthy of confession, that you might find in some way ties to your story. I was not completely honest with you on how I received this Golden Owl here." Which Doctor Farrow retrieved from the shelf and placed on the top of his desk as he now decided to stretch his legs. "The nerve of the damn thing, personally I haven't had a string of bad luck since. Of course, my wife. You see, I also could wish for things to be different but what good could ever come from that? I try not to make it obvious that I'm looking for something like you. To be honest, I am a lot like you." He said leaning over the top of his desk. "I don't care to tell people too much about my problems and I tend to come off defensive when I feel people pry to close to home but I should have been straight forward with you about myself and for that I apologize. I mean, I'm sorry. But if you would let me" he suggested glancing over at the clock that now said two-thirty "We still have some time left in our session, I would like to see if I can improve the both of our circumstances by shedding some light on my past." He said as he sat back down on his adjustable leather desk chair. "In my small circle it is not a secret I like to play cards, to an unhealthy extent. One might call it an addiction or a gambling problem, I call it a sure thing almost seventy five percent of the time. Makes it that difficult to pass up but I'd rather admit that I'm no different than anyone else, except the type of money that I risk to lose made it harder for my wife to sleep at night. What are you going to do in a situation like that? Make more money. Right. But that is not the reason why I stopped by this tumbleweed lounge that night. I got into it with my wife the night before about something so stupid I can't remember how we made up, but after all day of dealing with other people's shit, I thought I might retreat my shit with a few drinks on the way home. I wasn't feeling too guilty or too thrilled to race back to our South End apartment and walk right into round two. It's something that I'm working on, I believe the term is process. Well anyways it was one night leaving the office I stopped at a real hip replacement looking bar downtown, I wasn't too worried about where it came from, but I thought it was me in the moment and I just needed a drink. The inside was a real manly man cigar smoking type spot with good-looking waitresses, dim lighting, and free drinks for the regulars at the bar not playing pool or poker in the back. Here I am wearing a three-hundred-dollar suit in a smoked filled room with Ariana Grande singing something like *You Send Me* by Sam Cooke or if not, it was an Ariana Grande doppelganger performing live music. You know that Disney channel singer?" I knew who she was. "Well the whole scene was totally out of sorts, so I thought I probably wouldn't hang around too long, but I might as well grab me a drink and think of a line of strategy. So, I find my way to the bar and I grab me a henny on the rocks before walking back toward the darkest part of the room where nobody would see a man cry. The same time I headed to the back, I see this man freaking drunk as an Irish astronaut being kicked out of a table where there were three other men playing cards.

> "Hey sweetie! Let me get a Hero sandwich" one of the men gestured over to a nearby waitress happy to oblige to the man child's obnoxious appetite. "That's the sub that got blue killed" he said to the table as the waitress taking mental note of his order then directed her skills toward the two men on the other side of her.

>> "Last thing your wife needs is you to be stuffing your face with more deli meats" a man with a cigarette and a thin smoker's face said.

> "Listen, I aint plan on doing her no favors anytime soon and if anyone has a problem with that I'll make sure when they bury me, they bury me face down so you can walk by and kiss my ass" the heavier man closest to me responded.

"Anything for you gentlemen?" the waitress asked.

"Nothing for me sweetheart." The thin man said ashing the remainder of his cigarette into the small hole of the wooden table where normally a nail goes. Kinda looked like one of those outside picnic tables where you were sure to get a sliver if you were not fully committed and then even sometimes if you were.

"What about you?" she asked the remaining card player who with his back against the wall, disguised much of his face under a shadow.

"I'll have a Stinger on the rocks." I happened to overhear the man's drink of choice which was also cognac.

"Never stop, never settle!" I raised my glass to the man who apparently had some style and class.

"Why don't you make that a Royale, neat, in an old-fashion glass" he then conveyed to the waitress a change in style.

"We need a fourth" said the man with a gray handlebar mustache sitting at the end now paying attention to me with his sneaky eyes. The thin man in the middle wore sneaky eyes as well. I was not at all in the mood to play cards and my intention with this visit wasn't to meet new people but on the other hand, what caught me was the stakes that were laid at center of the table. What they were playing for. The best way to describe it was a large sum of cash and expensive trinkets that look like they needed a stamp from customs to be in this country. Apparently, they even had their own bouncer because the drunk guy who was being escorted out of the immediate area made room for me. I had a couple hundred in my wallet and a two thousand-dollar Shinola on my wrist.

"What's the game?"

"Black Lady."

The game of hearts was not really my game, I was more of a poker player. I did know how to plunder a crock pot with relative ease like a back burner on low. "Yeah I think I would like to join you men in this friendly game." The thin man in the middle kicked out from underneath the table a chair that I would be taking all their money from. What I did was I had to enable my gambling problem in order to mask my drinking problem. At least for the first couple games. So, I could keep my balance and keep what the kids like to brag about now adays in their music, you know a buss down time teller." Which I caught a glimpse of peeking out of the cuff of his sky-blue shirt. "Though my henny on the rocks was part of the plan, helping my fellow card player acquire this piece that is around my wrist might have been up for debate if not for some premeditated abstention.

"Can we hurry up and deal already" the man with the handle-bar mustache snarled.

"I understand the feeling when you just need that last player to get the game rolling."

"Are you going to bet" the mustache man's hungry expression reacted to the voice of the thin man in the middle who might have been better suited getting the game started before the mustache man's sandwich showed.

"I see your twenty and I'll raise you twenty-five."

"Do you know something that I don't know?" the man in the shadows spoke. To get more comfortable I dug my back into the unpolished chair when I heard a rumbling of thunder outside, above the short ceiling "Ok boys the score is up to 80," he declared as the waitress arrived with his hero sub than, which he let sit to the side only when he had not a hand to eat with. The rules are fairly simple, once a player reaches those total points the game ends and the player with the lowest score, wins. Thirteen cards were dealt to each player. The first hand is played to the left, next hand is played to the right, then across and so on and so forth. There are only two tricks to his game you really need to know to be successful. Number one always follow suite; hearts must first be broken before one can lead with hearts. Number two, before you supply the table with an education on how to dump hearts, maybe find out what rules the others are playing by. Except after two more henny on the rocks I cared less about anyone's feelings and more that my watch was now on the table.

I told them I was some schmuck lawyer from back east who hadn't the time to waste playing cards.

"Hold on a second, back east?"

Did I say back east, sorry I meant on the east side of town. Anyways, I saw two of the men had depleted funds written all over their face, so it was looking like this was going to be the last game. Besides that, it was late, and I had an early appointment the next morning. So, this last hand was pretty much all or nothing for everyone at the table and by the looks of the man with mayo on his cheek I made out just beyond his mustache and by the way the thin man and his two Pac marks were more focused on waitresses passing by, no other player left to my concern but the man in the shadows. Let me know if you haven't heard the proverb, bigger the risk the bigger the reward. When a player can successfully capture each penalty card, which is somewhat like reverse psychology, being that it is the opposite outcome you are striving for. If the said player can avoid detection by playing in the dark only long enough to deceive his counterpart so that he or she is able to, without fucking it up give the remaining player all thirteen hearts and four black ladies, than that player has successfully shot the moon and won the game. And that's exactly what I did. This was a legal rule, a standard of the traditional game of hearts. I would have been declared the victor any other night except this one.

"We don't play by those rules around here" the man in the shadow declared.

"Bullshit", I said "that is a standard way to play Hearts"

"Maybe back on the east side where you're from, but over here at this table, "We don't shoot the moon unless we mean it." the man which I could see dressed in black relocated his face from out the shadow while the thin man in the middle just then pulled out a Glock nine and placed it on the table for effect.

"What am I supposed to be intimidated?"

"Put the gun away" the man in black said before returning his upper half to the shadow. After a tense stare down with the thin man that was exaggerated to the point a second longer, we were either going to make out or end up killing each other.

"Nice going Nick! You are a real jerk you know that? What did you think you were going to invite a Rockstar to play a kids birthday party, and you weren't going to see a mother fucker! Remember that next time you're in need of a fifth" the thin man said with a smile as he stood and grabbed his only remaining possession off the table before walking away with it again tucked inside his shirt.

"I should have suspected you being a damn cheat once you told us you were a lawyer." The heavy-set mustache man said before he too walked away from the table. "Aww hell" he concluded by taking a big bite out of the last thing he had with him which was the half-eaten sandwich.

"I am not even real lawyer," I admitted.

"No, but a liar every other day," The mature voice from the left of me continued.

"Listen all I wanted tonight was cold drink and then you guys asked me to play so I thought I could be of service. I didn't know we were playing checkers or else I would have kept walking. Are those not the rules of the game?" I asked for clarification. "Let me introduce myself, my name is Dr. A.M. Farrow" I humbly stood to shake the hand of the last remaining card player at the table which apparently had no purpose to the emotionless silhouette of a man as my hand was quietly rejected.

"It means you're not as smart as you think you are pulling a move like that in this place. But maybe you are as smart as I need you to be."

"And where am I exactly?"

"I think you know, so why don't you have a seat" The man offered sounding serious.

I don't know man I just came in to have a drink, it's getting late I probably should be going.

"I wasn't asking, beside you haven't finished divvying up all your winnings."

As there wasn't anything left on the table for me to collect I thought, "Right well, what doesn't matter to someone the likes of you, happens to be important to someone like me" I said to the man in black whose left side came to the light, "And that is to go home."

"Use this moment to your advantage as you won't get another like this in your life." He advised while reaching under the table to reveal the gold creature that sits a top my desk to this day, which instead of seeing me walk out the front door right fucking then and there with the prize, in all reality it simply confiscate the remainder of my night.

"Okay so where is it?" I requested in reach of missing humor.

"This is what you want and all that I ask for is a couple more minutes of your time, as this here valued mascot comes with a story. After that, you're free to leave no problem." The way that bouncer investigated in my direction it seemed I did not have much of a choice.

"Welp I don't have all night" I resigned.

"Let me tell you the story of why we don't shoot the moon, something to help you remember." Ready to call it a night I reluctantly gave the man who loomed in the shadow my condescending but unbroken attention as he opened with,

The Hangman

It was the Summer of 1874, the city of Vicksburg where feelings of jealously tracked their feet on the inside with stains of war and the stench of industrial expediency. About ten years after reconstruction, in the bottomlands of the Mississippi delta, a beautiful piece of land to grow up on if you were say an America Goldfinch or a Red-winged Blackbird. But mostly if you were white. Though colored's moved forward with not much to look back at except love ones who they were forced to leave buried as they either escaped north where more and more blacks were being recognized away from the terror of organized posse's gathered, with their hounds and their torches to parlay unbeknownst, privilege by the moonlight hunting for progressive blacks in the south.

That same year down in the Delta school commenced for colored children under new laws that were supposed to protect our right to equal education. "I'll tell you what the problem was, all these years preaching equal education to us blacks as if we would be opposed to anything superior. The problem is we spend all the focus on the equal aspect and less or no emphasis on the education part. So, congratulations now were all equally stupid." I have disrupted the story. Anyways later that year proud southerners also got their first black sheriff elected to office. Which meant a cold day in hell for more than a few whites when a proud pickaninny took power but more important than having too much was never having enough when you've had so little for so long. How far we have come brought along with it doubt. Doubt in that we would be able to survive our own and doubt we should even have a say in this matter. "If we could just stay together while separating ourselves from those that want to do us harm all would work out in our favor." I mumbled as the liquor took control of my inhibitions. Only now there was more reason to hate. All the way down to the way you wore your hair which would be considered a threat that somehow would end for us back with shackles around your ankles. This period could be so harsh if one hadn't a dream and even than sometimes a dream easily can turn to a nightmare, and then there were the ones who wanted it that way. Solely motivated to live a life as one of the better obedient with disregard to the belief that colored people could truly be free. Believing you deserve better can also have its own consequences if we can't find the time to appreciate things already acquired. Are you with me turned into "where are you going?" which turned into, "I do not need anyone" for a little while until it turned into, "they'll be back, they always come back!"

"Listen to the lord!" one lonely freedman in denial of the changes to occur in front of his very eyes thought if he whistled while he waited for everything to go back to the way things used to be. It meant that he was the only one truly awake and every other son was riddled by mistake. Even when he knew he was doing wrong, longing to be accepted into the house, a brother dark as midnight couldn't ask for higher status then house negro where the food was never cold before it got to one's tongue and the cleaning of the horses stable was left to the undesirable, unbearable to the eye, the untrusting and unwilling to accommodate field nigger. So, you can image how difficult it was for him to accept that this was the end of the old webby road he traveled. It was on to greener pastors just over the horizon for many and many who could care less at what affect this had on Hudson but were sure to find reason in a white man's promise.

"They think they're better than me."

What was the man's name?

Well, the name given at birth was Hudson Kane, but this is the story of hangman. A wicked tale that starts back ten years earlier at the powerful hands of black man's earthly judgement, run dry as he had not followed behind the ones who loved him most. Putting in extra hours Hudson held on to the only thing that ever mattered after his wife and daughter, who were murdered as an example of what is to happen if a slave attempts to outsmart a white man. That which he had never thought of taking part in. Under the malediction of a new moon Hudson became impatient to the cards life had dealt, to the point he only wished to sleep in the same house as where the master slept, which would be the reward for the doing of evil deeds he was made to do, to survive on the nice misters plantation. Eventually which became more frequent as Hudson grew normal to the feeling that came with a colored man's death. Either that or the boredom he used as an excuse to rat on someone who might have been doing somewhat better than he was. That was until the only thing left more for him to lose was himself altogether.

A blessing disguised as talk of a promise land that Hudson knew didn't exist and that which he hadn't paid any mind to, where a few slaves decided to run off in the middle of the night one day because of rumors that had made it all the way up to the big house of a colored man's freedom just around the corner. To the extent that even some of the more fortunate slaves had decided to hightail it up north or than out west. Possibly for fear it might be considered cheaper to kill them all than to let them live free. The day Hudson was brought the news of his much-needed service inside the big house was the day he hoped and dreamed of wrapped in the deep blue eye of forever. The date was September 13th, 1862.

It was nine days later that President Lincoln would sign the preliminary documentation freeing forever the slaves in all thirty-four states, leaving Hudson and his dream of being a house negro shattered as his master could no longer afford to maintain the sizeable plantation without unobjectionable labor. For years Hudson continued to live off the land in one of his former overseers' outpost, a shack a quarter mile downstream from the big house which besides that and what totaled the hundred-dollar annual wage. For nothing more was provided to Hudson who now only looked to be comforted by impending demise as a cure for not being welcomed in the big house as a newly freedman. All the hope as fast as it appeared, crumbled as if fortune and death both conspire to forget Hudson.

What love on the other side of the world not next to southern swamps of self-torment, where out of sight if not for the light of the moon illuminating what now reign a symbol of affliction for all who passed by this depleted man who sat cold like the deformed tree stump underneath his ridged body of malice malcontent. It was often claimed if one were to listen closely while passing through the now desolated town, the whisper of Hudson could be heard cursing the day everything was different. "One better world, one better world, one better world." Life as it awaited so many others, passed right by him even some of the whites who could not understand why this negro had not taken advantage of the federal pardon. As the seasons cycled day in and day out Hudson alone waited to be thrown back into slavery if not to be lynched by a passing crowd of whites as a sign of mercy. Whites would lynch a black man just based off intrigue. They usually didn't need an admissible reason besides that they could, which he did not find much luck there either. Then Hudson figured he wasn't even worth the rope used to tie a man to a tree. I mean his mind was so twisted that If they gave him a list with the names of all the former slaves that use to live on master's plantation and told him to bring them back down to the south, that is exactly what he would have done. Except probably most fortunate for several free men this slave had not entered the masters house until toward the end of slavery, so he didn't learn to read or write much and he wasn't much good at tracking since his owner beat him so bad one time that he lost his sense of smell. "Can't smell so good boss." is how he explained it. Still, he found it in his heart to forgive him. Chalked it up to a bad case of the mistaken identity. See, Hudson was never one to make his master enraged if possible. So, if something was askew on the plantation and someone

was to receive punishment, sure enough he felt that whomever it was catching the brutal beating deserved it, including himself. For ten years this former slave sat on the same tree stump outside his previous owner's house every night. The hair on his head now like cotton and the wrinkles on his face matched the crack in his heart. Praying far behind paradise on twenty-five some acres of government owned land, Hudson who had stopped speaking all together as an example of someone already dead on the inside, under the spell of mother night he would demonstrate how dark his soul actually was with ghostly force and a solid black chin and a way to end it all while the punishment of doubt as to whether he really ever existed would remain lingering, especially present once again like a change in season. In 1874 the answer that came for Hudson in the form of the slightest dark cloud. If Hudson were to get any type of normalcy back into his world, he was going to have to do it himself. He knew of the perfect spot close by, one beautiful phoenix tree down by the water where Hudson decided he was going hang by the neck as to conspire against both fortune and death as he was prepared to watch all of the evil deeds he had done flash in front of his eyes. He fashioned himself some rope, extra-long as he wanted to find the biggest tree to support his wish. The rope now a noose hung around a sturdy branch high up so that he could look down on at this cruel world with bitter remedy, one last time. Only problem was as he measured the slip in the knot precisely to the size of his head, he hadn't remembered to fashion a big enough tree ladder so that he could get his neck up into the noose. Hudson knew of a property just south of his former master's plantation where some timid horses were possessed by a couple of white devils. Never in his forty-five years of slavery did Hudson ever imagine himself stealing from a white man. He would have rather seen himself hang, ironically, they were now one in the same, but this bizarre narrative would be creation by his own eminent doing. Early morning temperatures ripe with sounds of insect chatter, rose with the summer sun as Hudson strolled into a white man's barn with no regard to being spotted as if he were just some hired hand returning to the job. So as to prop his body up to the knot Hudson stole one of the horses that he learned to ride just before being cast aside by his owner. What I am saying is that, he knew how to take control of a horse. So as Hudson stood atop of the beast and while the beast remained still, I know some people who would have needed to have their hands tied around their back because naturally we are going to fight away death to our final dying breath. Instinctual preservation. We are who we are and that's all we are. Well when it was time to let the horse ride off into the sunset, to let Hudson hang until blood dripped from out his cornea and his bowel movements had released all the waste of this world while he believed his feet not to kick as the hurting passed through and touched igniting his heart, to awake Hudson from this horrific dream. Well the horse fucked that up. While Hudson kicked his heels to the flesh of dumb animal, it still hadn't moved. Hudson stood atop that steed for ten long minutes with a noose around his neck trying to get this horse to runaway so that he could leave the way he envisioned. "Lord God can't you do right by me just once." Hudson's soul dancing around spite finally gave into fate for he let go of trying anything and that meant even trying kill himself. All that was left was anguish or at least that's what he thought staring off into the clear pith of fresh waters that streamed sly out into the Mississippi. That's when he saw something crystal like shine from out the water, something he had never seen before, something that no one has ever seen before. It shined like gold one second and then the next with the colors of a Kaleidoscope as if the water became a catalyst for the immediate immortalization of Hudson's eye. A calm sensation washed over his soul as the ground shook and that's when the horse Hudson had been trying to send on his way for the past ten minutes took off leaving Hudson hanging like how he first intended. All went as planned right? Wrong! Whatever that was in the water distracted him long enough to rethink killing himself because just like the reason one might want their hands to be tied behind their own back was Hudson's natural survival instincts, which kicked in where he now attempted to slide his fingers in between the rope and his neck. None of that was of any consequence because what shook the ground and what ran the horse off right than was an impromptu earthquake. Large enough to take down the medium thick branch that Hudson was slung up under. The hard-southern ground caught his fall. In my opinion, now this is just my opinion but what seemed to be a series of fortunate events if one had changed their mind about killing themselves, a couple friends I told this story to awhile back still believe it to be simple gesticulation of plain luck but I believe it to be the sign of change, glory to lord for when what flashed in front of Hudson's eyes as he struggled to breath was not of his evil deeds but instead he recalled everything that had ever warmed his heart. Hudson's attention was no longer on the horse and he could have cared less about the convenient timing of the earthquake. Killing himself was not of his main interest at the moment but what lay in the water, had Hudson's unbound attention. Mesmerized by the diamond light at the edge of the bank, let calming waters flow like memories fading and returning around this frozen cerebrum. As God took the memory of sin from Hudson's mind. He was not the type to appreciate love the first time around, commonly it takes a duplicate feeling to resurrect Love. There was a moment in Hudson's life, before the end of slavery where he held life as a house negro as his highest state. Entangled between the strings of deceit, self-hate, anger, pride, was the creation God intended. He wouldn't have traded that moment for anything in this white man's world including this peace of crystalized legend that lay before his eye. For a man who was two seconds away from destruction to now all of a sudden experience complete euphoric bliss meant that this was to be no ordinary stone refracting light. Hudson had no intention to be possessed over the crystal because he was a changed man. Without fear before as most blacks in the south at that time hadn't feared death since death was thy neighbor on the plantation, who came a knocking every now and then to borrow someone's child. Let's just call it some sugar. Like a contact high of harmony, Hudson now sought what others could only wish to seek. Another level of love. It was like Hudson invited death inside and offered him a glass of water. For it was the long rope, noose, Hudson had tried to hang himself with that became shorter every now and then when he would have to cut it from around the neck of a white slave cropper who crossed paths with Hudson that day, evening or night. I know what you're thinking, Hudson now was out for revenge trying to kill every white man breathing before they killed him. This was not case. No, Hudson had no way out of a sanguine destiny see, nothing made him mad nor made him happy anymore because that would consist of Hudson becoming angry at times. No such emotion existing in Hudson anymore as he was simply now a mirror to others hate, anger, and greed. That was at least true if they dared to look him in the eye. Some say that before the unsuspecting locals hung themselves, they witness what was to be the home for every living creature but nobody really could be too sure since if your eyes were to meet Hudson's, you didn't live long enough to describe what you saw. Some locals who believe in Ghosts fled with their families, but it was still the south in the eighteen hundreds, I mean you can't have a black man walking around at night downing white southerners before the break of dawn. One at a time, sometimes two at a time. The white men would observe this mysterious dark figure walking along the road and would want to bring forth what they saw as repayment now coming over to them but for the sake of their lives it was best they kept to themselves and moved on. Beware of the Hangman, the children of the dead men use to tell each other. Well the way things worked out was every now and then Hudson would walk back and forth, down, and back south of that tree by the river again and then back north of that same sapling. Clasped in the large palm of his worn out slave hands, Hudson who spent most of his life in the shadows now eerily whistled an unnerving melody hummed most troublesomely when some unwary white men reaping what was sowed, was about to meet their demise. They'd take one look into his muddle brown iris which had gradually been immersed into the darkness of Hudson's dilated pupil, which I think the white folk must have seen some light or saw themselves for who they really were, where they really came from and where they were evidently going. Everything they needed to see in one lifetime. And then he was gone. Rumors of a mysterious hangman spread throughout neighboring communities. Children weren't allowed to play outside past four in the afternoon, for fear of one of the kiddos opening the door to the Hudson. Relatives and friends were advised to call out the person's name from behind their fence if they wanted to speak with them. These were turbulent times I would say for both a black man and white man in this stricken town. Use to be just a black man had to worry about was being lynched but even more so while this was going on. They would now just shoot at a black man instead, for fear of getting close enough to see the illumination of their eyes. Every other week they would find a poor white man's head hanging crooked over a decomposing body draped around a different tree branch. If these white men were in their sane minds themselves, they probably could have avoided untimely death. In any case their posse got bigger and bigger. Fuck the white hoods they said, we must be able to see this black bastard. A whole summer gave reason to fear the black man like never before. For the most part black men were clueless to the happening, at first. Whites figured if they murdered enough black men they would eventually get the one they had really been looking for and that's exactly what they did. I don't know how they didn't see him until now, but it took forty white slavers and fifteen broads to finally capture the Hangman with help by the light of the moon. I don't know if the Hangman's story would have been complete if he hadn't been called home, but it was these white farmers who would rest easy having sent Hudson to whatever hell he kept close to heart. High up in the same tree by the same calm water where the infamous legend of the hangman began, is where it also came to an end. For by the bottom of his feet the white folk gathered, a couple of black children as well watched in secrecy another black man being lynched. "Any last words before we kick the stool out from under you?" There was no stool just a white man's pulley. Hudson again found tranquility in the water that lay before him except this time there was no shimmering crystal in the apparent. As dusk inched the sky closer to a rosy hue, a persistent wind pasted over the scene almost releasing the men's hands and Hudson to hang prematurely. On a white man's shoulder rested a black cat and in the distance a Pharaoh Owl with present eyes wide, perched on a tree branch across the water to watch as the men let go of the rope and Hudson's body drop to the applauding crowd, swinging by the pivot of his neck. Hudson did not fight this. He didn't make a sound. He only stared into the eyes of the owl until all the life transferred out of Hudson's body. Story goes, Hudson's body was left to decompose for a week before mysteriously vanishing one day. But the lore is he transferred whatever maleficent powers he had inside him into the eyes of an owl, which then turned gold upon his death. "See this right here, it's yours. This is what you win for shooting the moon." I told him he could keep it as I stood up to leave but the room had a wicked spin to it, he grabbed my arm. "Tell me, how long are you willing to play in the dark, if it is the light that lies to unlock your truth." Said the man in black before he released my forearm.

CHAPTER 24

"Take it. You have no choice" he said as I again looked over toward the bouncer, "A bet is a bet." I said before I grabbed the winged curse off the bar table. "Something about finding an eye", Doctor Farrow said as he stood leaning at the edge of his desk. Where he then walked over and handed me a small piece of paper and then walked back to his desk as the office phone rang. Dr. Farrow answered, "Yes. I am in the middle of session." He looked disheveled as he then started fidgeting with the newspaper. The face he was making told me that this was an important phone call, something worthy of draining his melanin. While I was waiting, I indulged in a bag of peanuts I remembered to stuff in my pocket before leaving my house this morning. I saw he was beginning to doodle something on his notepad. "Well hopefully it's just Te" he stopped a moment before fully finishing his thought "Well hopefully it's just a temporary. A noble protest regardless the outcome is sure to make headlines", he let the other person on the line speak "That's Horrible. Right, right. mhmm" he continued. "Well, let them protest, there would be something seriously wrong if the people turned their back. Well Okay but somebody owes us, he paused. "I understand" he said before pausing again, we need to force their hand." After another pause, "all you can do is lock up, go put up a sign that says black owned business and hope they can read. "Take your time' he paused. "Okay be safe, talk to you in a little" he said before he hung up the phone. "Sorry about that Samori, the police just shot an unarmed kid in West Athens. They are starting to riot in front of my secretary's family business," he said with his eyes on the pack of cigarettes now next to the newspaper.

"Anyways I am telling you how I was drunk and just wanted to go home, so I grabbed the owl off the table "let the owl be your guide to either fortune or curse." Sounded like some mumbo jumbo. At first, I didn't mind having the owl around, it actually brought a nice touch of class to my world until bits and pieces of my balanced life started to go missing, also important papers, bills, a matter of my lively hood.

I couldn't understand why some of these things were happening when I am always very careful. I mean one of her idiosyncrasies was touching stuff while she was talking to you, but I did not believe her a thief or worse a mental case. My wife that is, the archeologist her name was Venetia.

"Was she really an archaeologist?" I asked in the right to reconsider everything this man has said.

"Yea that's right, her focused research was in Egyptian Artifacts, apparently leading her to one of the greatest finds ever, in her own words. It was what her and her partner thought about daily. Her partner with the excavation and all the appraising," he explained with his hands. "But I don't think any of us could have imagine the type of mystery that came with this object. As for me I had enough of looking at the damned owl. It was time for it to go. I wanted to get rid of the matter, but it seemed to be naturally mine as the darn thing came back each time. I had put it in a black trash bag when I threw out the rest of the garbage to the bin out in the back of my apartment. The next day, I catch my wife in her office cleaning it off with an excavation brush. When I asked her where she found it, she said she almost tripped over it as it laid on the kitchen floor with the rest of the trash.

"I know I threw it outside in the back. The only other explanation is the dogs from the Christmas Story must of ran through our house, unless you're messing with me?"

"You should know I wouldn't do that. You must have taken out the wrong bag and I don't even want to know why you would want to get rid of something that has this type of value. If anything, why don't you sell it?" we already had problems.

"I can't believe you right now Adam,"

"So where are you going?" I deliberately inquired.

"I am going to see my sister, she wanted to discuss her relationship troubles she's having. Is that alright with you?'

"Stay with me tonight. You can see your sister tomorrow."

"I guess it's not alright. She has been trying to speak to me all day and I've been putting her off to do things like pick up all the garbage off the kitchen floor."

"Let"s move to Montenegro! I'm serious." She laughed.

"Who are you right now?" she shook her head in disbelief as she told me she had to leave and not to wait up.

"So, you tried to sell it?" I asked.

Not that I started to believe that this figurine was cursed or anything of that sort, I just didn't think it was too good to let go of and I wasn't looking for whatever fortune followed. I wasn't going to pawn it if in fact it was actually cursed where the owner than would want to give it back to me. I wanted it to stay gone and thought if someone else were looking for it then maybe it wouldn't bother me anymore."

Only for five thousand dollars but I think the guy who I sold it to knew it was worth way more because he started to over think the purchase. I told him if I didn't have a fit of bad luck, I would have no luck at all. The reason why I couldn't afford to hold on to it. I had to work for everything I ever accomplished. A week later turns out the owner of the pawn shop fell down his stairs and broke his neck. And that is not even the crazy part. The crazy part is I guess the man had no close relatives to leave the shop to when he died so either by freak turn of events or possibly my indelible first impression, I received a phone call informing me of a newly acquired affluence. I now owned a pawnshop and everything in it. As I felt a tad guilty, I wasn't even brought in for police questioning and not even a summons to appear in court. All they did was hand me the keys to the shop. It felt as this might be a problem.

Oh, and then I gave her uncle Ray a job managing the pawn shop. What was going on? What they couldn't see every night at the same time, was me receiving a mysterious phone call with nobody on the other end. That was until I went down to the pawn shop in the middle of the night to retrieve the Owl. Now I thought about throwing it to the bottom of the Connecticut river but that would make me ignorant to what this Gold replica had in store for me. After that I embraced my destiny so much I brought it upstairs and put it back on the mantle of my blended Victorian style office right where I had it in the first place and then I went to bed. I'm not going to lie it was some of the best sleep I got in long time. I woke up like the last nigga on earth, more relaxed than I've felt in years, addicted to nothing. Birds were chirping as me and my wife made love the night before and now the smell of my baby cooking breakfast downstairs had antagonized me the good life. That's when I came to the top of the staircase where it smelled less like complimentary cooking and more like a last meal, like something burning. The top of the stove was on fire! Half asleep I almost threw water on top of the flame, but it was a grease fire so then the whole apartment would have gone up. I remembered we had just bought a portable fire extinguisher. So, I raced to the next rooms closet where it was still in the box, "Oh c'mon, idiot!" I said to myself. I then raced back to the kitchen just slowing before reaching the change of flooring. Just an exhale to display some composure before I went to put out the flame that had mysteriously extinguished while I was away grasping what I should of have done from the very beginning. All that remained was a dense puff of gray smoke that spread free throughout the room.

"How in the blue blazing hell did this happen?"

I called for Venetia but there was no answer. I walked into every room calling for my wife but still not seeing her brought on the panic of uncertainty rolling through my veins until I determined that I was the only one in my apartment. I stepped outside the door to my Boston brownstone in my satin dark blue bathrobe which now let bare my thick black chest hair, where I was to observe the world continuing to move but without my wife in the picture.

"Venetia vanished without a trace and I couldn't help but believe it had something to do with this Owl." That's all the information I've had until today. See I believe this Owl has led me to you, as unbelievable as that sounds, he paused. On the piece of paper, he handed me and what I am now just taking notice of

The word "Tetsuo?" Dr. Farrow who could not stop himself recited. "The word that you saw in your father's woodshed."

"Yeah, what does it mean?" I said sliding forward to the edge of my seat.

"Tetsuo! They are an International metal processing company who make and import iron, like such tools used to excavate through durable stone."

"But I thought the Owl was made out of Gold?" I said.

"I also believe it means wise man in Japanese, but this is the word you saw isn't it? "Tetsuo" the name on the contract?

"Yea that looks right." I agreed, still not fully comprehending how it related to us.

"Venetia's partner at the archeologist research center in Boston, the name of the company he worked for. Well remember that great discovery I told you about earlier that her and her partner made, her partner who happens to also work for a company, Tetsuo? We stored it inside the pawn shop."

"Well what does that mean?" I asked again.

"It means if we ever wanted to find out how exactly the word Tetsuo connects your story to mine, I have the one master key to both our problems."

CHAPTER 25

"So, let's go get it!"

"Wait a minute Sam. I know I said I have the key to the shop but that was two years ago, who knows what has been confiscated during that period. I am over here in Los Angeles. We can't just pick up and leave for Boston on a hunch."

"Doesn't your uncle's wife run the shop?"

"Yes, my wife's uncle run's it but," my enthusiasm told me now was the time,

"Do you trust him? Call him."

"Slow down. I haven't spoken to my wife's uncle since she went missing,"

"Did you ever think maybe your wife's coworker went missing as well. So, it could be just sitting there in storage waiting for us to retrieve it "What is the address to the pawn shop?"

"Sam, we don't even know what it is. What if it's not what we are looking for? And what if it is. What then?"

"Well we will never know if we don't do this one thing for sure! Don't you want to find your wife?"

"Sam, of course I want to find my wife, but I suggest we just slow it down and take some time to think through a plan before we make a move. It is three in the afternoon on a Monday and you want to catch a flight to Boston?"

"Just hand me the address I will go by myself" I said as we just stared at each other for a moment both not blinking seeing which one of us would be calling the others bluff."

"Fine, you want the address?" Doctor Farrow reluctantly wrote it down "Its forty-four Roosevelt street. If I find Ray's number, I will let him know you are coming. I hope you find it in you to let someone else know your whereabouts, so the police don't come shooting down my door in the middle of the night."

I was almost out the door when I heard, "Sam wait, here's the key to the cellar door. That's the only door that key opens but if it's like how I last remember there was a loose screw missing from the back window." I turned to leave and at the same time I dodged the coffee tray Sheila walked in with. Doctor Farrow called for her. "Hey Sheila, come here for a second. I need to whisper something in your ear, hopefully you can translate."

I was out the door, "Hey what are you going to do about money?" is the last thing I heard him yell. What was I going to do about money? I was going to spend the last of what my father left me as insurance. For life.

I caught a five-minute carpool to the busy Los Angeles International Airport. I took the face mask out of my pocket, the one that grandma Coral fashioned for me. Some things we can't take back no matter how bad you want to. I was traveling so lite I forgot my Raiders cap in Doctor Farrow's office. It really didnt matter as I was moving fast through the condensed airport, as fast as security would allow me for nobody was avoidant of the new health screenings. Before I got on the plane I removed the pinky finger size bandages that horizontally dressed some of the wound and the more tender stitches under my eyebrow in the airport bathroom, as it was another one of my bright ideas to look less like a bond villain and now apparently more of an actual security threat as the TSA felt no law abiding American could bleed this much from around their eye without some criminal activity having taken place. Once that was cleared up, I caught the three-forty-five Alaska to Seattle before it arrived in Boston. I found time to have a couple of night terrors on the almost twelve-hour flight. I texted my mother that I was in Boston and that I would explain why when I got home. I then arrived exhausted at Six o five am the next morning.

My father would talk about Massachusetts sometimes as if I needed to visit. Bottom line he hadn't taken me to visit, and on most days I woulda loved a grand tour of some colonial parchment. Maybe after I found my father, we could experience this rich city together just for the love of it. Here I was at the address that Doctor Farrow wrote down. It didn't look like a pawn shop, but what do I know about Boston other than what my father has told me. The front door was locked so I went around back because I remembered Doctor Farrow said that the back window would be ajar. He wasn't wrong, the window was basically standing up right only for appearance. I fell through the open window to a dark unfurnished kitchen pantry. It looked like someone's abandoned house, but I was almost positive this was the address. I was about to call Doctor Farrow when then I saw a man grabbing on to a woman who was laid out across the floor, who I thought coulda been the doctor's wife and her lover caught in the act. "Don't you touch her!" I emphasized. I saw yellow tape connected across a door frame. I put my phone away to stretch my body under the crisscrossed tape. "Freeze!" Usually when someone says that to you, they are pointing a gun. I wasn't about to make any fast movements to find out though. What I witnessed was stale blood stains on the white sheets, a mess at the end of the bed, drops of what looked like blood darkening the wood, a flower vase that had fallen to pieces and several Styrofoam cups placed in different parts of the room. Some I bet still had room temperature coffee in them.

CHAPTER 26

"By Julius Caesar Chappelle I think we found our suspect."

"Interlock your fingers on top of your head." This person was sounding more and more like a cop but that didn't make me feel any better. They were police officers reenacting a crime scene that I just moseyed on in to.

"We can add breaking and entering as well, wouldn't you say Officer Caravelli?

The officer with the navy trench coat cuffed my hands behind my back and turned me around to an Officer Caravelli holstering his pistol.

"Returning to the scene of the crime for some sick pleasure aye," said Caravelli.

"Wait a minute", I said as I needed a moment to swallow my pride, "this has to be a mistake, I thought this was 44 Roosevelt street."

"Holy fuck he even knows the address, we got him Jackie!" Jackie was Officer Jack Caravelli and apparently the lead detective. The officer who was doing all the informal talking was also the one that stood over the female officer playing victim as I stepped forward to get a closer look and he was also the same officer who cuffed me. His name was Officer Beckard.

"How did you Know the victim?" Officer Caravelli who took charge said.

"Victim? I thought this was a pawn shop."

"Do you usually break into pawn shops?" Officer Beckard asked me as if I was already found guilty.

"Take him to the car Officer Beckard, he can explain himself further down at interrogation." But that did not stop them from trying to interrogate me in the cop car. I told them that I was not from Boston and that was it.

Down at the precinct I was handcuffed to the chair inside the interrogation room "Who you got in there, Potato Head?" I heard one of officers say to his brother in blue who were separated by two divisions and what church they attended on Sunday but also how far away they were as they continued to have their conversation publicly, while officer Beatneck had one foot out the interrogation room and the other up my asshole.

"keep it down Smith," he flapped and whispered. "He is a suspect in the Christie murders."

"Get the fuck out of here, you got a confession?"

"Well why don't you just go to the fucking papers dude. I don't want it to get out, not until they get my side of the story. Let me do my job so you don't have to go broke while I'm telling you the story at Brennan's tonight, you hairy bastard."

He closed the door on the inside before it was open again by Officer Caravelli.

"You weren't thinking about interrogating the suspect without me now, were you?"

"I had just told Vernell to go find you." I was impressed with his ability to lie and chew gum at the same time. Officer Caravelli slid me over a Styrofoam cup of water.

"So, mister Waters, you not being from Boston and all, do you feel like telling us what you were doing breaking into a crime scene of an ongoing homicide investigation?"

"How did you get that nice cut over your eye?" Officer Beckard asked.

I didn't care how it looked or that I was being falsely accused for a series of crimes I knew nothing about only that it now interrupted my search to find my father and to find out what the key that I'm no longer in possession of unlocked.

I told them I wasn't going to say another word without my lawyer and if they had a problem with that, they could ask me again upstairs at internal affairs. Here we are three months later, and I am telling you how I lost everything even before I caught a case.

"Aye man your life is just like that movie where Tom Cruise has to wear a prosthetic mask because Cameron Diaz just couldn't let him get away. Where his face got disfigured and shit. No offense."

"Nah its cool I don't stress over the things I can't control anymore, somehow it will connect. That was then and this is now. But hey, you never told me what happen to your brother" I said in hopes of a happier conclusion."

"So anyways they were stealing from the customers, right. Hiking up the prices and skimping on the herb and just like I said they caught me, but they never found the money. The two brothers showed up before the cops arrived and everyone knows your supposed to walk up to the biggest guy in the room and strike him in the face with the barrel of a gun. Well I neither had a gun nor did I sock the correct brother, as I learned the hard way that sometimes big things come in small packages. And I guess they had me on camera throwing the bag out the window into the alley because I than was trapped inside, belonging to the shops every desire. Kicker is, when the cops recovered the bag a block away all they found was a couple towels and some hand sanitizer but no money. My guess is that someone walked by and scooped out all the cash really quick. They would have also come up on a sapphire if that's how it went down. I don't know who has a harder time keeping things off the record, the ones plotting to commit a crime or the one who finds out some spicy new information. Remember how I told you my cousin who would help with my brother when she did not have to work herself? Well bud tenders don't make as much as you would think. Apparently not enough to be involved in a robbery because the three ladies soon found new professions. While I'm in here my brother is staying with my cousin Judy. And you know what else? you wouldn't ever think us to be cousins on account we have different last names, and her skin tone is so much lighter than mine. As she even gets mistaken for a white girl sometimes. She always loved having Dawin around, so she didn't mind when it became her new job.

"He really figured out the combination to the safe?" I asked.

"17,19,63."

"Amazing."

I knew it had to be early morning since the story I told the inmate underneath me started last night. I am surprise he stayed awake. Sam was feeling pretty tired as well he knew the guards were going to shake us out of our cells at any moment. That morning he had one of those slumbers where you think your awake but can't shake your-self out of it as your exhausted not being able to remember the exact moment your two eyelids started to get heavy and what you thought you were doing prior but in an instant, at any moment and in any place the dream can reappear. It was not too long though for only twenty minutes later Sam could hear the guard with his familiar footsteps getting closer,

"Wake up!"

It was Sam's turn to wake up and it startled him so much that he fell off the top bunk, stomach first on to the cold cement to his roommate opening his eyes.

"Chow time Johnny boy. Let's go Putty nose, you got a phone call."

"Can't you see, we're Awake!" Inmate MA 23154 said before he walked pass the CO opening our cell.

I said, "The names McAndrew. And I Am Alive K!"

CHAPTER 27

"Are you okay?" That morning on the phone Sam asked me how his mother was doing and if she had been getting his letters. To make Sam's stay as bearable as possible, I of course told him that she was doing fine and that his aunt was helping out with his baby brother but the truth is, I have not spoken to the family for some time neither Eva nor Thomas Waters. That morning he told me about a dream he had just before being summoned to this courtesy call on the jail phone. Sam recalled that in his dream there was a man all in black with black tap shoes and a black disguise covering more than half his face. All but his actual eyes were covered as he tap danced up a plethora of glowing stairs where there was a man with a guitar playing heartbreak hotel all while the man in black's family and friends watched in silence off to the side. That's when the Man in Black blew the roof off the theater up in to the dark blue sky, as he grooved past a bell boy with menacing yellow eyes into an extravagant chapel where there were curvatures of women who's faces were replaced with mirrors. He time stepped and shuffled past the fame; the flashing cameras, the reporters, the lawyers, into a Maxi Ford right past the fortune, the dollars and the gold. The man in black quickly turned around lifting his mask for a moment to see his grotesque face in the mirror break down to cry one tear with his features, I couldn't make out in the dream. Children watched outside through a window, the man in black continue to dance until he reached a magnificent soul in a red dress without a mirror covering her beauty. The Man in black gazed upon her summertime smile before he took her hand and twirled her around for all whom he danced past to adore the woman in red as we would a winter wonderland inside a snow globe. He then let go of her hand to pan away, dismissing her pleads for him to stay. As it was a crucifix overhead that would bid him adieu. The Man in Black levitated and spun on to the crucifix, open palm hands and arms spread apart, curling his right tap shoe up to his slightly bent left knee. His head dropped.

"Is it still Sherlock Holmes?" Samori Water's requested more of my advice over the prison phone.

"Indubitably so" I said.

"Do you know what it means?"

"Sam it could mean a lot of different things at this point. It could mean you are a victim of inherent circumstances, the everlasting effects of true love. In a place where there is only our misconception of love like a belief the stars in the sky are not the brightest stars of them all, especially after dark. Anything other than God being fair would not do the heart Justice." Sam slowly started to respect my opinion as time went on, while jail only made him more persistent in finding out how far back our paths linked to each other's, but truthfully if he had any scattered idea, I mean I didn't mind that he digressed. I found it quite interesting. "You need to look out for yourself in there Sam, be on your best behavior. We are going to get you out but it's going to take some time, please be patient. Your family needs you. I need you." I did need Samori thanks to his father Thomas Waters, and his forfeit of this abstract gift I now grudgingly cherish instead of my absent wife. The motive, I am a dedicated health professional with an obligation to each of my client's no matter how impervious to transparency I had become. Well in the end it all comes full circle and only when we're able to understand how the game goes, can we finally begin to play it the way it is supposed to be played. So, there can be no end but to be continued at a later date. I had realized that at some point near the conclusion of Samori and I's session, his words as pertinent and captivating as they flowed from out of his mouth, were apt to become my words in my new book just as his loss had led to mine. Something in the way I told the end of the story was specifically tailored for Sam's emotionless state, as what really happened while I was living in Los Angeles on March 20th was only for me to make public. It was earlier in the night when I had stopped for a couple of drinks at this downtown dive bar where I was persuaded into a high stakes card game by none other than Thomas Waters himself, enabling me from the shadows which I figured out was him by the evidence Sam provided me. For it was this Owl, Sam's story and the fact that what Thomas Waters had done when he grabbed my forearm as I tried to make a fast exist, was slip a piece of paper into my palm with the word Tetsuo written on it, as I did for Samori. As it was Thomas Waters, who told me the story of the Hangman before I was to be burdened by this troubled enigma. And I sit here on my five-wheel flame retardant office chair, satiated by the hot tea that my secretary was nice enough to pick up from my favorite Chinese Tea shop. I can recall the moment I understood the meaning of the word Tetsuo. See you might not agree with everything I say or do, but I can assure you there is a need for people like me. Nobody knew this better then Thomas Waters when he chose to disappear the same night, he invited me to support his existence. It was right before my secretary called me on the office phone when something clicked in my head. I knew what had to be done and I knew it was something Sam had to figure out for himself. Samori skipped breakfast that morning to return to his cell where he then got down on both knees to recite a prayer. "Dear Lord father, while you remain ever present in my life, I thank you for not letting my heart succumb to the loneliness that wants to invade while I am away from home. I shudder to think where I would be if you had given up on me while so many continue to choose to do this for themselves. Though I am condemned to servitude for what you have kept a secret all the days until you vanished from this world. I have yet to take responsibility, for without the deeds of my past I might not be having to miss you as I do to the second. To truly rectify my wrongs, the only purposeful cure for what continues to be all my fault and all my love to be again reunited in one day, this I swear. Amen. "Whereas there can be no stone left unturned, what we tend to find underneath its ruin exposes the nature of our creation. The backward snuff and the long faces they would fear if they were left to marvel at the infraction marked in the stone. I would not have strayed, If I didn't care and you wouldn't have left me the antidote, which the time has come to set in motion. Regardless the intent if we play our cards right. All alone I sip on the intoxicating lip of my special Yin Hao Jasmine tea and I find myself able to relax knowing the revelation is conditioned to loom by what is unconditional. Setting myself up for the biggest kick back of my career. If I could help it. If I may quote the Ink Spots, "You see, I don't want to set the world on fire honey, I love you too much. I just want to start a great big flame in your heart."

A Divination of the Dog

Printed in the United States
By Bookmasters